WHISKEY SOUR

AN ADDISON HOLMES MYSTERY (BOOK 2)

LILIANA HART

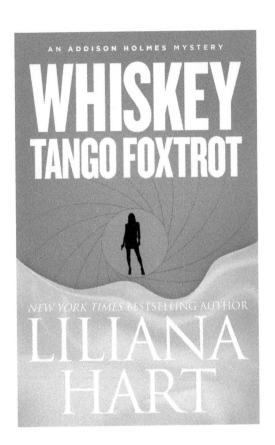

Coming April 26, 2016
WHISKEY TANGO FOXTROT
Order Now

AN ADDISON HOLMES MYSTERY

WHISKEY SOUR

NEW YORK TIMES BESTSELLING AUTHOR

LILIANA HART

OTHER BOOKS

The MacKenzies of Montana
Dane's Return
Thomas's Vow
Riley's Sanctuary
Cooper's Promise
Grant's Christmas Wish
The MacKenzies Boxset

MacKenzie Security Series
Seduction and Sapphires
Shadows and Silk
Secrets and Satin
Sins and Scarlet Lace
Sizzle
Crave
Trouble Maker
Scorch
MacKenzie Security Omnibus 1
MacKenzie Security Omnibus 2

Lawmen of Surrender (MacKenzies-1001 Dark Nights)
1001 Dark Nights: Captured in Surrender
1001 Dark Nights: The Promise of Surrender
Sweet Surrender
Dawn of Surrender

The MacKenzie World (read in any order)
Trouble Maker
Bullet Proof
Deep Trouble
Delta Rescue
Desire and Ice
Rush
Spies and Stilettos
Wicked Hot
Hot Witness
Avenged
Never Surrender

JJ Graves Mystery Series
Dirty Little Secrets
A Dirty Shame
Dirty Rotten Scoundrel
Down and Dirty
Dirty Deeds
Dirty Laundry
Dirty Money

Addison Holmes Mystery Series
Whiskey Rebellion
Whiskey Sour
Whiskey For Breakfast
Whiskey, You're The Devil
Whiskey on the Rocks

Whiskey Tango Foxtrot
Whiskey and Gunpowder

The Gravediggers
The Darkest Corner
Gone to Dust
Say No More

Stand Alone Titles
Breath of Fire
Kill Shot
Catch Me If You Can
All About Eve
Paradise Disguised
Island Home
The Witching Hour

Books by Liliana Hart and Scott Silverii
The Harley and Davidson Mystery Series
The Farmer's Slaughter
A Tisket a Casket
I Saw Mommy Killing Santa Claus
Get Your Murder Running
Deceased and Desist
Malice In Wonderland
Tequila Mockingbird
Gone With the Sin

M att Savage was two hundred pounds of solid muscle. I knew because he had me pressed against the wall of a teeny tiny closet in a suite at the Marriott. His muscles had muscles, and I was pretty sure it wasn't his gun pressing into my belly.

Soft light seeped around the edges of the closet door, and his eyes gleamed like black fire against the darkness of his skin. He was fifty percent Native American and a hundred percent raw sex. His face had been chiseled by Michelangelo—prominent cheekbones and a sharp blade of a nose—his lips were full, and the white scar at his chin kept him from being too perfect.

Did I mention I was only wearing two small scraps of lace to cover my lady bits?

If there hadn't been a dead body less than ten feet away with more holes in it than Swiss cheese, then I'd be in a hell of a moral predicament.

My name is Addison Holmes, and I was no stranger to moral predicaments. I was also no stranger to dead bodies, which was why I was gasping for oxygen instead of gasping in pleasure. If it weren't for the fact that I had one too many men in my life at the moment, I'm almost positive my morals would have known what the hell to do in this situation.

I was in danger of hyperventilating, and I couldn't quite decide if I wanted Savage to kiss me so I could forget that I'd just witnessed a man being blown to smithereens, or let him give me CPR.

"Relax," he whispered against my ear. "And be ready to move on my say so. Someone else is in the room."

He pushed me harder into the wall, his body shielding mine, as he brought the gun in his hand up and pointed it at the closet door. I bit my lip hard enough to taste blood, and I took comfort in the way he put his free arm around me. I fit against him easily—too easily—and it was something I'd have to consider later. Preferably when I had clothes on.

I heard the crunch of glass as someone made their way across the room. Then there was nothing but silence, and I knew whoever was out there stood just on the other side of the closet door. Savage and I both held our breaths as the knob jiggled once before it turned.

Light flooded the closet and I squenched my eyes closed against the glare, not having any desire to actually see my death up close and personal. I waited for the sound of gunfire and for hot metal to rip through my skin, but there was nothing but tense silence.

I cracked my eyes open one at a time and immediately wished I'd left them closed. Nick Dempsey stood in the doorway, his weapon pointed steadily at Savage as his glacier blue eyes met mine. I should have ignored the slow flush of guilt that worked its way up my body. But considering I was all but naked in a closet with a man Nick had once threatened to cut the balls off of, and my leg was somehow wrapped around that same man's waist, I could see how Nick might get the wrong impression.

"It's not what it looks like," I croaked out. "I swear."

"Gee, doesn't that sound familiar." His voice was harsh, and the lines of his mouth were pinched—a mouth that had the ability to turn me into a puddle of jelly when it touched my skin. "Just remember that payback's a bitch, sweetheart."

If looks could have killed, I'd already be six feet under. Nick and I had a tumultuous past, and from the looks of it, we were going to have a few road bumps in our future.

Nick sure as hell knew how to hold a grudge. It's not like I meant to shoot him. My finger just slipped on the trigger. I swear.

Wednesday—One Week Ago

CRIMINALS ARE MOSTLY DUMB. AT LEAST IN MY EXPERIENCE. And Walter Winthrop III, Noogey to his friends, was no exception to the rule.

I squatted behind a group of dumpsters at the Lone Ranger Trailer Park, ignoring the flies that swarmed around day old Hamburger Helper and dirty diapers. I was hard-pressed to tell the difference between the two and reminded myself to get my birth control prescription filled as soon as possible. Not that I was having a lot of sex or anything lately, but I didn't want to take any chances. I wasn't ready to be responsible for a child. I was barely responsible for myself.

Summer in Savannah wasn't forgiving, and it sure as hell wasn't for the faint of heart. It was barely eight o'clock in the morning and heat roiled in invisible waves off the pavement beneath me, baking the soles of my flip-flops and frizzing my hair, as the temperature pushed triple digits.

The air was thick with syrupy humidity. The breeze non-existent, the moss covered trees completely still. I hadn't heard a bird chirp in more than twenty minutes. I was pretty sure they were all dead—either from the heat or the stench—I couldn't be sure.

The Lone Ranger Trailer Park was located on the northwest side of Savannah, away from any tourists who might accidentally discover that not every part of the historic city was picturesque. The trailers were parked on a cleared off gravel lot, and if there was grass anywhere I'd yet to see it. Just miles of dirt and cement. The trailers sat haphazardly, a patchwork quilt of tin and rust, and bags of trash and old car parts littered the area.

I'd had no choice but to hide behind the dumpsters. The park was almost completely open unless I wanted to venture into the trees and marshland and set up camp— which I didn't, because twelve year old me knew from experience it wasn't fun to have a snake slither down your blouse.

Sweat gathered in places best left unmentioned, and I'd reached the point that the smell of my body no longer made my eyes water. Even raising the Long Range Nikon in my hands exerted more energy than I had left to give. Noogey Winthrop was going to have a lot to answer for if I ever got hold of him.

Six months ago, Noogey had been living the high life. He'd owned a mansion in Miami, a two hundred year old plantation house in Savannah, and three other homes across the world. He'd driven expensive cars and bought outrageous jewelry for his mistress. He had stocks and bonds and a thriving company, and he'd just gotten permission from NASA to have his ashes shot into space. But somewhere along the way, Noogey's luck changed.

When Noogey's wife caught wind of the mistress, she filed for divorce and decided to take half of everything he owned and then some, since there had been no prenuptial agreement. They had three kids between the ages of twelve and seventeen, and Mrs. Winthrop was going to make Noogey pay. More power to her. In my opinion, Noogey was lucky she hadn't run him down with a car or gone Lorena Bobbitt on his ass.

Unfortunately, getting taken to the cleaners wasn't sitting too well with Noogey. All of a sudden, his company wasn't turning a profit, his cars were being repossessed, and his debt almost doubled his net worth.

The theory going around was that all Noogey's money was really being siphoned into offshore accounts, and his wife had hired us to prove his guilt. My job should have been simple: Find evidence that Walter Noogey Winthrop was spending above his means. But I'd learned over the past months that hardly anything about my job was ever simple. At least when I did it.

Noogey was a tough nut to crack, and he and his mistress had moved into the Lone Ranger Trailer Park so their story would be more convincing. I had to admit I was pretty convinced. The smell alone would have made me confess to any crime after ten minutes.

I had a perfect view of Noogey's trailer from my crouched spot, and I'd gotten a couple of good shots of the primer gray rectangle. The knob on the front door hung precariously and a hole had been kicked in the bottom of the door. Their patch of concrete was empty except for a late model hatchback with a missing bumper and an oversized weathervane that looked as if it had fallen off the roof at some point.

I knew Noogey wasn't home. Kate McClean, my boss at the McClean Detective Agency and my best friend, had told me Noogey had left on an early flight to the Caymans on business. And he hadn't taken along Marika Dubois, his current ladylove.

I pulled out my phone and dialed Kate, hoping above all else that she needed me to come into the office and start work on another job besides this one. One that was more sanitary. And maybe one with sexy naked men.

"This job sucks, Kate," I said by way of greeting. "I'm going to have to bathe in bleach to get the smell off."

"I hear it's good for the skin. Kind of like arsenic. What's happening with Noogey?"

If I'd wanted a sympathetic ear, Kate was the last person I should've called. We balanced each other pretty well for the most part. I was prone to high drama and she kept me grounded (mostly). Sometimes keeping me grounded was like pissing in the wind, or so my mother liked to say. I liked to think I brought a little adventure to Kate's life. And I kept her in homemade baked goods when I felt like the scales were becoming unbalanced.

"Noogey's gone and there's been no sign of the girlfriend."

"She's still in there," Kate said. "Though rumor has it she's making Noogey pay for the inconvenience. I need you to get close to the trailer. See if you can get some shots of the inside through the windows. I bet the inside of that trailer looks like a palace."

"Sure thing, boss," I said, rolling my eyes. "I'll just mosey on up and see if my x-ray camera lens can somehow see through the dirt coating the windows. No one will notice me skulking around in broad daylight."

"That's the spirit. I'm sure you'll think of something to get her out of there."

I sputtered in disbelief as Kate disconnected, and when I stood up to shove my phone back in my pocket I felt the squish beneath my feet.

I sighed and probably would have cried if I hadn't been so dehydrated. "At least it was the Hamburger Helper instead of the diaper," I said. Sally Sunshine, always looking on the positive side of things. That's me.

I pulled Noogey's file from my backpack and thumbed through it, hoping an idea of how to get Marika Dubois out of the trailer would magically appear in my mind.

Marika was a former model who was used to creature comforts. I knew without a doubt that the only thing keeping her around was Noogey's promise of the millions he'd somehow stashed away. A woman like Marika wouldn't live like this unless the payout was worth it.

A list of Marika's acquaintances were listed in alphabetical order on the back page of her profile. Kate was nothing if not efficient. An idea popped into my head and I picked a name at random. Sometimes my cleverness astounded me.

I grabbed my phone and dialed Marika's cell number, moving further behind the dumpsters just in case there were any nosy neighbors or Marika got suspicious.

"What?" Marika barked out, her French accent heavy with irritation.

"Marika, darling! It's been too long," I gushed, trying not to gag as I inhaled something especially foul.

"Who is zis?" I was still trying to figure out what *zis* was while she kept talking. "Zis is ze private number."

"It's Honey Rhodes." I thickened my accent to magnolia blossom proportions since I knew from the file that Honey was a local. "Don't tell me you don't recognize my voice. I'll just be crushed."

"I zought zou were in rehab. I haven't zeen zou in months."

I rolled my eyes, trying to interpret her sentences and wishing I'd taken French instead of Spanish. But any teenage girl would have made the same decision. The Spanish teacher at my high school had looked like Ricky Martin and he'd worn tight t-shirts that had barely fit around his biceps. My fantasies of him pretty much got me through high school.

I thought quickly, trying to decide how I wanted to handle the rehab news. "I've been back a few days," I said with a dramatic sigh. "I just needed to get away for a while. Life just gets crazy sometimes with all the parties and the social whirl. I figured rehab was the one place no one would bother me."

"Zen it's not true about ze story I read in ze paper? Zey said zou had cocaine and crashed ze Ferrari into ze pool."

Son of a bitch. I would have to impersonate the one friend on the list who'd had a high profile brush with the law.

"It was all a misunderstanding," I reassured her. "Now enough about me. I have rehab skin, and I think we need to treat ourselves to a day at the spa and a little shopping. We owe it to ourselves to stay beautiful for our men."

I hoped to God I wasn't overselling it, but the only examples of socialites I could think of were Paris Hilton and Kim Kardashian, and I'd assumed it wasn't all that hard to be shallow and vacant.

"I'm not zeposed to shop," Marika said. "Ve have to be poor for a little while. Ze government is paying attention to our spending."

I made a sympathetic noise, trying not to gag. "Oh, sugar. It'll be my treat. I'm sure you need the break more than I do. I can't imagine having to live like a poor person."

"It is very difficult," Marika agreed. "Zey have nothing. No sexy cars or hot tubs. No body scrubs or shopping sprees. It is a dismal life. I'll be glad ven ve can collect our money."

I restrained the urge to march up to her front door and put my hands around her throat after her comments about being poor, choosing the mature route by making notes in the margin of the file about she and Noogey being able to collect their money soon.

"That's just terrible," I drawled. "How much longer are you going to have to live that way?"

"Not long, I zink. Walter promised me we'd be in Rio zipping zhampagne by the end of the month."

"Ooh, then you definitely need a spa day, sugar. You can't go to Rio with the smell of poor following you around."

"Zes, zou are right. I vill meet you at ze Green Door in half an hour."

Without so much as a goodbye, Marika disconnected and I shuffled my way back to the edge of the dumpster so I had a better view. I'd have to report the trip to Rio to the authorities. The judge hadn't demanded Noogey's passport because his lawyer had claimed Noogey needed to be able to deal with his foreign businesses in person, but this information would likely change that.

I smiled as the trailer door opened and Marika came trotting out in tiny shorts that showed off miles of tanned legs. Her long blond hair was pulled back in a ponytail and her breasts held up a halter-top of shimmering violet. Her feet were in strappy heels and a Yorkie stuck his head out of an oversized purse. I could see the disgust on her pouty lips from where I sat as she made her way to the hatchback with the missing bumper.

I shook my head in disgust. It was the most terrible

11

attempt I'd ever seen at subterfuge. Marika made the worst poor person I'd ever seen. She kicked the tire once and let out an oath ripe enough to make a sailor blush. I zoomed in on the rock decorating her ring finger, taking several quick shots of the tacky diamond. It had to be at least ten carats, though she was wearing it on her right hand, so it wasn't an engagement ring. If Noogey and Marika were truly in financial trouble, that ring would have been the first thing to go.

Marika threw the car in reverse, the gears grinding and tires squealing, before she sped out of the trailer park. I waited a good five minutes to make sure she was gone before I unfolded from behind the dumpsters. The sun was brutal, and I could feel the burn on the back of my neck and my nose. I needed ice cream, a bottle of water and a shower. In that order.

The surrounding trailers were quiet as I crept toward Noogey's, most of them having left for work bright and early. The flimsy knob and hole in the front door were a nice diversion, considering it also had two sturdy dead-bolts and the door was thick as a tree trunk. The windows were a heavy, double-paned glass, and I was willing to bet they were wired with a hell of a security system. They were coated with grime, dirt and a black film to keep anyone from being able to see in. Noogey was protecting something, that was for sure.

I walked the perimeter of the house and found a broken dog kennel by the back stairs that looked like it had been ground in a garbage disposal. I pushed it up to the window carefully, avoiding the sharp pieces of metal, and I climbed on top. I held on to the windowsill for balance, distributing my weight on each corner of the kennel as it creaked and wobbled beneath me.

My heart pounded in my chest and adrenaline coursed

through my veins as I lifted the camera above my head. All I needed was a weak spot in their security and this job would be done. Maybe the camera would be able to see something I couldn't. I started clicking the shutter as the wobbling below me increased, and I found it harder and harder to keep my balance.

I'd just decided to get down and try another window when the face of a beast crashed against the window—snarling jowls and strings of snot hanging between razor sharp teeth.

I screamed as the kennel collapsed beneath me and I went sprawling on the concrete, my arms wrapped around the camera to protect it. I hit on my back with a *whoomph* and the air was knocked out of me. Something sharp had pierced my leg, but I barely noticed, my eyes wide and unfocused as I focused on getting my breath back.

"Ouch," I croaked out.

The growls intensified and the window shook as the beast rammed its head over and over against the glass. If that was a dog, it was unlike any kind I'd ever seen before. Unless you counted Cujo.

I inhaled air painfully into my lungs and rolled to my hands and knees, looking around to make sure no one had witnessed my latest disaster. Granted, I'd gotten better at my job in the last few months, but that was probably along the same lines as telling Forrest Gump he was being promoted to remedial math.

The beast kept ramming its head against the window as I got to my feet. I gave it the middle finger because it made me feel better, and then I turned to head back to my car I'd left parked in a ditch near the marshland about a hundred yards away. My leg throbbed and blood coated the bottom part of my jeans. Good thing I'd already had a tetanus shot.

The growling and head butting stopped as suddenly as

it began, and I breathed a sigh of relief. It was short lived, because the door of the trailer shook with a mighty force as the beast rammed against it. Apparently, he didn't like being flipped off, because his determination only seemed to intensify.

I shook my head in pity at his stupidity and kept limping in the direction of my car. The trailer house doors were reinforced just like the windows, and there was no way that dog was breaking through. Noogey was definitely hiding something inside that trailer.

I heard a yelp and then silence, wondering if the dog had knocked himself out, and then I heard a different kind of noise. One resembling a can opener peeling back a metal lid.

"Oh, shit," I said, staring wide-eyed as I realized what the beast was doing. Maybe he wasn't so dumb after all.

The doors and windows to the trailer were reinforced, but the trailer wasn't. Teeth ripped through plastic siding and insulation, and I saw the metal on the outside of the trailer bulge and bend grotesquely, reminding me weirdly enough of when the alien was trying to burst out of Sigourney Weaver.

I started to run, the adrenaline and fear masking the pain my body was in, and I didn't look back as I heard the metal give. Vicious barks and snarls gained on me with alarming speed. My car came into view—an old white Volvo that had about 300,000 miles on it.

I'd left the windows down because the air conditioner didn't work and I was tired of the cracked leather seats cooking my ass. I'd never been so grateful to see that stupid car in my whole life. I dived head first into the open window and turned back to roll it up just as the beast hit the side of my car.

Seeing him in his entirety was completely different

then seeing his head through a window. He was the size of a horse and built like a monster truck. His fur was black with blotches of brown and gray and his paws were the size of dinner plates. It was safe to say the beast hadn't been neutered, considering he was half sprawled on my hood, humping the shit out of my side view mirror while he tried to eat his way through the metal to the inside of the car.

He changed positions and the passenger door caved in under his weight. I was trapped inside the Volvo oven, paralyzed with fear. Slobber and snot coated the car window, and all I could see was miles of snapping teeth and beady black eyes I'd see in my nightmares. My hands shook as I dug out the keys from my pocket, and it took me three tries before I was able to get the key in the ignition.

The car started easily, and I rammed it into drive, peeling out in a cloud of dust as I kept my foot on the accelerator. When I looked through the rearview mirror, the beast was still standing where I'd left him, his eyes intent on my car. With my luck, he was probably memorizing my license plate.

I rolled my windows back down to let the hot air out and decided I really needed a beer. Maybe a lot of beers. Unfortunately, there wasn't a drive-through beer store in the Savannah area. I was in no shape to go in anywhere. I'd have to settle for ice cream.

———

THANK GOD FOR DAIRY QUEEN. I WAS FINISHING OFF MY second Oreo Blizzard by the time I found a parking space in front of the McClean Detective Agency offices.

Kate had bought a corner building just across from Telfair Square. It was three stories of red crumbling brick being overtaken by the ivy that seemed to grow on every available surface in Savannah, and it was shaded by willow trees that looked as if they'd been there since the dawn of time.

I remembered to turn off the car and managed to get the door open without falling flat on my face into the street. I was fading fast. Maybe it was the adrenaline, maybe it was the blood loss, but I knew if I stayed out in the heat for another minute they'd have to scrape me off the hot pavement like a fried egg.

I focused on putting one foot in front of the other until I got to the glass-paned front door. A cold blast of air hit me in the face as I stumbled inside and I stood there in the entryway with my eyes closed, savoring it.

The agency was made to look like a comfortable home. The front entryway was large. Warm golden tiles sat in a diagonal pattern across the floor and rugs that picked up the color were scattered around. The walls were painted a lighter shade of gold and a leather couch and two matching chairs were placed in front of a large stone fireplace that never got used. A massive walnut desk sat in the center of the room, and the person who sat there guarded the inner sanctum of the agency with an iron fist.

Lucy Kim was technically the agency secretary. But I had a feeling she had some other duties as well—like ninja or vampire—but that was pure speculation. She was about five foot four—a few inches shorter than me—but her posture was rigid enough that she looked much taller. She was exotically beautiful—her Asian/American heritage giving her the best features of both—and her black hair was straight as rain down to her waist.

In the few months I'd been working for the agency, I'd never once seen any sort of emotional expression cross Lucy's face. I'd pretty much decided she wasn't human, but the look on her face now completely blew my theory out of the water.

She'd stood so fast when I came in that her ergonomic chair had rolled across the tiles and toppled over when it hit an electrical cord. Her hand was clasped over her nose and her black eyes were round and watery. She made small gagging noises before she finally gave up and ran down the hall.

I guess just because I could no longer smell myself didn't mean other people couldn't. No wonder the girl at Dairy Queen hadn't charged me for the ice cream and shoved the two sundaes at me through the drive-through window.

"What in the name of all that's holy is that smell?" I heard Kate yell from her office.

I heard office doors opening and footsteps shuffling as everyone searched for the offensive smell. I had a hand on the doorknob ready to hobble back to the car when Kate came into the lobby.

"Oh, it's you," she said, wrinkling her nose. She stuck her head back through the door and yelled, "It's all right. It's just Addison."

Heat rushed to my face as I heard the unhappy grumbles and office doors slamming closed.

"Sorry," I mumbled. "I'll go."

"No, stay right there. You're hurt," she said, her worried gaze zeroing in on my leg.

"It's not too bad." At least I didn't think it was too bad. I was going with the theory that if my leg was still attached, I was in no immediate danger. "It turns out Noogey has a big ass dog in his trailer."

"Noogey's a wily kind of guy," she said, her lips quirking slightly. "Let's get you cleaned up and then we'll talk when you're in better shape. I've got a new job for you."

"Will I have to hide in a dumpster?" I asked pathetically as I followed Kate down the hall to the large bathroom that was for agency use only.

"I doubt it. The FBI isn't fond of dumpsters."

I raised my brow at that bit of knowledge. I'd never worked with the FBI before. Kate usually gave those jobs to her more experienced agents, and quite frankly I was more than happy to let the more experienced agents take them. I wasn't even a real agent. I was a contract employee hired to do surveillance work. Period.

"I'm not meeting with the FBI contact until tomorrow, so don't hurry your shower," Kate said, putting a first aid kit on the sink, her hand still covering her nose. That was Kate code for *scrub more than once, preferably with bleach and a sander.*

I sighed and hoped I didn't drown. I wasn't feeling all that great and the day's events were starting to catch up to me. The good news was it was barely ten o'clock in the morning, so things would more than likely get better.

Kate left as quickly as possible and closed the door behind her. I had to peel my jeans away from the wounded area where the blood had dried, and I whimpered as I saw the deep cut in my calf. It oozed blood sluggishly, but I was pretty sure I could get away with bandaging it up myself. I wasn't a fan of stitches. Mostly, I didn't want to have to make another trip to the emergency room. The doctors there knew me by name.

I looked under the sink and found a thick black trash bag, the kind that wouldn't leak if you put a dismembered body inside, and I stripped out of my clothes, putting them in the bag and tying it tight.

On one side of the wall was a row of cubicles that held

personal belongings any of the agency employees might need. This wasn't the first time I'd had to use this shower, and I was almost positive it wouldn't be the last, so I had my own selection of soaps and lotions in the cubicle marked with my name. I grabbed shampoo, soap and a loofah and stepped under the hot spray of water.

I hissed as the water touched the cut on my leg and went through every curse I'd heard repeated in my thirty years of living. I grew up in a house with a cop, so I knew a lot of curses. The last thing I remember after I'd washed my hair and scrubbed my body twice was laying my face against the cold tile of the shower.

I think I might have fallen asleep because the next thing I knew, someone turned the water off and was lifting me out of the shower.

I inhaled a familiar scent and snuggled closer to the hard body that held me. Nick Dempsey wasn't the kind of man a woman forgot. He was a little over six feet. Whipcord lean with the body of a swimmer. He looked amazing with his clothes on and even better with them off. His hair was black and cut short, though it had a tendency to curl some on top when it grew out, and his eyes—sweet Jesus those eyes were a miracle. They were pale, arctic blue with silvery flecks. When he was aroused, they darkened a shade so it looked as if the ice were melting. When he was angry they could freeze you where you stood.

"Does this mean you're speaking to me again?" I asked.

"Let's not get carried away."

He wrapped a towel around me and set me down on the counter next to the sink. I finally gathered enough courage to look him in the face and wished I hadn't. His eyes were fixed on the cut on my leg and his lips were pinched with anger. He opened the first aid kit and rummaged around, kneeling in front of me as he made quick work of doctoring the cut and bandaging me up.

I tried my best to think about my grocery list and the piles of laundry I had waiting for me instead of the fact that Nick's face was about twenty-four inches away from a part of my body that wasn't wet because of the shower.

I breathed a sigh of relief when he stood back up, but the relief quickly turned to worry as he slapped both hands on either side of me, effectively trapping me against him. His face was like granite and I knew I was in for it.

"Are you mad about my leg or because I shot you?" I asked.

His gaze snapped to mine and I tried to pull the towel tighter around me, but it was caught under his fingers.

"I have a list that grows longer every day," he said. "Your job is to take pictures from a distance. How in the hell do you keep ending up looking like a crash test dummy? Your palms are scraped, you've got bruises all down your back, your leg is cut bad enough that it might need stitches, and you're so sunburned I can feel the heat coming off your body from here."

Now that he mentioned it, I was starting to feel the aches and pains of my other injuries. Nick's voice got softer and softer the longer he kept talking, and I knew his temper was about to reach explosive proportions.

"I had to start taking blood pressure medication," he said. "Every time I got a call I was afraid someone was going to tell me you were dead. And believe me, after all the stunts you've managed to involve yourself in, I get a lot of calls."

I narrowed my eyes and remembered exactly why Nick had no say in my life anymore. We'd had a rough relationship since we met three months ago. We'd been hot enough to set each other on fire. For a while. Then I caught him with another woman, and I was hot enough to do something drastic. This was the first I'd seen of him in weeks.

"You have no right to get mad over anything," I said, slapping my hand against his chest, the towel forgotten. "You made it perfectly clear that we're not in a relationship any more, and you have no say in my life."

He growled low in his throat and I could feel the rumble from his chest against my hand.

"I have every right to be mad. You fucking shot me in the ass with a tranquilizer gun."

His teeth were grinding together so hard I was surprised he could get the words past his lips, and a tiny vein bulged in his temple.

The anger I'd been trying to repress the last few months was coming to the surface in a hurry, and I didn't do the quiet voice when I got angry. I became a firestorm of waving arms and Arsenio Hall whoops, and I channeled every antebellum ancestor I'd ever had, so my accent grew thick as honey.

"It's not like I shot you with bullets. You're overreacting. Though you're damned lucky I didn't have a real gun on me or I might have. You were with another woman. At a motel. In the middle of the day. What the hell else was I supposed to think? All I know is that one minute you had me naked and panting, and you were finally about to be inside of me, and the next thing I know, your cell phone is going off and you're running out of my apartment like your pants were on fire. And then twelve hours later I see you at a motel talking to a woman who was trying her best to get you to turn your head and cough. What was I supposed to think?"

"She was an informant." Exasperation tinged his voice. "I've already tried to explain this to you, but you're too stubborn to listen. And that doesn't excuse the fact that you shot me with an elephant tranquilizer."

"Are we done here?" I asked, pushing against him so I could slide off the counter.

My knees gave out and Nick caught me around the waist, holding me close to his body until I got my balance. I sucked in a breath at the contact and closed my eyes to savor the feel of our bodies touching. I looked up and saw his eyes smolder with pleasure as he brought me closer, so we were completely aligned. The towel had dropped to the ground and my nipples hardened to pebbles as they pressed against his chest. His mouth hovered just an inch away from mine so our breaths mingled, and I wanted nothing more than to take a bite of his full lower lip.

The chemistry between us was definitely still there. Too bad I had lousy taste in men. If we started kissing now it would be hard to stop, and as much as I wanted to taste him, we had too many unsettled issues between us. I pushed away from him and bent down to grab the towel, wrapping it around me securely.

"What are you doing here?" I asked, not meeting his eyes this time. I felt his sigh and wanted to give one of my own. We were a mess.

"I brought you some clothes. Kate said to burn the ones you were wearing. You must have smelled pretty bad. The entire lobby reeks of disinfectant."

"It wasn't one of my finer moments. Thanks for the clothes. You can go now."

He smiled and heat shot straight to my loins. "Don't think you're going to get rid of me so easily," he said. "We're going to be seeing a lot of each other over the next few weeks. I'm the lead detective assigned to work with the FBI on the case Kate mentioned to you. It made it easier since I already act as media liaison through the department."

Nick's a detective for the Savannah PD, and last I'd heard he was working homicide. He'd been assigned as media liaison because he had the patience of a saint and the looks of a movie star. I couldn't imagine what type of case would involve a homicide detective, the FBI and a P.I. agency, and I wasn't sure I wanted to know.

I propped my fist on my hip and glared at Nick. "Ununh," I said, shaking my head. "There's no way I'm working with you. You'd probably get distracted by all your *informants* trying to stick their tongues down your throat, and then I'd get arrested for killing you."

Nick fisted my towel in his hand and pulled me toward him, making my breath catch at the dangerous look in his eyes. He was either going to throttle me or kiss me, I wasn't sure which.

His lips touched mine gently, though I could feel the anger vibrating through his body, and his tongue caressed mine as if he were tasting his last meal. By the time he pulled away I was breathing like a steam engine and I was pretty sure the towel had disintegrated from the heat my body was giving off. My female parts were screaming, *this one*, and my heart wasn't too far behind. Luckily my brain had better sense. My heart had already been trampled on and was in no mood to repeat the process.

"I like it when you're jealous. And despite you shooting me up with tranquilizers, the only person I want to stick my tongue into is you."

My eyes almost crossed at the imagery that one statement brought to mind. I knew from experience that Nick's tongue was a miracle.

"Looks like I still know how to shut you up," he said. His eyes gleamed with unconcealed humor and his dimples fluttered briefly as he opened the bathroom door to make his escape.

I grabbed a hairbrush from one of the cubicles and launched it at his head. It thudded against the door as he slammed it shut, and I could hear his laughter from the other side.

"You sure know how to brighten a man's day," he yelled through the door.

I tried my best to get the stupid grin off my face, but damned if he didn't make me feel the same way. All of a sudden, I was really looking forward to the new job Kate had for me to do. I was going through Nick Dempsey withdrawal. That man had been driving me crazy for months, and if I had to wait even another day to feel him naked against me it was a day too long.

I looked at myself in the mirror and barely contained a screech of horror. My face was the color of an overripe tomato and my dark hair was drying in tangled tufts. My eyes were bloodshot and my pupils so dilated I could barely see the small ring of brown.

So maybe I'd have to wait two days to get him naked. I could be patient.

2

B y the time I'd gotten dressed and out of the bathroom, Kate had been called away from the office. She'd left a note on her door for me to come back early the next morning so she could brief me before the meeting. I was clueless as to why she'd want someone with my limited abilities for this particular assignment—unless they needed cannon fodder—which was highly probable.

My hometown of Whiskey Bayou was a ten-minute drive south of Savannah. By the time I passed the *Now Entering Whiskey Bayou, The First Drink's On Us* sign just on the outside of town, my seatbelt felt like it was strangling me and my fingers were gripping the wheel so tight my knuckles were white.

Don't get me wrong, the town is picturesque in a Pleasantville meets Deliverance kind of way, but it was an adjustment. And I was still adjusting after thirty years of living there.

It was an island of sorts and built on boggy ground, so the buildings shifted and looked as drunk as the town founders had been. The Walker Whiskey Distillery squatted short and fat in the center of town, run down and vacant for more than forty years. The bank, gas station, sheriff's department, and other assorted businesses sat around the square, paying homage to the sinking historical albatross of the distillery, stuck in 1942 forever.

Going home always made me want to drive into the marsh. Especially since I was now living with my mother. A couple of months back, my apartment building had been condemned and bulldozed to the ground. I'd finally decided I could afford a tiny one-bedroom apartment in Savannah when I got the news that Veronica Wade, my archenemy and supreme bitch of the universe, had decided to sue me because one of her breast implants had popped during a fight we'd gotten into. It had been a doozy of a fight, and we'd gotten a first page write up in the Whiskey Bayou Gazette. I'd also gotten stun-gunned on the ass, so I preferred not to think about the fight too often.

I'd like to say I was ashamed of myself, but that would be a lie. It had felt damned good to take out years of hostility and abuse by getting physical. Veronica had been the bane of my existence for more than twenty-five years. She'd been the one who stole my lunch money, and she'd been the one who'd put super glue on my oboe reed. I liked to think that karma had my back this time around with the whole implant explosion. Except for the lawsuit.

Fortunately, there had been enough cops around as witnesses that her suit had been dismissed in court, but I'd still had to pay all the court and legal fees. Which was why I was driving a twenty-year-old Volvo that had a hole in the passenger side floor instead of my sweet little 350Z. The car was only one of the numerous setbacks I'd had over the past few months.

I was a ninth grade history teacher, I was thirty years

old, and I was living with my mother. That translated to *deadbeat loser* in the eyes of most people. And if the gossip mill was right, I was about to be an unemployed deadbeat loser. Which was why I had no choice now but to kamikaze my way through the cases Kate kept handing me.

I'd managed to live with this down in the dumps feeling hanging over me for the last six weeks—a combination of desperation and wondering when the axe was going to fall and lop off my head. I was getting an ulcer, though I'd somehow managed to survive my current trials and tribulations without jamming a fork in my eye. But the urge to self-mutilate was becoming stronger every time I pulled into the driveway of my mother's house. I was going to have to find another place to live. Soon. And maybe change my name and hair color. I've always wanted to be a blonde.

I waved at Mrs. Meador as she swept the walk in front of The Good Luck Café—a thankless job since the clapboard sidewalk never seemed to be free of mud and sand. I wound through the crooked streets of Whiskey Bayou and turned left off of Main Street onto Shot Glass Drive, and then I took another left on Tumbler Street until I came to my mother's house.

It was a small, cottage-style house made of gray stone with a dark shingled roof, and it was the last house on a dead-end street of similar houses. The front door was painted bright red, and magenta and yellow flowers sprang up out of the planter boxes beneath all the windows.

It was a cute house, and it probably would have been a nice place to grow up if there'd been more than one bathroom. As it was, the thoughts of my childhood home brought back memories of pounding fists on doors and screaming matches between me and my sister.

My mom's Dodge Charger, an exact replica of the General Lee from the Dukes of Hazzard that she'd bought off eBay with the insurance money from my dad's death, was missing from the driveway. She was a huge fan of the show, and she said driving the car through Whiskey Bayou was a great way to keep the old people out of her way because the engine sounded like it came from a monster truck or Hell's Angels, and you could hear it coming a mile away.

I breathed a huge sigh of relief that I'd gotten lucky and had beaten her home. I didn't need her to see me in my current condition. Not that she'd lecture me or anything about being careful. My mom was a free spirit and didn't often think of things like safety or taking preventative measures. More likely she'd give me suggestions on how to do better and insist on accompanying me on my next job. It's happened before. And as much as I hated to admit it, I had a sinking suspicion that I was a lot like my mom.

What I didn't expect to see was the bright yellow Volkswagen Beetle parked in front of the house. I was starting to wonder if I'd done something to piss off God, because it really felt like I couldn't catch a break. I mean, there was that one incident where I'd almost had sex in a church crypt, but I'd felt really bad about it afterwards, so I figured I'd been forgiven. Apparently not.

The Beetle could only belong to one person—Rosemarie Valentine.

Rosemarie taught choir in the room next to mine at James Madison High. It wasn't easy teaching about the Battle of Little Big Horn over the constant sound of Rosemarie's warbling contralto. I kept a bowl of earplugs by my door on test days and frequently wished I could keep Jack Daniels in my desk drawer. She was a nice woman, but being with her was like herding toddlers or small dogs. I lacked the energy.

The Beetle's engine shut off and the door was flung

open, birthing Rosemarie from its interior with a lot of groans and flailing arms and legs. Her curly blonde hair was somewhat wilted by the heat and only added about three inches to the circumference of her head instead of the normal five. Rosemarie wasn't a small woman, and I could almost feel the Beetle giving a sigh of relief at her exit.

I shook my head and blinked my eyes as I got my first full view of Rosemarie's outfit. It was a one-piece short suit made of terrycloth—something I normally didn't see on anyone but two year olds or Snooki. This one was bright orange and strapless, and the only thing holding it together was well sewn seams and a prayer. My mouth dropped open in shock as the elastic band trying to contain Rosemarie's breasts gave up the good fight and snapped down to expose a pair of the whitest mounds of flesh I'd ever seen.

The elastic snapped so hard I was surprised her breasts didn't bounce up and put an eye out, but Rosemarie shoved those puppies back in with all the determination of a woman at an *All you can cram in a paper bag for $5* garage sale.

I finally found the courage to get out of the car, my muscles protesting and my movements slower than normal—not that that was saying much. I noticed Rosemarie pulling a giant basket of fruit from the car and my curiosity at her arrival went up a notch. All she needed was a Carmen Miranda style hat and she could have been the spokesperson for Chiquita Banana.

"Yoohoo, Addison," Rosemarie warbled, as if she had to catch my attention for me to see her. "How are you holding up, dear?"

I looked down at my borrowed black athletic shorts

and lime green tank top, the stark white bandage on my leg and my bare feet and said, "I've been better."

"Well, just keep your chin up. Everything will work out okay. You've got your friends to see you through."

I was beginning to wonder if someone had died and I'd just forgotten as we made our way to the red front door. It was unlocked, because Whiskey Bayou was still the kind of town where the older generation still felt safe leaving their doors unlocked, even though I knew some of the kids I taught would probably end up in prison in the next few years.

I ushered us into the air-conditioned house, immediately falling to the orange and brown velour sofa with mutant flowers my mom had bought when she and my dad first married. I was pretty much out of southern hospitality at this point, but Rosemarie just acted like nothing was out of the ordinary and set the fruit basket on the coffee table.

"What's with the fruit basket?" I asked.

"All of the teachers took up a donation, and this is the best fruit basket money can buy. I read the statistics about how those who lived in poverty were most likely to get scurvy, and I thought this would help with your health."

She beamed at me, obviously trying to keep things upbeat, the two perfect dots of pink rouge on her cheeks quivering from the strain. A sinking feeling of dread began to curl in the pit of my stomach and I slowly sat up on the couch.

"Why would all of you think I'm at the poverty level? What's going on here?"

I mean, technically I probably was at the poverty level with all the debt and fees I'd had to pay recently, but everyone knew it wasn't polite to tell someone they were considered poverty stricken to their face. That was something done behind a person's back.

Rosemarie gasped and her cornflower blue eyes practically bulged out of their sockets. "Don't tell me they haven't told you yet," she said, pressing a hand dramatically to her breast. "Those cowards. They know there's going to be backlash because you had quite a crowd of parents and students there to support you at the school board meeting last night. You are a good teacher after all. You just sometimes make poor decisions. And really only the once. Or maybe twice," Rosemarie amended, finally winding down.

"They fired me?" I asked, the reality of what that meant finally sinking in. "I didn't really think they would."

I was chilled from the inside out, and I shivered violently, unable to decide if I wanted to break down into tears or throw up. I think my bodily functions were confused because it turned out I could do neither, so I just laid back down on the couch and stared at the ceiling.

Of course, they'd had grounds for letting me go. I knew that as soon as I'd made the mistake of taking a job as a stripper at the Foxy Lady. It didn't matter that I'd only had the job for thirty-two minutes or that I was really bad at it. I'd been in desperate need of money and I'd made a bad decision. Not one of the better moments in my life. And I'd qualified my reasoning by telling myself that me making a little extra money on the side was no different than Marylou Waldrip, who taught economics, giving piano lessons after school, or Peter Newberry, the football coach, working at the Piggly Wiggly when his wife left him high and dry.

I'd even made it a point to go into Savannah for the job. I never could have imagined that I'd see my principal in the audience during my brief career in exotic dancing. And to compound the problem, I'd found him dead in the parking lot shortly after. Luck hadn't been on my side, and I knew I'd have to face the consequences of my actions. I just never expected things to go this far.

"Now you can't let something like this get you down," Rosemarie said, too cheerfully. "You've got to look at this as an opportunity. This is your chance to be whatever it is you've always wanted to be."

I watched as she dug around in her giant orange Vera Bradley purse until she came out with a pen and pad.

"We're going to make a list of everything you've ever wanted to do, and then we'll find you a job. No offense, but you're not likely to find a man now that you're living with your mother, and you're getting to that age that's the point of no return as far as getting married."

I realized the low growling sound was coming from me and made an effort to relax. Rosemarie was only trying to help. It wasn't her fault she had the subtlety of a neutron bomb.

"Okay, I'm ready," she said, clicking her pen. "Tell me everything you've ever wanted to do in your life."

"Well," I said thoughtfully, "I wanted to be a rock star when I was fifteen because I had a crush on Billy Lee Gentry and I was sure he was going to make it in the big time, but I found out early on I didn't do well with leather pants," I said, remembering the sound my thighs made every time I tried to walk. "Not to mention it's never a good idea to wear leather this far south. The chafing isn't pleasant."

"Not to mention you can't sing a lick," Rosemarie said, making notes on her pad.

I narrowed my eyes, and the only thing keeping me from launching myself at her was the fact that she was right.

"What else?" she asked.

"It's a long list. I had six majors in college before I finally decided to teach history. My interests are varied."

My father had liked to say that I'd lacked focus. My mother had always countered that I was just trying to find myself. I was starting to lose hope, because I still wasn't all that sure I'd found myself. I'd just stuck me in a rut and kept paddling to make it seem like I was in control of things.

"I've also wanted to be a potter, an interior designer, a shoemaker, a trophy wife, an archer, a spy, and have my own show on the Travel Channel. Do you think there's a job market out there for any of those?" I asked.

Rosemarie stared at me with her mouth hanging open, as if I were the one with my breasts exposed this time, and I looked down just to make sure I was still covered.

"There are barely job openings right now for people who want to be bank tellers or receptionists. I'm not sure this list idea is going to work after all. Maybe you just need to get used to the idea of not being a teacher for a little while. Go file for unemployment, and then you can research your options."

"You know," I said, sitting up as a brilliant idea came to me. "I've really enjoyed the work I've done for Kate these last few months."

"Except for the maimings and embarrassing mishaps—"

I glared at Rosemarie and she made a sign like she was zipping her lips.

"I bet I could make a lot more money if I became a full-time private detective. I could get my license and carry a gun and everything. I could be just like Jessica Fletcher, without the pastel sweater sets, of course."

I didn't think Rosemarie's eyes could get any bigger but they managed.

"That's a great idea," she said, bouncing a little on the

chair across from me, the seams of her onesie stretching to epic proportions. "Maybe I should take the classes with you. It'd be good to have a fallback if teaching doesn't work out for me. I don't want to be stuck in a situation like you with no career to fall back on. Do you think they'd want me to lose weight? I know I'm a curvy woman, but I could probably bench press a truck if I had to. Men like curves, and I'd hate to be forced to waste away to nothing just so I could be a spy. It seems to me that the best disguise is my own self."

It's true, I thought. No one would ever expect a spy to go around in an orange terrycloth jumpsuit. I cleared my throat and tried to think of something polite to say, but I was at a loss. Though it wouldn't have mattered because Rosemarie was now on a mission. Full steam ahead.

She gathered her purse and pushed herself out of the chair. "Make sure you tell me what we need to do to become real private eyes. I'm gonna go shopping for spy clothes. And don't worry, I'll get something for you too. I know spy clothes won't fit in your budget right now and you can't go around dressed like that," she said, waving her hand in the general direction of my borrowed clothes.

I closed my eyes when I heard the front door snick shut behind her. Getting my private detective's license was the most logical step to take, considering my current situation. Kate was going to have kittens when she found out this was what I'd decided to do. Nick would probably have a coronary.

But as crazy as the idea was, it felt like the right decision. I'd decide what to do about Rosemarie later. Much later. I drifted off to sleep with the image of Rosemarie wrenched into a black leather corset, knives strapped to her arms, and a Zorro mask tied over her eyes. Even my subconscious knew that things were probably about to get very interesting.

I WOKE TO THE OVERWHELMING SMELL OF ONIONS AND SOME kind of fried meat. My mom had never really gotten the hang of cooking, but it never stopped her from trying. She hadn't killed any of us yet, and usually there was something salvageable on the plate to tide you over until you could sneak back to the kitchen for a bowl of ice cream or Chef Boyardee.

Voices spoke in low whispers from the kitchen, and I buried my face into the couch cushions when I realized who was talking to my mother. His name was Vince Walker, and he'd been my dad's partner for a lot of years up until my dad died about a year and a half ago. Dad had been too young to die, but he'd had a massive heart attack while watching a Falcons game and was gone in an instant. No warning or early symptoms. It had taken us all by surprise. I missed him terribly.

Vince was a good cop and very distinguished looking, his dark hair threaded with silver and his shoulders broad and muscular—kind of like James Brolin on steroids. He was a distant relative of the Walkers who owned the whiskey distillery our town had been founded around, and he'd been hanging around at the house a lot lately. His interest in my mom was plain for anyone to see, and she blushed like a schoolgirl whenever he was around. But my dad's death was still too recent for me to deal well with another man in the picture. Yet another reason for me to escape the house as soon as possible.

I dragged myself off the couch and into the bathroom to splash water on my face, and then headed into the kitchen. My mom was at the stove doing something scandalous to potatoes and Vince was standing entirely too close behind her, as if the secret to frying potatoes was related to the movement of his hips. I narrowed my eyes and went straight to the fridge to get a beer.

My mom broke out of his embrace and came over to give me a hug. "I heard about your job when I was buying groceries this morning. It's all that stupid Stella Larson could talk about standing behind the register. She never did have a lick of sense."

I put my head down on her shoulder and just took a minute to bathe in the comfort of her arms like I was a little kid again.

"Well, she has good reason to talk," I said. "This should keep mouths running for a few weeks at least."

"Nonsense," my mother said, patting me once on the back before going back to the potatoes and draining them. "As soon as Mitch Clumsky gets arrested for beating on that poor wife of his again, everyone will forget all about you."

For as long as I'd known Mrs. Clumsky, I wasn't sure I'd ever heard anyone call her by her first name. Everyone always called her Mitch's poor wife, since he'd been drinking away his paychecks and taking it out on her their entire married life. She would never press charges and she refused to take help from the neighbors who kept trying.

I grunted in agreement and went to set the table. The three of us sat down and I looked at the meatloaf and the surrounding bowls of food, congealed and lumpy. Vince put on a brave face and started dishing out the food. He must have really liked my mom, and it made me smile a little at his determination.

"So have you thought about your other options?" he asked, trying to cut through the meatloaf with his fork. He finally gave up and went to get a steak knife out of the silverware drawer.

"I have, actually," I said, tackling my own meatloaf. "Maybe you could give me some pointers."

"Sure, what do you have in mind?"

"You know I've been doing surveillance work for Kate, but I figure I can make twice as much money if I become an actual agent. I've decided to get my private investigator's license."

The piece of meatloaf Vince had finally managed to get into his mouth fell out onto his plate and he covered his face with his napkin as he started coughing. Before he could say anything about it one way or the other, my mother piped in.

"That's a terrific idea," she said, clasping her hands together. "Don't you think, Vince? She's done such a great job bringing down those lowlifes. I saw her with my own eyes. She'd be a natural. Just like Jessica Fletcher. But without the sweaters."

Vince had the wild-eyed, panicked look of a man whose woman had him by the balls, and he nodded reluctantly.

"Do you know the requirements for the state of Georgia?" I asked Vince, a full smile coming to my face for the first time that day.

He cleared his throat and said, "Kate can probably give you the specifics, but as far as I know it's a written test, and then you'll have to go through the Citizens' Police Academy. You might want to see what Kate thinks about this. All of her agents are either current or former cops. They've got a lot of experience, which is why her agency has such a good reputation."

"Kate's going to think this is a *great* idea," I lied cheerfully.

In reality, Kate was going to think this was one of the

worst ideas I'd ever had, right up there with the time I'd decided to give the both of us home perms and burned our hair off to the scalp.

But I knew Kate. She was the best friend I had in the entire world. She'd bluster and try to talk me out of it, but when push came to shove, she'd be there for me because she'd know I needed the help.

After dinner and the dishes were done, I headed to my childhood room with a sense of peace I probably shouldn't have felt considering the situation. The house was a perfect square—living room, dining room, and kitchen at the front of the house, and three bedrooms and a bathroom at the back. The master bedroom was in the middle and the two smaller bedrooms on each side. It was always best to keep me and my sister separated whenever possible, so there had been a modicum of peace in the house during our teenage years.

My room was still decorated with yellow walls and white lace Priscilla curtains. A full size bed sat in front of the window and a chest of drawers was pushed into the corner. There were still Nirvana and Pearl Jam posters on the wall, a shelf filled with books and trophies, and pictures tacked to a bulletin board of me and Kate and me and my dad.

The room was comforting and terrifying at the same time, but now instead of seeing myself living out the rest of my days in this room, I saw the possibility of something else. I had a purpose. I was making the right decision. *A good decision.* I was an intelligent human being. Surely I could become a competent agent over time. Maybe all I needed was the right mentor.

The thought had Nick's face flashing through my mind, and I fanned myself with my hand like an adolescent girl. Maybe Nick and I had needed a few weeks of cooling off.

It had been instant attraction between us, but we'd slowly been getting to know each other when the tranquilizer incident happened. And if I hadn't seen red the moment I saw him with another woman—another woman who had no business touching him the way she had been, informant or not—then we would have already been sleeping together.

Maybe now that I knew what I wanted to be when I grew up, it was a good time to rekindle things as far as my love life went. With that settled, I turned my iPod on random and Patsy Cline's Crazy came on first thing. I shook my head and went to bed, wondering if the Fates were also in charge of the soundtrack of my life. I couldn't seem to turn my mind off, so I lounged on the bed, staring at a poster of Marky Mark above my head.

I'd lost track of the time somewhere, and maybe I'd actually dozed for a while, but my eyes popped open when Def Leopard's Pour Some Sugar on Me came on, accompanied by an unusual and atonal noise that didn't belong. At first I thought someone had broken into the house. I reached into my nightstand drawer to grab my nail file just in case it was an axe murderer, while I felt around in the dark for my cell phone so I could call 911.

My eyes widened as the sounds became more familiar and the need to retch violently became most prevalent in my mind. Apparently Vince had decided to stay the night. From the animalistic sounds coming from the room next to mine, and the rhythmic thumping of the bed hitting the wall, I was guessing he was planning to stay *all* night.

I'd spent eighteen years in this house growing up, and in all those years I'd never heard those sounds coming through the wall. Not that I didn't think my parents had sex or anything. But I'm pretty sure they never had the kind of sex that my mother was now having with Vince.

Come to think of it, I'm not sure I've ever had that kind of sex.

I shook my head violently to clear out the images that were bombarding my fragile psyche. This was not something any daughter should have to listen to, no matter how old. And there was no way in hell I'd be able to face either of them in the morning.

I slapped a pillow over my head and tried to suffocate the sounds out, but they were hitting their stride and nothing but death was going to keep me from hearing. I waited patiently for half an hour, thinking surely it would have to end soon, but they were still going strong and I couldn't take it any longer.

I got dressed quickly in denim shorts and a stretchy tank top and slipped on my flip-flops. I shoved a few belongings into an overnight bag and was glad I'd opened the window earlier so my escape didn't make unnecessary noise. I'd perfected the art of sneaking out during my teenage years, and I hadn't lost the touch.

I jumped in the Volvo and waited to close the car door until I'd pulled out of the driveway and was down the street. Not that I thought Mom and Vince would stop what they were doing to listen to my escape, but I didn't want to throw them off their stride.

The problem with escaping in the middle of the night was that I didn't exactly have anywhere to go. I could call Kate, but she'd done enough for me lately. I didn't want to get her out of bed in the middle of the night. I could call Rosemarie, but I'd have to share the guest bed with her two Great Danes. My third option was Nick, but he'd have my clothes off by the time I crossed the threshold, and I was still sunburned and in pain. My last option was the agency. I had a key to the outer door, and I'd have access to the shower and the lounge, which had an overstuffed couch I could sleep on.

With the decision made, I headed toward Savannah. And the first chance I got, I was going to look for another place to live. I had enough to make a deposit, and if I ate like I was in college again I could probably pay most of my bills every month. Maybe every other month.

3

F*riday*

"WHAT DO YOU KNOW ABOUT VINCE WALKER?" I ASKED Kate the next morning.

She hadn't looked surprised to see me asleep on the couch when she'd come into the office a little after seven. Nothing much surprised Kate, so I rolled off the couch and followed her into her office, my clothes rumpled from sleep.

Kate's boxy linen suit was already creased with wrinkles and her hair was still damp from her shower. She'd pushed it back with a black headband, and her face was free of makeup except for a touch of mascara. Kate was one of those women who didn't need makeup. Her skin was flawless, her cheeks naturally rosy and her gray eyes wide and clear. She had a cute little button nose and delicately arched brows a shade darker than her blond hair.

43

She hadn't changed much since high school—mostly she was a little fuller in the hip and a lot more cynical.

"He's a good cop," she answered. "Solid reputation and someone who's looked up to in the department. No smirches on his name or badge. I'd think you'd know all that considering he was your dad's partner for ten years. What's going on?"

"Yeah, well, sometimes it's hard to know what a person's really like until it's too late. Especially when they ruin a perfectly good song." I'd forever associate Pour Some Sugar on Me with debilitating gorilla sex.

I watched Kate go through her morning ritual—hang ugly suit jacket on the coatrack by the door, lock gun in desk drawer, turn on computer, get messages out of the box that had arrived after she'd left the office. Kate was very regimented. It was an impressive sight to see, and I wished frequently that I could be more like Kate.

I sighed and went to the Keurig coffeemaker she kept on a sideboard, making us both a cup and doctoring it the way she liked—with too much sugar and a third of a cup of milk. I'd never seen the point of drinking coffee at all if you were just going to turn it into dessert. I sat in the chair across from her massive walnut desk and waited for her to sit down, staying unusually silent.

Instead of taking the chair behind her desk, she sat in the one next to me and gave me an arched look.

"Spill it, Addison. What do you know about Vince that I don't?" she asked.

"You have to promise not to laugh. And you can't tell anyone."

She rolled her eyes at me. "I won't tell anyone."

"Let's just say that Vince doesn't seem to have a problem with premature ejaculation. And the walls of my bedroom are thinner than I thought."

She tipped her head back and laughed until tears rolled down her cheeks.

"You promised not to laugh."

"No, I promised not to tell anyone," she hiccupped. "Jesus, Addison. That is not something I needed to have a visual of. So your mom is doing the nasty with Vince, huh?" Kate's grin was evil and I shot her a dirty look.

"Either that or he was giving her a hell of a pelvic exam."

"All women should be so lucky."

The bitterness in Kate's voice had my head snapping up and my eyes zeroing in on her face, but Kate was really good at not showing anything she didn't want to be seen. A hell of a poker player was Kate.

She'd been married for a handful of years to Mike McClean, another Savannah cop, and I'd never gotten the impression that anything was wrong in their relationship. In fact, I would have described their devotion to one another as damned near perfect. Before I could ask if anything was wrong, she changed the subject, and I knew whatever it was, she wasn't ready to talk about it.

"The FBI will be here at ten to meet with us about the case," she said. "It's very high profile and they're trying to keep it as quiet as possible, so everything said in this room is privileged information. Understood?"

I made an X over my heart and tried to look trustworthy and unassuming. The secrecy was my least favorite part of the job, considering most women in the south cut their teeth on gossip.

"No offense, but I can't imagine why you'd need me for this job. It doesn't seem like the sort of thing you'd use me for."

She smiled and moved out of the chair next to me and into the one behind her desk. "Normally you'd be right, but we're dealing with professional criminals in this case, and professionals can sense a cop a mile away."

I straightened my shoulders and examined the cuticles on my nails. I needed a manicure, only that was one of the recent budget crunches I'd had to make.

"I've decided I'm not going to take offense at that statement," I said. "I'm going to pretend like you need me because I'm so good at blending with my surroundings."

"Yeah, you blended right in with the bushes when you fell out of that tree on your last case."

Kate opened a thick file on her desk and pushed it toward me. The photo on top was gruesome enough that I felt the color drain from my face and a clammy sweat pop out on my skin.

"Geez, Kate. Warn a girl, would you?"

"Sorry. This whole mess started when a man named Christian DeLuce was the highest bidder for a package of loose gems during a series of auctions the Russian government was holding to raise money. The gems supposedly belonged to the Romanovs, and DeLuce bought them sight unseen."

"Christian DeLuce, jewelry designer for the stars? That Christian DeLuce?" I asked.

"The one and only."

"Why would he buy gems sight unseen?"

"Apparently, that's all the rage right now among jewelry designers. It lends a little mystery, as well as history, to whatever pieces they design. Countries in need of actual cash are making a killing doing auctions this way. They state only how many loose gems are in the package—not what kind or the carat. They promise the gems came from a specific time in history, and were worn by specific historical figures. The bidding wars normally exceed six figures, sometimes seven. The jewelers in turn easily make that back ten fold because the story is often more lucrative than the actual gems. Though to be fair, all of the gems auctioned so far have been of good quality, if not especially large."

"Nice," I said, turning the photo of the mutilated corpse over since I couldn't seem to stop staring at it. "I assume the body that looks like it's been through a meat grinder and left in the sun too long is important to this case somehow?"

"DeLuce made the money transfer from his bank after he won the bid on the gems per the auction rules, and the package was opened via Skype so he could see what he'd gotten out of the deal. Turns out there was an engraved emerald the size of a baby's fist inside that hasn't been seen since the reign of Catherine the Great."

I let out a low whistle and looked at a photocopy of the emerald. "The Heart of Ivan," I said, recognizing it immediately. "Lots of rumors about the emerald's origin, but apparently Ivan the Terrible procured it through dubious means from China's Jiajing Emperor."

"No one cares about Ivan the Terrible," Kate said, getting up for more coffee. "It's the Romanov legends that send all the crazies out."

I gave Kate an arched look. "As I was saying, Ivan's first wife, Anastasia Romanovna—"

"Oh," she said sheepishly. "Sorry. You know I could never stay awake during history."

"Anyway, Anastasia became ill not long after she and Ivan married. She was very young, early thirties if I remember right, and she was really the only one able to truly keep Ivan's temper under control. The sickness tore through her body for weeks, leaving her frail and unable to eat. Ivan reportedly never left her side and was out of his mind with worry because he really did love her."

I sighed a little because I'm a romantic at heart. I cry at commercials and sappy greeting cards, and despite the hand fate's dealt my love life, I believe in happily ever after. Kate shook her head at me and I knew she'd read my mind.

"Ivan somehow got word about the emerald and that it supposedly had healing powers, so his men took it from the emperor of China, and Ivan brought it to her while she was in the last hours on her death bed, hoping for a miracle."

Kate's eyes were starting to glaze over, and I shook my head in wonderment that the two of us could be so different. Tingles were shooting all through my body at the excitement that a new piece of history might be discovered, and Kate looked like she was about to bury her cat.

"I take it the emerald didn't do the job?" she asked.

"Nope. It turns out poor Anastasia was poisoned, so there wasn't anything that could have been done for her. She died anyway, and what little sanity Ivan had left died with her. His reign of bat shit insanity started shortly thereafter, and accounts say Ivan wanted to have the emerald ground to dust, but the Romanov family had a clearer head and put the emerald away with the rest of the family jewels until Anastasia's grandnephew, Mikhail, took over the Tsardom."

"Huh," Kate said, shaking her head. "Anyway, after the sale was completed and DeLuce gave the approval to transport the gems, a courier was dispatched with the package to the United States with plans to hand them over to DeLuce here in Savannah."

"I didn't realize DeLuce was from Savannah," I interrupted.

"He's an implant," she said with a shrug. "Said California drove him crazy and he likes to make the celebrities come to him as some sort of power trip. He's known for his eccentric behavior, and for being a bit dramatic. His shop is only a few blocks from here. Very exclusive and expensive."

"I take it DeLuce and the courier never met up?"

"Bingo," Kate said. "The courier didn't show up. Turns out he'd been shot point blank in the face and shoved in a waste barrel for a couple of days, so he was unable to attend the meeting. Then DeLuce calls Russia and gives them some of his temper because his gems didn't show up and he's out half a million dollars. Russia's pissed because they say the emerald was never supposed to be in the package in the first place and the courier never should have left the country to deliver it."

"So it's a complete clusterfuck is what you're saying."

"Oh, yeah. The FBI is involved because this is considered international gem theft. Also because the jewels that had been in the briefcase attached to the courier's arm were removed—along with the arm—and because the body was moved across state lines into Savannah. The Savannah police are involved because they discovered the body at the docks. And we're involved because Christian DeLuce has hired us to find his gems and get them back to him before someone from Russia can get here and whisk the emerald back across the ocean."

"And I'm here again, why?" I asked. This sounded so out of my league I didn't even know where to start.

"Because you work for me and the FBI told me to find someone they could use that didn't look like a cop. The FBI also wanted someone young and female for what they have in mind. And no, I don't know why," she said just as I was opening my mouth to ask. "I'm sure Agent Savage will tell us why during the meeting."

"Agent Savage? Seriously?"

"That coming from someone with the last name Holmes," Kate said.

"Touché, my friend. Very good." I stood up and grabbed my purse. I had a little over two hours until the meeting. It was enough time to grab a quick shower and start looking for another place to live. "I'll be back in time for the meeting."

"Where are you going?"

"To look for apartments. I can't survive through another night of Vince porn. I'm pretty sure I won't even be able to look my mom in the eye again until after Christmas. I've been traumatized."

"How are you going to afford an apartment?"

By the way she asked, I could tell she'd already heard the news about my recent unemployment.

"Who told you?" I asked. "Why didn't you say anything?"

"I still live in Whiskey Bayou," she said, which was explanation enough. "I found out the minute I pulled into my driveway last night. Mr. Lester stopped watering his roses long enough to hightail it to my car before I even got the door open. I thought he was going to break his neck, all bony arms and legs, his gardening hat flying off and the hose soaking the bottom of his trousers."

"Hmmm," I said for lack of anything better.

Mr. Lester's wife was on the school board, so he'd probably been one of the first to know. Part of me was hoping his roses died sometime soon. The other part still felt sorry for him for having to be married to Mrs. Lester. She had a full mustache and a goiter on her neck the size of a cantaloupe.

"And I didn't say anything because I kept expecting to get a distraught phone call sometime during the night and it never happened. Then when I saw you this morning, I started to wonder if you'd even heard the news."

"Oh, I heard the news," I said, thinking of Rosemarie.

Kate was right. I should have called her and told her about the problem, but as soon as I'd made the decision to get my private detective's license, I stopped worrying about the unemployment issue. It had all been settled in my mind. And maybe I wanted to avoid talking to Kate for a while until I figured out how to tell her about my decision.

"Well, you're certainly taking it well," she said, narrowing her eyes at me. "You want to fill me in on what's going on?"

I started to edge toward the door, hitching my purse higher on my shoulder in case I had to get ready to run.

"I thought of a plan," I said, opening the door a crack.

"Why do I get the feeling I'm going to hate this plan?"

"Oh, you'll totally hate it. At least at first. But I think if you give it a chance it might grow on you."

She was shaking her head at me. Her ability to assess the situation was already giving her a clue what I had in mind.

"No way, Addison. You need to think this through. I cannot have you running around half-cocked on the streets with my agency's reputation at stake."

"That's the thing," I said. "If I get my private detective's license, I'll be running through the streets full-cocked. I'll know all the rules and strategies that you guys use, and I'll be able to close cases on my own instead of turning over information I collect for another agent to take credit for. How much do you pay your agents?"

"Thirty percent of the contracted fee," she said hollowly.

"See, that's great," I said even more determined. "I've

seen some of your invoices. You're damned expensive. And I can get my permit to carry concealed so you won't have to worry about my safety anymore. You're always saying how you need more agents."

"Oh, God," Kate said, her mouth opening and closing repeatedly.

"I mean, I know you still feel guilty about giving me that tranquilizer gun, but really, it wasn't your fault. You were just trying to give me a way to protect myself, and I take complete responsibility for shooting Nick. You couldn't have known he'd be at that motel with another woman, though in all honesty, you know me well enough to know that I'm not one to take that kind of treachery lightly. Not after what happened with Greg and Veronica."

Greg Nelson had been my fiancé for a short time. Unfortunately, we'd had different ideas of what monogamy meant, and he'd left me at the altar to play hide the salami with Veronica Wade in our honeymoon limo. A few months later, he'd run out in front of my car during a downpour and he'd bounced off my windshield. It turned out I wasn't the one to kill him—someone did that with poison—but that just goes to show you that karma is a bitch. I still had nightmares about running him down. No one deserved to die that way. Not even Greg.

I'd run out of positive things to say about why I should become a private detective, and Kate had fallen back in her chair once I'd mentioned the incident with the tranquilizer gun. She was reaching in the bottom drawer of her desk for the whiskey she kept there for the occasional medicinal purpose.

"Please, Kate. I'm desperate. I need the work, and the surveillance stuff is good for a side job, but it's not enough to survive on every month. If I get my investigator's license, I'll be able to work full time and make more money. Please don't say no. Just think about it for a while. I'm begging you. I promise, I'll take it seriously and do the best job I can do. I won't embarrass the agency."

Her gray eyes were round in her face with shock and she tossed back the amber liquid like water. When she was silent for a full minute, I took it as a sign that she needed a little bit of alone time and I escaped her office and closed the door behind me.

"That could have gone much worse," I said to comfort myself. "Things can only go up from here."

AFTER I'D SHOWERED AND TAKEN ANOTHER SURVEY OF THE damage from the day before, I decided I wasn't as bad off as I'd originally thought. My back muscles were sore from where I'd fallen and the cut on my leg looked like hell, but the sunburn had faded so I only looked slightly rosy instead of belonging in the fruits and vegetables section of the food pyramid.

I slathered on moisturizer and pulled my hair back in a loose ponytail, bothering with only minimal makeup since it would melt off by ten o'clock anyway. I dressed in a short khaki skirt and white stretchy top so I'd look respectable and like I could pay my bills when I talked to potential landlords, and I slicked on extra Burt's Bees lip balm because I liked the taste of mango.

I took a cup of coffee to go and swiped the *Residential* section of the Savannah Times from Lucy's desk while she was in a meeting with Kate. The outdoors felt like a sauna and I hurried over to the Volvo, thinking it might be a good idea to buy a couple of ice packs to put on the leather seats to keep my backside from melting.

I'd just bent in to put my coffee in the drink holder

when a black pickup truck pulled in beside me. Nick slid out of the driver's seat looking like no man had a right to. He was dressed for work—in a pair of neatly pressed khakis and a white button-down dress shirt. His tie was silvery-blue and his face was already stubbled, even though I could tell he'd shaved by the little nick in his chin. His gun was in a holster at his side and his badge was clipped to his belt.

I mentally girded my loins and tried to remember it was best if we took a break from each other to see if what was between us was real, but this sudden rash of appearances after we'd spent so much time apart was wreaking havoc on my common sense.

"Wow, twice in twenty-four hours," I said as he made his way to my side. "Something must be going on. You've avoided me like the plague for weeks."

"Well, you shot me in the ass. I was angry." He held up his hands in defense when I opened my mouth to start the same argument we kept having. "I don't want to fight. I'm willing to chalk it up to a misunderstanding and move on."

"Big of you," I said, arching a brow. "But that still doesn't explain your sudden reappearance in my life."

"There's no sudden about it, babe. I've tried calling for weeks and you wouldn't talk to me. I've been giving you the space you obviously wanted." He smiled and moved closer so my back was pressed against the car. "And then I saw you naked in the shower and decided you've had enough space."

Nick was right. I'd been the one putting distance between us. Not him. He'd tried to explain several times what I'd seen in that motel parking lot, but I hadn't been ready to listen. The truth is, I'd put on a good face after Greg had left me at the altar for Veronica. I'd returned gifts with polite thank you notes and kept my head held high at school and around town, but that experience had pretty much destroyed me emotionally.

Not because Greg was the love of my life, but because I'd realized that he was the man I'd picked to spend the rest of my life with and he was untrustworthy, he lacked honor, and he'd never once made me feel like he was willing to make sacrifices for our relationship. That made me doubt myself.

Obviously, I couldn't trust my own judgment when it came to finding someone I could give my heart to. And seeing Nick in that parking lot, no matter how innocent, had only driven that fact home. It wasn't even until I was faced with the situation that I realized I hadn't felt for Greg a fraction of what I felt for Nick. And that had made it hurt all the more.

So to protect myself, I'd distanced myself entirely from Nick, even though I still wanted him with an intensity that terrified me.

"Oh," I said, my heart thudding wildly in my chest.

"Yeah. We've wasted all this time, and we could have been doing this."

He bent his head and kissed me softly, his lips rubbing hypnotically against mine until I realized I'd stopped breathing at some point. I put my hands against his chest and he leaned back to look at me while I gulped in air and tried to get my brain cells working. Nick was a pretty good kisser.

"I'm sorry I shot you in the ass," I said. "It was a gut reaction."

He smiled and took a step back. "I guess I should be flattered. You want me bad."

"Conceited much?"

"Not really," he said. "But I do find myself feeling rather possessive all of a sudden. I can understand where you were coming from. If I saw a man doing those things to you they'd never find all the pieces."

"Geez." I needed to get a grip. Possessiveness shouldn't be a turn on.

"Now, as much as I'd like to keep kissing you on the street, if any of the guys happened to drive by they'd never let me hear the end of it."

He looked down at the newspaper I'd crumpled in my hand and slowly unfurled my fingers until he could smooth it out.

"What's this?" he asked.

"I'm apartment hunting. Living with my mother isn't going to work for me anymore."

Nick laughed and skimmed his knuckles just above the neckline of my shirt. "I heard a rumor going around at the station that Vince Walker is making time with your mom. That wouldn't have anything to do with your sudden desire to move, would it?"

"Maybe."

He leaned in close again and whispered, "It turns out I've got an empty side of the bed I'd be willing to let you rent for a reasonable rate."

Spots danced in front of my eyes, and visions of the methods of payment Nick would demand flitted through my mind.

"I'm not sure I can afford your rent," I finally managed to get out.

"That's okay. I'm sure we could come up with some kind of deal that would be mutually satisfying to both of us."

He paused a minute to kiss me, his tongue stroking mine in a way that told me Nick would be the type of man who left no stone unturned when it came to bedding a woman. He'd be a vaginal Magellan.

"Very satisfying," he said, breaking the kiss.

His breathing was slow and measured, but I could see the pulse drumming in his throat. The blue of his eyes had darkened to the color of a stormy sky, and I could feel him hard and ready against me.

"I think I need to go now," I said, backing into the open car door until I fell into the driver's seat. I could barely remember my name, much less about my plan to find a new apartment. If I didn't get out of here soon, I'd be renting Nick's empty side of the bed after all.

"Chicken."

"You bet."

I started the car and pulled out of my parking space while Nick gave me a smile that had all my lady parts dusting off the cobwebs and primping in front of a mirror. It had been a while since I'd had a lover, and I hoped I could even remember what to do. Staying away from him would certainly keep me from a potentially embarrassing situation. Or maybe I could just get him drunk first. There was nothing quite as daunting as going to bed with someone for the first time. Not that I wasn't willing to try.

4

It turns out Savannah is an expensive place to live.

By the time I got back to the agency, I was glistening—because southern women don't sweat—and I was wondering where all the decent slumlords were in the world, because it sure as hell wasn't here.

I'd walked through some of the most hideous excuses for safe lodging I'd ever seen—which was saying a lot considering my previous apartment building—and the prices for rent were sky high. I'd also been propositioned twice and pinched on the ass by a man who had fur coats growing from his armpits and a piece of spinach stuck between his two front teeth. At least I hoped it was spinach.

When I entered the front door of the agency, Lucy Kim stared at me as if she expected the plagues to follow me in, which in all fairness, I probably deserved. But to me, a little garbage stink wasn't quite on par with being devoured by locusts.

"Morning, Lucy."

Lucy never bothered with unnecessary conversation.

She was the strong, silent type, and she jerked her thumb toward the door telling me to go on in to Kate's office while she continued typing away on her computer.

"Always nice talking to you," I said as I headed to the inner offices.

I stopped halfway down the hallway and felt the sudden urge to kick Jimmy Royal square in his baby maker. Jimmy was an ex-cop like Kate who'd only put in a few years on the force because he'd gotten tired of all the political bullshit and red tape. He was second in command here, and normally he was a decent guy. Except he lived to torment me. If we'd been in grade school I would've thought he had a crush on me, but he was happily married with a couple of kids, so I knew that wasn't it.

Cops were a strange breed, with a sense of humor that took some getting used to. It's why so many of them ended up divorced. They were kind of high maintenance on a personal level, but since I'd been around cops since the womb, I was used to the oddities.

"Jimmy Royal," I yelled through his office door after I'd twisted the knob to find it locked. "You get out here and take this sign down."

There was a chalkboard hanging on a nail just outside his door that said:

It's been $\underline{0}$ days since Addison Holmes had an accident

Jimmy had been putting the board up since I'd started working for Kate, and I even got up to seventeen days once. The board was like a game for Jimmy, and we'd fallen into a pattern. He kept hanging it in different places all over the agency so there was a better chance for everyone to see it, I'd bitch about it as soon as I found where he'd hung it, and then he'd take it down and move it somewhere else.

"I mean it, Jimmy," I said again, this time pounding on the door. "Do you hear me?"

"Everybody can hear you," Kate said from her office a couple of doors down. "Jimmy's out on a job, so your wrath can't be appreciated properly." She looked down at her watch. "Get in here. Agent Savage will be here in a few minutes, and I want to give him the appearance that this is a legitimate place of business."

I nodded as Kate went back inside her office, but I'd already thought of the perfect revenge for Jimmy. He'd made the mistake of leaving a little piece of chalk in the holder, and I was going to take full advantage of it.

I dug around in my purse until I came out with a tissue, and I erased Jimmy's idea of a joke, replacing it with one of my own. Jimmy would probably be pissed, because he seemed like the kind of guy who liked to dish it out but couldn't really take it when the joke was at his expense. But I didn't care. Jimmy deserved to have his manhood taken into question.

I dusted my hands off and stood back to examine my handiwork. If luck was on my side, I'd be out of the building before Jimmy got back. I headed into Kate's office and saw Nick lounged on the leather couch in the sitting area she used to make clients feel more comfortable. He looked perfectly relaxed, but I could see his body was tightly coiled, ready to spring into action if needed. Come to think of it, I'm not sure I've ever seen Nick completely relaxed.

"I recognize that look," Kate said. "You always get that little smile whenever you've just done something you shouldn't have. What gives? It makes me nervous for you to have that smile in my office building."

I rolled my eyes and looked back and forth between the empty spot on the couch next to Nick and the small chair on his other side. He arched a challenging brow at me, knowing the debate going on in my mind. If I sat next to Nick on the couch, there was no way I was going to be able to concentrate on anything anyone was saying. And heaven forbid we accidentally touched thighs or something. It had been so long since I'd had an orgasm I was afraid I might spontaneously combust.

I wisely took the chair next to the couch, and Nick whispered, "Coward," out of the corner of his mouth. I would've thought of something clever to say, but Agent Savage picked that moment to walk into Kate's office and I lost all train of thought. At least I assumed he was Agent Savage. He certainly looked like he could live up to the name.

He was a couple of inches taller than Nick, making him close to 6'5", and he was broad and muscled. Everywhere. He looked like the love child of The Rock and Pocahontas. He took up every bit of space in the doorway, and not even his conservative black suit could hide the power beneath. His skin was the color of copper and his hair was black as coal and cut stylishly. His face was like a work of art, sharp angles to make it interesting, and full lips that brought nothing to mind but sin. His dark eyes were framed by lashes that I'd have paid good money for.

Even Kate was rattled by the sheer magnetism of the man, and Kate was never rattled about anything. I snuck a look at Nick and saw his eyes were narrowed menacingly at the new arrival. I could already feel the tension crackling in the air, and I was pretty sure it was the testosterone. Two men like Nick and Agent Savage couldn't be in the same room without there being cataclysmic results. They probably shouldn't have been inhabiting the same planet.

"Agent Savage," Kate finally managed to say, extending her hand to shake his. "It's good to meet you in person. I'm Kate McClean."

"Nice to meet you. Your agency has a great reputation. I've heard it's the best," he said diplomatically.

Savage's voice was even and deep, betraying no accent or inflection that would give me a clue about him. He couldn't have been from Georgia. It was hard for anyone to get rid of the southern drawl once you'd been here long enough. I was guessing Yankee, but mostly because he had that formal politeness that belong to people who live on the northern side of the Mason-Dixon Line.

"We work hard to keep it that way," Kate said. "Let me introduce you around."

She walked over to us and Nick and I both came to our feet. I wasn't going to lie, Agent Savage was a beautiful piece of man, but there was something about him that scared the bejeezus out of me. He wasn't the kind of man I'd ever be truly comfortable around, and there was something in the black pits of his eyes that made me think he could pull the trigger of that giant gun he had hidden under his suit jacket and never bat an eye.

He also looked like the kind of man who could pleasure a woman for hours, and I snuck a glance at the thigh muscles bulging against his suit pants. I had the sudden urge to fan myself, being surrounded by all that hot male glory, but then I caught a glimpse of his eyes again and the fantasy disappeared. Nope, I could appreciate from afar because I wasn't dead, but that was about it.

"This is Detective Nick Dempsey," Kate said, motioning to Nick.

I watched as Nick and Agent Savage shook hands, their

grips tight enough to have veins popping out on the back of their forearms and their smiles brittle with tension as they sized each other up. I wouldn't know who to put money on if they ever came to blows, but damned if this macho display wasn't entertaining.

"Thanks for being here, Detective," Savage finally said, releasing Nick's hand. "I understand you're the lead investigator on Sasha Malikov's murder. You're running a tight investigation."

I had no idea who Sasha Malikov was, but I was assuming he was the courier who'd been stuffed in the barrel. Nick nodded at Savage and his stance relaxed marginally. They'd come to some silent understanding, and I realized Nick's tension was because he didn't want the FBI to come in and take over his case.

"And this is Addison Holmes," Kate said, directing Savage's attention toward me.

As soon as those black eyes met mine, I had a pretty heavy premonition that things weren't exactly what they seemed with Agent Savage. My mind flashed *Danger, Danger* even as my ovaries jumped up and begged for him to be a willing sperm donor.

I had no clue what was wrong with me lately. It's like once I hit thirty all I did was scope out men to be potential sperm donors. I didn't even *want* to be a mother at this point in my life, but I couldn't seem to help myself. Almost as if my body was making the decision for me and leaving me out of the equation.

Savage's eyes didn't leave mine, but I had the feeling he'd somehow managed to check me out from head to toe anyway, and from the tingles in my nether regions, I was wondering if he could somehow see through to my underwear as well. One corner of his mouth tilted up in a smile and his hand reached out to take mine. His grasp was cool and dry, his palm and fingers holding interesting callouses.

"Nice to meet you Ms. Holmes. I've heard a lot about you."

"Addison," I told him. "And probably everything you heard has been exaggerated."

His smile grew a little wider and it reached his eyes this time. I could practically feel Nick vibrating beside me as Savage kept hold of my hand a little longer than he should have. I pulled out of his grasp and took a step back, and he went to the other empty seat across from me as if nothing awkward had just happened.

I appreciated being scoped out as much as the next girl, but I had plenty of testosterone in my life at the moment. I didn't need more, and there was a part of me that wondered if Savage had somehow sensed there was something going on between me and Nick and was just being overly admiring to get a rise out of a potential rival. I was pretty sure FBI agents were trained to pick up subtle clues. Men were known to get involved in pissing contests over the stupidest things. Not to mention Nick's threat about never finding the pieces echoed in my mind.

"Can I get you a drink, Agent Savage?" Kate asked, breaking the tension.

"Coffee if you have it. Black," Savage said. "Thank you."

Kate brought the coffee back and we all settled back in our seats. Savage's pants rose as he sat back and I got a glimpse of the most colorful socks I'd ever seen. They were such a clash with his staid suit that all I could do was close my mouth before he caught me staring. They were multi-colored stripes of bright blues, pinks and purples, and yellow skulls were printed right over the ankles. The socks didn't make Agent Savage less dangerous, but they sure made him a hell of a lot more interesting.

"I assume everyone has been brought up to speed," he said, handing out new file folders to each of us. At our nod, he took out photos of the gems that had been in the package Christian DeLuce had purchased and laid them out on the coffee table. It was hard to look at anything other than the main attraction—the Heart of Ivan was stunning, even in a photograph.

"Along with the emerald," Savage said, "There were dozens of first quality loose diamonds that totaled more that forty-two carats. There were also assorted colored gems that bring a lesser value, but were still of good quality. I've given you an itemized list, and the short of it is that Christian DeLuce got a hell of a deal here."

"Do you suspect him?" Nick asked. "I'm assuming if the gems never reappear then DeLuce won't be out the cash?"

"You're right," Savage said. "And we've run an initial check on him, but he appears to be clean. It'll take some time to dig deeper. Did you suspect him for the Malikov murder?"

"At first. But if he claimed the gems were stolen and collected his fee back, he'd never be able to use them in his designs. A man like Christian DeLuce isn't one to let his creations sit unnoticed. Besides, he had a rock solid alibi. Thousands of people saw him in Salt Lake City at an international jewelry expo. We also haven't found anything inconsistent with his financials suggesting he might have paid someone to do the deed."

"I'll be honest," Savage said. "We're leaving Malikov's murder up to you guys. We don't have the time or the manpower. It's the gems we care about. This has the potential to be an international pissing contest if Russia doesn't get that emerald back. But we're going to have some overlapping in the investigations, so it's probably best to work together."

"Fine with me," Nick said.

Savage nodded and continued. "For two weeks we've kept in touch with pawnshops and some private collectors who keep us informed of underground auctions, but we haven't heard anything about the gems being sold. It's like they never existed, which means whoever killed the courier and took them didn't do it for money. At least not initially. They can afford to sit on them and wait until the right time to unload the product."

Savage took another picture out of his folder and tossed it in the middle of the other pictures. I sucked in air and my fingers tightened on the edge of my seat at the sight of another body. This one was of a woman, and she hadn't met death easy.

She'd been beautiful before her life had been taken. Her dark brown hair was long and silky, spread out like eerie tentacles on the gray carpet beneath her. She was young—really young—maybe a year or two over twenty, and her skin was smooth and flawless. Her dark eyes stared sightlessly and were filmed over with a cloudy substance, and her arms and legs were splayed at an odd angle. She was nude, so the single gaping slash across her throat stood out all the more grotesquely.

"Up close and personal," Nick observed dispassionately. "Who is she?"

"Her name is Amanda Whitfield. A twenty-year old undergrad at Emory. She comes from a white-collar family, and on the surface she's everything a normal college girl should be. With the exception that she turned up dead in a suite at the Ritz two days ago, and underneath her body was a diamond of the first water, and an exact match for one of the stones the Russian courier brought over."

"How do you know that?" I asked.

"All of the gems were museum quality goods, and they've all been marked with a serial number invisible to the eye."

"Handy," I said.

"So Amanda Whitfield wasn't who everyone thought she was," Kate said, looking at the picture more closely.

"Why would you say that?" I asked. One thing I always noticed about cops was that they immediately thought the worst of everyone, with the theory being that people always had something to hide. "Maybe she was just in the wrong place at the wrong time."

"Nice college girls don't end up murdered in a three-thousand dollar a night suite, surrounded by enough sexual paraphernalia to start their own business, and lying on top of stolen gems," Savage explained. "But if I told you she was a high-priced call girl, the picture starts to make a little more sense."

"You could've just said that in the first place," I grumbled.

So I had a lot to learn in private detective school. Sue me. Savage grinned at me and I narrowed my eyes in his direction. A pretty face would only get him so far.

"What did her financials say?" Kate asked.

"That she was very popular in her profession. She received direct deposits of $25,000 every two weeks for the past year and a half. She was barely eighteen when she started."

"Was it traceable?" I asked and everyone turned to look in my direction. "What, I'm not allowed to ask questions?"

Nick winked at me and turned back to look at Savage, and I was so distracted by the uncharacteristic display of affection I'd completely forgotten the question by the time it was answered.

"It took some digging," Savage said, "but the money has

been traced back to a company known as Sirin Incorporated. It has its fingers in a lot of pies—"

I snorted out a laugh at the unintended pun—you know, call girls and fingers and pies—and cleared my throat. "Sorry," I said. "Please continue."

"And it's the parent company for Sirin Escorts," he said as if I hadn't interrupted. "I haven't gotten any names as far as who its Board of Directors are, but the one name that kept popping up in conjunction with the company was a woman named Natalie Evans. She's listed as CEO and president."

Savage tossed another photograph out on the table and we all looked at the most stunning redhead I'd ever seen.

"Natalie is a forty-eight year old divorcee with no children and an unlimited bank account. She has connections from A-list Hollywood all the way to the White House. She pays for her girls to be educated, most of them getting advanced degrees in things like political science or international business so they can be well informed on different issues, and she also requires they be given lessons in etiquette and languages. The girls have to be in top physical condition, and according to the official propaganda of the company, sleeping with clients is grounds for termination."

"Damn, maybe I should be an escort," Kate said.

I was thinking the same thing. "That woman does not look forty-eight."

"I need to moisturize more," Kate added.

"Women are so strange," Nick said. "This woman is the Heidi Fleiss of the South and all you can talk about is how good she looks."

"That's not all," I said. "She also has great taste in shoes."

I saw Savage take a quick drink of coffee to hide his smile. Apparently, badass FBI agents weren't supposed to have a sense of humor. Savage regrouped and looked directly at me.

"We have no grounds to shut her down because we can't prove her escort service is a prostitution ring," he said. "Everything on the surface is above board, and she has enough clout and high profile support that we've already been getting calls from the governor and two senators to back off. If there weren't a dead body involved we'd be out of this completely, and I don't know how long we're going to be able to hold on to that."

"The official statement from Ms. Evans is that Amanda wasn't scheduled to work that night, therefore she must have had plans of her own. We don't have proof otherwise to dispute the fact. Just a body and a stolen diamond. But I can't think of a reason that girl would have the gem unless someone who had the means and opportunity to know what it was gave it to her."

"So what do we do?" It hadn't gone past my notice that Agent Savage had been solely talking to me for the last little bit. I was starting to get the feeling Nick and Kate were superfluous in this conversation.

"I'd like you to apply for a job with the company, or if that fails, make friends with some of the other girls. You're a little older than they like to hire, but you don't look your age. You could pass for early twenties. You have the look of the kind of girl Ms. Evans likes to employ, so you have a shot."

"You've got to be out of your mind," Nick said incredulously. He leaned forward and put his hands on the coffee table, intimidating the hell out of me but not doing much for Agent Savage. "Do you realize the risk you're putting her in? She's not trained for this."

"Which is why I need her to do it," Savage said calmly. "There's not an agent or a cop out there I could put in undercover without them sniffing her out. I need an outsider. Ms. Evans has been in this business for a long time for a reason. She'll know how to spot a plant."

"What happens if they don't hire me?" I asked.

"It's not the end of the world. You're used to doing surveillance, so you can stick to that in the meantime, checking out the girls and documenting any suspicious behavior. Your involvement is just another avenue for us to take in this investigation, because right now we have nothing except two dead bodies and a fortune in missing gems. What do you say Ms. Holmes?"

"Addison," I automatically corrected. "Who's paying me?"

"You'll temporarily be on FBI payroll as a consultant. Any other fees are between you and Kate."

"I'm in," I said, before I had the chance to think it through too much. I needed the money, and beggars couldn't be choosers.

"Addison—" Nick growled.

Kate hadn't said anything, so I turned to look at her so I wouldn't have to see the death glare Nick was giving me. She looked contemplative and a bit pensive, but she wasn't issuing a protest. She shrugged her shoulders at me and sighed, and I knew she'd help me do whatever I needed.

Savage gathered up his files and looked at his watch. He knew when to retreat. "I've got another meeting scheduled for today. Can you meet me tomorrow afternoon? Around three o'clock? I'll talk you through everything and show you what I want you to do."

"Sure, you can pick me up from here." I figured that would be easiest, considering I was practically living here for the moment.

"Tomorrow then," Savage said and gave me the full power of his smile.

Oh, shit. I could have just made a very big mistake. That was definitely interest in his eyes, and I could tell he'd thought he'd won this round with whatever the hell was going on between him and Nick.

"Nice to meet you, Ms. McClean," he said, nodding first to Kate then Nick. "Detective." And then he was gone and I was left in the room with two people who had so much to say I could practically see the words bubbling out the tops of their heads.

"I think I need to check in with Lucy and see if she has any important messages for me," Kate said, looking back and forth between me and Nick.

Nick was glaring at me, so I stood up as if I were going to head out with Kate.

"Don't you dare walk out that door," he said. "I want to talk to you."

"Not if you're going to use that tone of voice," I said. "I'm a grown woman. Not your lapdog."

"I think I'll take a long lunch while I'm at it," Kate interrupted. "Really, use my office for as long as you'd like."

Neither of us paid attention as Kate left. I backed away as Nick stalked toward me until my hip hit the edge of Kate's desk.

"He's using you," Nick said. "And you're so blinded by his looks that you're not taking any time to think this through. This isn't a game. It's dangerous."

"Wait a minute," I said, poking my finger into his chest. "I'm not blinded by anything. I'm not an animal in heat who heads toward whatever alpha male is left standing after a fight. I'm doing this because I need a job. You probably haven't heard, but I'm currently unemployed."

Nick winced and I watched the anger drain out of him. "The school board fired you?"

"Right the first time."

"Shit, Addison. I'm sorry." He pulled me into his arms and just held me for a minute. It was everything I could do to keep from crying.

"It's okay," I said, pulling back far enough that there was space between our bodies. "I've got a plan."

"I've heard. It involves you sticking your nose into business you're not trained for and possibly ending up in a hotel room with your throat slit."

I waved his concern away. "You'll keep me safe. And anyway, I've got a new plan. I'm going to get my private detective's license. That way you won't have to worry about me anymore."

"Jesus," he said, shaking his head. "It's like the world is conspiring against me."

"Hey—"

"No, I'm fine with it. Really," he said, holding up his hands as a peace offering. "I've known you long enough to recognize that stubborn tilt of your chin, and believe it or not, it might be good for you. The process of getting your license isn't an easy one, and you'll at least learn to keep yourself out of trouble. Hopefully."

Nick looked off into the distance as if he couldn't believe what he'd just said. I was having a hard time believing it too.

"Who are you, and what did you do with Nick?"

"Very funny. I mean it," he said with more enthusiasm. "This will be good. You need a strong dose of caution in your life, and this is the way to get it."

"You know," I said, moving back into his arms and dropping my voice so it rasped with sultry charm. "You might not know this about me, but I'm pretty competitive."

Nick's eyes twinkled with laughter as he backed me up against Kate's desk. "I never would have guessed that about you."

His fingers dug into my hips and he lifted me up so I sat on the edge of the desk. He settled comfortably between my thighs and I sucked in air as I felt him hard and ready against me.

"I'm going to want to be the top of my class, and I think the only way to do that is to get a private teacher to show me the ropes. You wouldn't happen to know anyone, would you?"

I nipped at the corner of his mouth teasingly and reveled in the power as I watched his eyes go dark with lust and his body tighten against me. I wrapped my legs around his hips and twined my fingers into his hair as his mouth ravaged mine. I moaned as he licked into my mouth and whimpered as he ground himself against the most sensitive part of me. I was a hairsbreadth away from climaxing in the middle of a busy office building in the middle of the day. And I didn't give a damn.

"Damn," Nick said as he broke away. "I'm supposed to be on duty. I've got to go back to work."

"Right. Kiss me again."

I gripped his shirt and pulled him back towards me, fitting my lips against his. He didn't put up much of a fight, but eventually we were going to have to take this to the next level and I knew this wasn't the time or the place.

"Tonight," he said. "We can hold off for—" He stopped and looked at his watch. "Another five hours. And then we finish this. Once and for all."

I shuddered against him, so close to the edge it felt like someone was sending electric shocks across my skin.

"Right. Tonight," I panted. "I can wait five hours. No problem."

He unwound my legs from around his waist and took an unsteady step back. I hated to tell him, but there was no way he could go out into the hall in his condition. Someone was bound to know what we'd been up to.

"Christ, I feel like a teenager."

"You sure don't look like one," I said, my eyes glued to the bulge in the front of his slacks.

He laughed and closed his eyes for a few seconds, trying to get himself under control while I hopped off the desk and went to grab my purse and the file Agent Savage had left.

"I'll leave first. You look like you need a little time to—" I motioned my hand toward the area that had decided to impersonate the Hulk and felt the heat rushing to my cheeks. "You know," I finished lamely.

I opened the door to Kate's office and looked back at Nick. "I'll see you tonight."

"Addison," Nick said, the seriousness in his voice completely at odds with his swollen lips and disheveled hair. "If Agent Savage has any plans of taking my place as your mentor tomorrow, I swear to God, I'll rip his balls off and shove them down his throat."

"Okeydokey," I said, wide-eyed. "I'll send him the memo."

I closed the door behind me and practically ran out of the building. I had to kill four hours and fifty-six minutes. I figured I might as well get some work done while I was waiting to get my world rocked.

5

Summer was a slow time of year for the agency. It was too damned hot to do anything that required a lot of energy, so adultery was down and fraud was up, since you could usually do that sitting in the comfort of your La-Z-Boy with a computer in your lap and a stolen credit card.

That being said, I only had one other case on my plate right now, and that honor belonged to Noogey. I wasn't in the mood to go another round with dumpsters or rabid dogs on steroids, but I didn't get paid if I didn't put in the hours, so I had no choice but to jump head first into the DeLuce case. At least that was how I was justifying it.

My phone rang and I saw my mother's name pop up on caller ID. I immediately switched it to go directly to voice mail and waited until she'd left a message. I could already feel the headache brewing behind my right eye. Maybe I had a tumor.

Addison, this is your mother—

I rolled my eyes hard enough to make the throbbing start behind my other eye.

You left the house this morning so early I didn't get to tell you

I'm leaving town for a few days.

She giggled like a schoolgirl and I could hear Vince mumbling something in the background.

Vince is taking some vacation time and we're going to the Bahamas. Isn't that exciting! I've left some casseroles in the fridge for you. Gotta go. Love you.

The message ended and I felt a little lighter of heart. I wouldn't have to face my sex fiend of a mother, and I'd still get to sleep in my own bed until I found a new place to live. Life was good.

I dug the file Agent Savage had given me out of my bag and flipped it open, bypassing the photograph of Amanda Whitfield and going straight to the page about Natalie Evans. She had seven escort services under the Sirin name, starting in California and moving east to Washington D.C. The Savannah office was the flagship office and where Natalie spent the most time since one of her homes was here.

I put the Volvo in drive and wound my way through the streets, waiting patiently for tourists to cross and pretending I was back in my Z instead of a boat with wheels. Natalie owned a home in Forsythe Park in the Victorian District. That wasn't a neighborhood that would hide used Volvos with rusted bumpers, but I could probably get away with checking out her house if I acted enough like a tourist.

I stopped by the drugstore and grabbed a few essentials —a disposable camera, a new pair of sunglasses, a cap to help hide my face, trail mix, a diet coke and a forty-eight pack of condoms. Nick had seemed pretty desperate, and I believed in being prepared.

The thing about me and disguises was that I pretty much felt invincible whenever I wore one. I got a huge burst of courage and a little extra attitude, and all of a sudden my Volvo was the equivalent of the Batmobile and I was Magnum P.I.

I popped in an Amy Winehouse CD and cruised towards Natalie Evans' home like I was her new neighbor. The old Victorian was in prime condition, painted the traditional three colors of cream, olive green and yellow, and there were two turrets and a widow's walk up on the third floor. A black, wrought iron picket fence surrounded her corner lot, and two huge magnolias shaded the entire property. The front gardens were lush, and even now, there were two men tending the flowerbeds and pruning shrubs.

I took a side street so I could glimpse the back of the house, but it was hidden by a ten-foot privacy fence. The three-car garage was shut down tight and the driveway was empty of cars. It never hurt to get a feel for how people lived. And it never hurt to become familiar with places in the daytime that you might have to scope out at night. Those were only two of the many lessons I'd learned the hard way over the past few months.

I did a sharp U-turn and was heading back toward the city when my phone rang again. I almost ignored it because it would be just like my mom to keep calling until I answered so she could make sure I wasn't lying by the side of the road in a ditch somewhere, which always seemed to be a fear of hers for some reason.

I didn't recognize the number, so I took a chance on answering.

"Hello," I said.

"Addison, I need your help." Rosemarie's voice was choked with tears and hysteria.

"What's wrong? What happened?" I automatically headed the car back towards Whiskey Bayou.

"It's Baby. I was out walking her by the old highway and

a rabbit streaked right in front of us. You know she can't control herself," Rosemarie sobbed. "She took off after the rabbit and got hit by a car."

"Oh, no," I winced in sympathy. Rosemarie's two Great Danes, Baby and Johnny Castle, were like her children. Really, really big children that had a tendency to eat the furniture and poop old shoes, but children nonetheless.

"I'm stuck here by the side of the road. I don't have my car and I can't pick Baby up to carry her to the vet. The bastard that hit her just kept on driving, but I got a partial plate number. After I get hold of the culprit, they'll be pissing blood for weeks."

My eyes widened and I pressed my foot harder on the accelerator. "I'm on my way. Just stay calm. Baby will be okay."

I kept Rosemarie on the line so she wouldn't commandeer some poor schmuck's car and leave him by the side of the road while she went to get help for Baby, and followed her directions until I saw her.

It was hard to miss Rosemarie, especially in hot pink bike shorts and a matching sports bra. Her hair was disheveled, and black mascara ran down her apple dumpling cheeks. Baby was sprawled across her lap, panting wildly with big eyes filled with pain. Blood covered her back legs.

I dug around in the trunk of the car and came out with an old quilt that was good for picnics or rescuing bleeding dogs and I laid it in the back seat. I went over and knelt down next to Rosemarie.

"This dog has to weigh a hundred and fifty pounds," I said, trying to figure out how we were going to get her in the car.

"She likes her bacon, don't you girl?" Rosemarie crooned.

I thought about the pair of shoes and matching handbag Baby ate the last time I was at Rosemarie's for dinner and thought the bacon was the least of her weight problems.

Baby whimpered and raised her head enough to lick Rosemarie right in the mouth. I scrunched up my nose and gave a mental *eww* as I watched Rosemarie return the kiss with delighted fervor. It was probably a good thing Rosemarie was single.

"Okay, I've got it," I said, going back to the car to get the blanket. I spread it out on the ground beside Baby. "We just need to get her on the blanket and then we can lift her without hurting her leg too much."

"Right," Rosemarie said. "Good plan. Get on the blanket, Baby. Can you do that for mama?"

They went into another kissing fest and I got on the other side of Baby to help move her over. Baby growled and turned her head to nip at my hands, and I jerked back quickly, having no desire to be Baby's version of raw bacon.

"Baby! Don't do that," Rosemarie chided. "Auntie Addison's just trying to help. Now lets get on the blanket and we'll get you all fixed up."

Rosemarie shifted and we both pushed gently until Baby was sprawled half on the blanket. I was sweating like a pig and my hair fell limply in my eyes. Rosemarie was huffing and puffing like a steam engine, and her face was nearing the color of her spandex.

"Come on, Baby. Just. Get. On. The. Blanket," I gritted out. We shoved a final time but couldn't budge Baby.

"Mama will cook you up a whole package of bacon if you get on the blanket," Rosemarie said in a singsong voice.

Baby's head perked up and damned if that dog didn't crawl on her front two legs until she was in the middle of the blanket. I rolled to my hands and knees and gulped in great gasps of air, trying to find the energy to get Baby into the car.

Rosemarie wasn't doing much better, and I vowed there and then that I'd have to get in better shape if I was going to become a serious private detective. Something besides hot yoga and kickboxing, both of which I only did with mediocrity. Those were two activities that were only good for putting yourself in potentially embarrassing situations. Mostly I went because the instructor was hot and we got to work out to 80's hair band music. There was nothing like rocking out to Motley Crüe while stuck in the downward facing dog, trying not to pass out because the hairy Italian man next to you smelled like used condoms and asparagus.

"Come on," I panted. "We'll die of heat stroke if we stay out here much longer."

Rosemarie had a manic look in her eyes and I felt a pang of sympathy for whoever hit Baby. She was a step away from going vigilante on their ass, and I didn't have the strength to pull her back into reality. Come to think of it, I'm not sure I wanted to. Only problem was I couldn't afford to bail her out of jail in my current financial situation.

We stumbled to our feet and each grasped a corner of the blanket, lifting Baby up with what was surely a feat of superhuman strength brought on by desperation. We got her settled in the back seat of the car and I drove them the rest of the way back into Whiskey Bayou to Doc Wilson's clinic.

It took almost two hours to get Baby and Rosemarie stabilized and all the paperwork filled out. I'd found an uncomfortable chair in the waiting area, and was reading up on at home dog enemas and how to survive your pets' terrible twos when Rosemarie finally came out. She looked like someone had stuck a pin in her balloon and deflated her completely.

"Doc says Baby's gonna be okay," she said, smiling bravely. "She needs to stay here for a couple of days, but I can come back Monday and take her home. If you hadn't gotten to us in time, Baby could have died."

Rosemarie started crying again and I felt the initial panic bubble inside me whenever tears appeared. I wasn't one of those people who dealt well with tears. They made me feel useless and uncomfortable, and I never really was sure about the best way to respond. I wasn't one of those naturally nurturing people like some. Usually I just stood around looking like an unsympathetic idiot, even though I truly felt bad for whoever was suffering.

"It'll be okay," I said quickly, patting her awkwardly on the shoulder. "Let's get you home, and I'm sure you'll feel better after a nap. And maybe a bottle of wine. I know I will."

I drove the three blocks to Rosemarie's duplex and got her settled inside with a Robert Downey Jr. marathon, Junior Mints and a box of wine. I needed to go home and shower and do the sex preparation ritual—it takes a lot of work to look casual and sexy and like you're not trying all that hard, while choosing appropriate clothing that's accessible without making you look too easy. Being a woman was fucking complicated.

I pulled the car into the driveway and let myself into the house, basking in the silence and my aloneness. I had the sudden urge to jump on all the furniture and run around in my underwear, but I restrained myself and headed straight to the shower.

I was staring at how giant my pores were in the magnifying mirror and waiting on the water to warm up when my cell rang. Nick's number popped up on the screen and I tripped over the toilet to turn the water off, bruising my shin in the process.

"Hey," I answered only slightly out of breath. I was revved and ready, the anticipation of what was to come as much of a turn on as any other foreplay I'd ever had. "My mom is off cavorting with Vince for a few days so the kitchen table is all ours. Of course, I'll never be able to eat dinner there again after what I plan to do to you."

I listened as Nick sucked in a sharp gasp of air and smiled. Men were so easy. The silence held a little longer than what seemed appropriate and I started to wonder if Nick was fibrillating on the floor. Maybe I'd come on too strong.

"Nick? You there?"

"I've got bad news," he said.

"How bad is bad?"

"I just caught a double homicide. I'm going to be a while."

"How long is a while?"

"Maybe next Tuesday. It's hard to say."

There was an awkward moment of silence as I went through a litany of curses. This was pretty much par for the course. Every time Nick and I had horizontal mambo plans, someone ended up dead. As of yet, Nick wasn't part of the body count.

"Not a problem," I finally said. Taking the mature road was a pain in the ass. "Good luck with your—bodies. Or whatever."

He paused for a minute. "Thank you. That's very adult of you. I'll call when I get a chance."

He hung up and I tossed the phone on the counter and hopped into the shower. On the positive side, it no longer mattered how big my pores were and I could have that bottle of wine after all.

It turns out wine in the middle of the afternoon is a bad idea for me.

I woke up just before six o'clock on the couch. My clothes were non-existent and something thick and furry coated the inside of my mouth. I staggered into the bathroom to brush my teeth and then stumbled into the kitchen to drink a bunch of water and rehydrate.

I was mostly sober, so I pulled on a pair of boxer shorts and a tank top and grabbed my Mac Air from my desk and flopped down on my bed. I pulled out the Sirin Escorts file and started reading, spreading the papers out on the top of my bed. I did a few Internet searches and printed out a few things I thought might be pertinent. I was a champion researcher.

There was nothing even remotely controversial written about Natalie Evans that I could find. She was the most squeaky clean madam I'd ever heard of—not that I had a massive amount of experience with madams or anything, but you'd think they'd have a blip *somewhere* on their record. Natalie had dated the Sexiest Man Alive a few years back and she was currently dating a Junior Senator from Massachusetts.

The Sirin Escorts website was very tasteful—just a picture of a silver fleur di lis on a satin background telling interested parties that all business must be conducted in person. They listed a contact number and an email address and that was it. The site looked tasteful and expensive, and there was no gossip on any forums or chat rooms I could find. Sirin had a very good troubleshooter, whoever he may be.

I finally found the courage to look at the picture of Amanda Whitfield's body again. She didn't look any better the second time. Nick had mentioned the attack being up close and personal, and from the cursory notes Agent Savage had jotted down, he suspected that the killer was someone she'd felt comfortable with. This wasn't a run of the mill escort job.

According to the report, Amanda and her guest had shared an intimate dinner and expensive champagne as if they'd been celebrating. The police had found two used condoms in the bathroom trashcan, but they'd also found evidence of semen in the victim, making me think Amanda might have known her attacker *really* well to let him get away with something like that when they'd been so careful before. There hadn't been any bruising on her body, so evidence showed all sexual activity was consensual.

The FBI had only done a cursory background check on Amanda so far. It didn't really tell me who Amanda Whitfield had been. I picked up the phone and dialed Kate.

"McClean," Kate snapped.

"What's wrong?" I asked.

There'd been something off about Kate the last couple of days. I couldn't put my finger on it, but I knew by the way she kept avoiding much direct conversation that she didn't want to talk about it.

"Nothing. Long day. What do you need?"

I was silent for a few seconds, a little hurt that she didn't feel like she could tell me what was wrong. We'd shared every event in our lives from the time we could walk. We'd never had secrets from each other before. I regrouped and decided to give her a little longer to stew.

"Can you have someone run a deep background check on Amanda Whitfield? I've got the basics, but I want a list of her closest friends and contacts, and I don't want to wait to get it from the FBI. The exclusivity of Sirin makes me think the girls might need to keep their circle of friends from within the company itself just out of necessity. It's easier to keep secrets when your friends have the same ones. Less of a chance of slipping up."

"Good thinking," Kate said. "I'll get Wally on it. He's in between cases at the moment. I'll email it over once it's complete."

There was another awkward silence on the phone. Another first for us, and I wondered what the hell was going on. I was starting to get worried.

"So I've been thinking about what you were saying about getting your P.I. license," Kate blurted out. "And I think it's a great idea. You should go for it."

"What?" I asked, holding the phone out from my ear and staring at it as if it could tell me what the hell was going on. "Have you been drinking?"

"Stone cold sober. Unfortunately. I think taking the classes will be good for you. And I'll make you a deal. If you finish at the top of your class I'll hire you here at the agency full time. But you'll need to be able to pass the conceal to carry test as well as the written test."

"How hard can that be?" I asked. "You just point and shoot."

"Right. I don't know what I was thinking. I'll write a recommendation for you to get into the class and the agency will take care of any fees since it's considered an investment on our part. The next Citizens' Police Academy starts next Thursday, and you'll need to do that on top of the classes for your license. You'll also need to be able to pass a physical fitness portion of the test. Just like a regular cop."

"I don't suppose that involves lifting donuts to my mouth?" I asked.

"Buck up, Buttercup. If everything goes as planned, you should have that license in the next six to eight months. Barring disaster, of course. Which come to think of it—"

"Be nice. I've done pretty well at averting disasters lately."

"True. And your eyebrows are growing back nicely from when Danny Gorman tried to barbecue you with that flamethrower."

I made a note to myself to remember to go by the unemployment office to see about benefits. Hopefully, they'd be sufficient enough that I could afford to go without a full time job for six to eight months. Otherwise, I was going to have to sell Slurpies and condoms at the nearest 7-11. Not that there was anything wrong with that, but the 7-11 in Savannah had been held up three times in the last six months and I had an aversion to having my head blown off.

"Thanks, Kate. You'll see. I'm going to ace the shit out of that test."

Kate laughed her real laugh, and some of the tension melted between us.

"And Kate," I said. "When you're ready to talk, I'll be here day or night. Whatever you need."

I heard her take a deep breath on the other end and knew from habit that she was letting it out slowly as a way to control her emotions. Kate didn't get emotional. She was steady as a river in winter.

"I know," she said. "Thanks."

She hung up the phone and I knew there was nothing left for me to do until she emailed me the information on Amanda Whitfield. I flipped the TV on to a Friends marathon and settled into bed. I needed a good night's sleep and a clear head to face Agent Savage tomorrow afternoon.

6

S *aturday—barely*

A POUNDING AT THE DOOR WOKE ME SOME TIME AFTER midnight. I'd been a cop's daughter long enough to know that usually wasn't a good thing. A million different scenarios raced through my mind as I tried to untangle myself from the covers—my mom had been in a plane crash, Kate had been in a shootout, Rosemarie had been eaten by her dogs—the list of possibilities was endless.

I tripped over the hall runner and banged my shoulder into the doorframe, racing to some unknown catastrophe. The house was completely dark, but I didn't stop to turn on the lights.

I flipped on the porch light and checked the peephole, becoming even more upset when I saw Nick standing there. What if the double homicide he was working was someone I knew? Or worse, what if I was being accused of the murder? It wouldn't be the first time.

"I didn't do it!" I said as I opened the door.

"I hope not," Nick said. "I just got here. I'd hate to have to kill anyone."

"What are you talking about?"

"What are *you* talking about?

"If you don't know, then never mind," I said, standing back to let him in.

I flipped on the overhead light and got my first good look at him. He looked dead tired. His face was shadowed with heavy stubble and his eyes were drawn and shadowed. Whatever he'd seen today must have been really bad. He looked sad, but at the same time he was practically crackling with anger. He had a shitty job sometimes, but he was damned good at it.

"What are you doing here?" I finally asked, noticing the bag slung over his shoulder for the first time. He was wearing his off duty clothes—old jeans that were worn thin in places and a black t-shirt that clung to every muscle in his chest and arms.

"I've got exactly five hours until I have to be up and back at the station," he said, dropping the bag where he stood and giving me a look hot enough to melt butter. "Sleep is overrated."

The light bulb clicked on above my head and I licked my lips and swallowed nervously as he came closer.

"Umm—"

"What? No response?" he asked, smiling a little.

He put his finger beneath the strap of my tank top and pulled me closer until I was flush with his body. His lips teased and nipped at my chin and down my throat and he backed me up until I hit the edge of the dining room table.

"Bedroom," I moaned as he pulled my tank top off over my head and his mouth latched onto my nipple. "Condoms. Bedroom." My speech was reduced to Neanderthal level, and then his fingers found their way up the wide leg of my shorts and I stopped thinking all together.

"I've got the first round," he said, pulling back and digging in his pocket. He threw a condom down on the table and lifted me so I sat on the edge. All I could think was that I was glad my dad had insisted on buying good solid oak. Otherwise this could have been an embarrassing situation.

"Right," I said, pulling his t-shirt from his jeans and jerking it over his head. "I've got forty-eight more in the bedroom. Just in case."

He pulled back and stared at me incredulously. "I hope you're not planning to use them all tonight. I have to be able to walk tomorrow."

I laughed and frantically tugged at his belt buckle, and he sucked in a breath as I finally took the hard heat of him in my hand.

"Jesus," he groaned. "I've been waiting too long to be inside of you. I'll be lucky to last five seconds."

"You'll have to make it up to me."

He kissed me hard, sliding his tongue against mine in a dance that had every nerve ending in my body ready to detonate. Sight and sound had stopped working at some point, and all I could do was feel—the cool wood of the table beneath my back and the scrape of the denim of his jeans against my thighs as he pushed them past his hips.

He settled himself between my legs and then he was pushing inside of me. I forgot to breathe and immediately spasmed around him.

"Oh, God," I said, as my eyes rolled back in my head.

He clasped his hands with mine and rode me through the wave, burying his head in my neck and calling my name as he followed.

AN ALARM SOUNDED SOMEWHERE IN THE DEPTHS OF MY subconscious, so I rolled over to turn it off except there was an obstacle in the form of a hard male body in my way. He turned toward me, draping his arm across my waist, and I could tell he was awake in more ways than one.

"Why do I hear bells?" I asked.

"I set an alarm. I've got to get back to work." He nibbled at my neck and hiked my leg over his hip, probing against me.

"Hey! I'm trying to sleep here," I said grumpily. "I thought you had to go to work."

"I set it early so I'd have time to do this."

His fingers worked some magic that made my eyes cross, and I decided maybe I could learn to be a morning person. "It's a good thing I like you."

He laughed and rolled me to my back, sliding deep inside of me and hitting my new favorite place, and I forgot all about being sleepy.

THE NEXT TIME I OPENED MY EYES IT WAS AFTER NOON. I didn't remember Nick leaving, but considering I'd all but been a puddle of jelly by the time he'd finished with me, my unconsciousness was pretty understandable.

I rolled out of bed, wincing as my muscles protested in remembrance of what they'd been doing all night, and I hopped into the shower. I jumped out again just as quickly and pulled on a royal blue strapless sundress and black flip-flops with giant flowers on top. My skin was healthy and glowing, my eyes were bright, and I had a stupid grin on my face. I looked like I'd spent a day at the spa. Apparently amazing sex was the next best thing.

I checked my email and was happy to see Kate had sent me the information I'd requested on Amanda Whitfield. I printed it out while I popped a hazelnut coffee blend pod in the Keurig and made some toast. I was a step away from bursting into song I was so cheerful.

"Ouch, shit," I said, blowing on my burned fingers as I pulled out the toast and buttered it. I took my breakfast to the table and had a hot flash as I remembered what Nick had done to me there. I gathered my stuff and went into the living room, but I was also having hot flashes about the sofa, the upright piano, and most of the walls. It had been a busy night.

I shoved all the papers into my oversized purse and poured my coffee into a to go mug. I figured I might as well head into the agency and use one of the spare conference rooms.

Whiskey Bayou was pretty active on Saturday mornings. I weaved in and out of traffic, mostly women hitting their weekly garage sales, and pretended not to notice when a few students and their parents pointed at my car and turned to each other to whisper.

I thought the gossip was bad after I'd exposed John Hyatt—pillar of the community and bank president—for being a cross-dressing murderer, but I had a feeling being fired was going to take the cake.

The people in Whiskey Bayou thrived on gossip when another person's life was spiraling down the toilet, heading for imminent destruction. They were like piranhas waiting to devour every scrap of soul crushing news until there was nothing left but bones.

I needed to get the hell out of this town. The Holmes were sixth generation in Whiskey Rebellion, so we had *a lot* of mishaps marring our family tree. We hadn't even been allowed to mention Uncle Jimmy's name when I was a kid.

If I had anything to say about it, I wouldn't be contributing to the continuity of the Whiskey Bayou population. The Holmes were a dying breed. Unless my sister Phoebe decided to move back from Atlanta after she found herself, but there was a pretty slim chance of that happening. She hated it here more than I did.

My fingers unclenched from the wheel and I let out the breath I'd been holding once I got on Harry Truman Parkway and pressed my foot to the floor. The Volvo lurched and maxed out at fifty-five, but it was good to put distance between me and insanity.

It was almost two o'clock by the time I found a parking spot in front of the agency. Lucy was manning the desk, the phone to her ear, typing rapidly on her keyboard. She didn't spare me a glance as I waved and walked past her. I didn't hear her actually conversing with anyone on the other end of the line. Maybe she was using her ninja powers.

I peeped through the glass window into the conference room and saw it was empty, so I went inside and made use of the giant table, spreading out all of the papers I'd printed out on Amanda Whitfield and opening my laptop. I grabbed a yellow writing tablet from a shelf in the corner and a pen and got to work making notes.

On the surface, Amanda seemed like any normal twenty year old kid. She was originally from North Carolina and was attending Emory on a full academic scholarship. She'd been first in her high school graduating class and she'd been Miss Teen South Carolina. The money trail from Sirin led back to October of her freshman year of college, and I wondered if Sirin specifically recruited her for the job. With the promise of that kind of money, eighteen year old girls would do just about anything. I could see how the lure would be attractive.

Amanda visited her family for a week at Christmas every year, but that was the extent of her contact with them, though it seemed like they'd been close before she hooked up with Sirin. There was no hint of drug abuse in her medical records, and she'd been tested every six months by a Dr. Isobel Lee for venereal diseases.

I made a note to get more information about Dr. Lee. It would make sense for Sirin to use one doctor for all the girls. I read through Amanda's emails, but they were all very generic, not referring to anything they shouldn't, but I matched the email address of her correspondents to a couple of names in her file. Becca Gonzales and Andi Bachman were two of the last people to speak with Amanda before she was killed. There were a couple of mentions of a third friend—Noelle Price—and I jotted her name down as well. It definitely wouldn't hurt to follow up with these girls.

My head jerked up as I heard a knock on the door. Agent Savage stood in the doorway and it took me a minute to remember that he was supposed to meet with me this afternoon. I looked up at the clock and saw it was five after three. I'd lost track of the time.

"Sorry," I said automatically, my mind still fuzzed from being buried in papers for the last hour and a half. "I was just getting to know Amanda Whitfield a little better."

"Not a problem," he said, coming in and taking the chair across from me.

He was back in another black suit, white shirt and black tie, and I snuck a glance at his ankles to see if the socks from yesterday had been an aberration—maybe he'd been out of clean laundry—but today's socks were just as crazy.

They were lime green and decorated with little martini glasses. I wasn't an expert on the FBI, but I was pretty sure socks like the ones Agent Savage wore weren't in the dress code.

"So what's the plan?" I asked, gathering up all the papers. "Are we going to do a stakeout? Throw our weight around? Capture a couple of Natalie Evans' goons and practice our torture techniques? This is exciting stuff. I never got to do this teaching history."

Savage looked slightly horrified, but he seemed like a man that wouldn't break under pressure. "I thought we'd take it a little slower. We'll work our way up to the torture. Also, we might have a few obstacles in our way during this investigation."

"Like what?"

"Like the fact that the FBI has been ordered off the Natalie Evans investigation. We're still supposed to find the gems, but we can no longer explore the lead that Sirin or anything associated had anything to do with the theft of the gems and the murder of Sasha Malikov. The order came from pretty high up. Not even my Director could question it."

"At least you know you're on the right track. You're making someone nervous."

"The question is why," he said. "I've got a theory."

"You seem like the type of man who has them."

His lips quirked in a semblance of a smile. "Natalie Evans has political clout and influence. We can't find out anything about her. There's nothing even remotely interesting in her FBI files, which I have my own theories about. Asking questions about her sends up enough red flags to have a dozen bulls chasing you down. She can't be touched. But I think she's involved in this. The only thing that can explain why one of the Romanov diamonds was found beneath one of her girls is if she were using her company to find buyers. After this many years in business, she'd have a select number of clients she could trust. Those will be the ones she tries to sell them to."

"Only someone got greedy and decided he didn't want to pay for the merchandise after all. Which means Natalie Evans knows exactly who killed Amanda Whitfield."

"Bingo," Savage said softly, leaning closer as the excitement of the chase was closing in. "More than likely Amanda had brought dozens of the gems to be inspected for purchase, but the one beneath her got away from the killer without his notice. Slitting a throat is messy business. Evidence in the room shows the shower was used, so he probably took the time to clean up and redress before he left the hotel room."

"Geez, that takes balls."

"And a high degree of sociopathic tendencies."

"So you're thinking politician for the culprit?"

"Ha, very funny," he said.

"I have my moments."

"So I've heard."

I narrowed my eyes. "What's that supposed to mean? I only stripped for money that one time. I don't care what anyone else said."

"What? Why did the conversation just take a one-eighty?" He stopped and stared at me for a minute as my words finally penetrated. "You used to be a stripper?"

"I told you. It was just that once, so not really. I wasn't very good at it. Why are you changing the subject? Weren't we talking about slitting throats and stolen diamonds?"

"We were, but I've been told to lead the investigation elsewhere."

"Oh, right." I scrunched my nose in concentration. "So what are you going to do?"

"Fortunately, private detective agencies don't fall under the same rules as the federal government. So you're going to help me out."

"Won't you get in trouble?"

"I'm not much of a rule follower," he said, smiling.

"I could tell by the socks."

"You should see my underwear."

Whoa! Now that he'd planted the thought in my head I was trying desperately to not imagine what he had on underneath those regulation black pants. I'd just spent five hours having the best sex of my life, and all of a sudden it was raining men. Life was cruel.

"No! I really shouldn't. See your underwear, I mean. I'm kind of in a relationship." Though come to think of it, Nick and I had never sat down and talked about what kind of relationship we had. "I think," I added as I pondered the question. I needed to find out. Was this an exclusive relationship? Was he only interested in the sex?

"Let me know when you find out for sure," Savage said. "You seem kind of conflicted. And Detective Dempsey doesn't strike me as the type of guy to be patient when it comes to waiting for his woman to make up her mind."

I *hmmmed* appropriately but didn't say anything else. I didn't need to make up my mind. I wanted a relationship with Nick. I was pretty sure. We just didn't know each other all that well and the physical side of things was a little overpowering at the moment. Maybe I was worried that once the chemistry wore off a little, we wouldn't be left with very much substance.

Savage sighed and stood up. "Come on. I'll fill you in on what I want you to do. Have you had lunch?"

I don't know why those four little words felt like he was asking me the equivalent of dancing naked under the light of a full moon, but it did.

"This isn't a date, is it?" I asked, shoving the folders into my purse and following him out of the agency.

"Definitely not."

I hiked myself up into the monster Expedition, trying to be graceful while keeping my skirt pulled down and the stretchy top of the dress pulled up. I wasn't having a lot of success and snuck a peek at Savage, but he had his eyes dutifully ahead.

"You'd know if this was a date," he continued. "I'd want to start things out slow. Maybe catch a baseball game and a burger on our first date. Mexican food and a movie on our second. The third date would be more romantic. Maybe a candlelight dinner and an art museum. The Georgia Museum of Art is doing the Pharaohs of Egypt exhibit."

Oh, man. I *loved* that exhibit. This guy played dirty, but I had a stronger constitution than that. I had feelings for Nick. Strong feelings. And I wasn't a cheater, though that wasn't going to stop the occasional fantasy from sneaking through. I had to leave room for Johnny Depp.

"Of course, the museum trip might have to wait for our fifth date," he said, navigating the Expedition through the old Savannah streets with efficiency. "It's a long drive to Athens. We'd have to make it an overnight trip."

My skirt was knotted in my hands and my palms were sweaty. This guy was a professional at torture techniques. I hated to see what he was going to do with Natalie Evans if he ever got a hold of her.

"Well," I chirped. "Tell me what you want me to do about the investigation."

He laughed and a satisfied grin settled on his face. "First of all, tell me what you found out about Amanda Whitfield. My investigation is being monitored now, so I haven't been able to dig as deep as I need to."

"My impression was that Sirin sought her out once she

got to college. Amanda was a very intelligent girl and she had the physical characteristics they needed for her to be a successful escort. She made a lot of money working for them, but she all but cut ties with her family. I also have the names of two friends she seemed closer to than anyone else—Becca Gonzales and Andi Bachman—ages twenty-one and nineteen respectively. I need to do a deeper check on both of them and a third friend that was mentioned briefly."

Savage tapped his fingers in an unknown rhythm on the wheel, his brow furrowed in thought. He parked the Expedition on Broad Street, and then turned the air conditioning up a notch so it was blasting cold air into our faces.

"That's the building Sirin owns," Savage said, pointing to a six-story square of smooth gray concrete. It looked sterile and modern sandwiched between crumbling buildings that had more history in one square foot than the Sirin building could ever hope to have.

"It lacks character," I said.

"So do its inhabitants. The top floor is Natalie's office. I'm not sure what the middle levels are used for. We weren't able to get very far when we went in to question the staff, but my best guess is they're used for training the girls and for apartments. It's hard to know since we don't have a full employee list. There's also a full time security team—two by the front entrances and then more on a rotation schedule."

He pulled a pair of binoculars from beneath the seat and handed them to me. I couldn't see anything about the building more clearly than I could without the binoculars. The windows were tinted with reflective glass on every floor and a guard stood in front of the door, so I couldn't even get a tiny glimpse inside.

"Damn, that just makes me more curious," I said.

"I know the feeling."

"I'm willing to bet Becca and Andi are also Sirin employees," I said. "Do you think we can check their financials to see if they look like Amanda's?"

"You can," Savage said. "I'm just along for the ride."

"Maybe you can tell me how to go about investigating while you're riding along. I'm kind of new at all this. I'm more likely to fall off the bike in the middle of a busy highway and get flattened by a semi."

"That's the thing about riding," he said, arching a dark brow and giving me a slow smile. "The more you do it the better you'll be."

"Jesus, you're a piece of work, you know that?"

"And here I've been on my best behavior with you."

"Lucky me." I turned to face him fully, ready to get this all out in the open to save myself the trouble of having to knee him in the balls later. Or worse, having Nick remove them permanently.

"Listen. You're an attractive guy. You obviously know this because your ego doesn't have a lot of room left to inflate. Yes, you're dark and mysterious, you have the body of a god and your socks make you interesting. But there is absolutely no chemistry between us. Not even a twinge on my end of things. The only reason you're bothering with the full court press is because you and Nick rub each other the wrong way for some reason and you're trying to make a point. So just stop all the innuendos and lets do what we're here to do."

His face was serious as he gave me a short nod of agreement. "Fine. Nothing but business between us."

"Fine," I said, nodding in turn. "Which brings us to another problem. If security at Sirin is that tight and the way they hire their girls that carefully monitored, then there's no way they'll even consider hiring me. That plan is not going to work. And thanks for the flattery, but passing as a nineteen-year-old call girl isn't in the cards for me. They'd laugh their asses off if I told them that lie."

"Don't worry. I've already thought of a different plan."

"Why does that make me nervous?"

"It's your own fault. You shouldn't have mentioned your past as a stripper."

"Dammit, I told you—"

"And just so we're clear on things—" Savage said, leaning over and placing his mouth on mine. The zing went straight to my lady bits and sent electricity to every nerve ending I had. He kept his hands to himself, which was a good thing considering the reaction I was having with just a touch of his lips. He was damned thorough, and by the time he pulled away, my eyes were crossed and kneeing him in the balls was the furthest thing from my mind.

"No chemistry, huh?" he asked. "I guess you're just cold."

I looked down at my nipples and was surprised to see they hadn't cut through the windshield. I shot Savage a dirty look and crossed my arms over my chest.

"Don't do that again," I said. "Never again." I nodded my head sharply so he'd know I meant business, and he just smiled and pulled into traffic.

"Never is a long time, sweetheart. Why don't we start with twenty-four hours and see how it goes?"

It must be my punishment in life to be attracted to smartasses.

"Never," I repeated, realizing I was trying to convince myself more than him.

7

A gent Savage dropped me off back at the agency, and I practically fell out of the car and hit the ground running before he could find a parking space. He yelled something at my back about being in touch soon and I shot him the finger. I decided to ignore his laughter. Engaging would be a bad idea.

I stormed past a blank-faced Lucy and down the hall towards Kate's office, still unsure if I was madder at Savage or myself. I was *not* a cheater. Especially since I knew how it felt to be on the other end. But he hadn't given me a choice. He'd just taken over and swooped in. Savage was a stealth kisser, and I'd have to be on my guard at all times.

He was also a genius at locking lips—I mean, he was the fucking Stephen Hawking of kissing. No—nevermind— that does not bring an attractive picture to mind. We'll just say he knows what the hell he's doing. Just swapping tongues with Savage would be enough to ruin most women. Fortunately, I'd been swapping tongues with Nick too, and I wasn't so easily swayed.

The sign was gone from outside Jimmy Royal's door, so

I figured he'd received the message I'd sent him loud and clear. Kate's office door was wide open so I went in and threw myself face first on her couch.

"How'd it go with Savage?" she asked, coming over to take the chair beside me. She was in her Saturday work clothes—jeans and a white t-shirt—and I took a quick glance at the time, wondering what she was still doing in the office. She usually just worked a half-day on Saturdays.

"I don't want to talk about it," I said. I rolled over and up into a sitting position, reaching for the files in my handbag. "I need to get a couple of more background checks."

"I'll have to do it. All my agents are busy at the moment, and I'm up to my eyeballs in work. I got a visit from the governor's aide this afternoon. He's concerned that our involvement in the investigation for Christian DeLuce would be potentially harmful to such an upstanding citizen as Ms. Evans. He'd hate for my agency's reputation to be hurt. He suggested we might try another avenue in looking for the gems."

"Oh, did he?" I asked. "Agent Savage got that memo as well. Only the FBI has been ordered to drop the investigation into Amanda Whitfield's murder completely. It had nothing to do with Sirin and they have no idea or connection to the diamond found under her body."

"These guys are really starting to piss me off," Kate said.

"If you're backlogged with work, show me how to use the search programs."

Some of the programs the agency used to do background on people were pretty invasive, so only her agents had clearance. But Kate's business was expanding by leaps and bounds, and more often than not, her agents were out of town working cases in different cities because word of mouth about the business had travelled that far. She only had two agents that worked local cases. Nick was one of them, but he had a full time job catching killers, and the other agent had been a cop since Moses was born and wasn't moving around as good as he used to.

"You know what?" Kate said, standing. "To hell with the rules. Come on. I'll show you what to do."

"Wow." I followed Kate to the office next door. "That governor's aide must have really pissed you off if you're breaking the rules. That's usually my job."

"Every once in a while, it's nice to be able to be the person who gets to do whatever the hell they want to."

"Hello?—" I raised my eyebrows and felt like I'd missed something significant.

"This is Carl Janson's office. He's out with a herniated disc for six weeks, so you can use it whenever you need to."

I wondered briefly if Carl had gotten his decorating ideas from the caveman channel. The walls were white and bare of any decoration. There were no plants or family photos. The only evidence that anyone had ever inhabited the office was a mug with handcuffs on it that said *I'm good at detecting pussy.*

"Cozy," I said.

"I've always thought so. And probably if you wash it, Janson will let you use his mug."

"I'll pass. I've never been that good at detecting pussy. It would be false advertising."

Kate sat down behind the computer and turned it on. She pulled out a notepad and pen from the drawer and started writing. "These are the passwords you'll need. The first one is to login to the computer. The rest are for the different search programs we use. You can just login as me, since you don't have an account. It'll raise less questions."

I leaned across the desk and watched as she typed in passwords. I was pretty technology savvy because of school, so I wasn't completely lost with what she was doing.

"I'll use you as an example so you can see how it works," she said, typing in my name and state. She showed me how to use clue words to narrow the search, ferreting out social security numbers and bank accounts, and possible relatives, both alive and deceased. It was like separating pieces of a puzzle and putting them back together until you had the final picture.

My mouth dropped open as my entire life was displayed on the page. "What the hell? How is this even possible?"

"Looks like your Banana Republic payment is past due and it's been more than a year since your last pap smear."

"This should be illegal. You can do this with anyone? Is nothing sacred anymore?"

"Not much. Certainly not the government's interest in knowing everything there is to know about anyone. Big Brother is definitely watching. That's why I only have a cell phone for work, I don't have a personal email account, I still pay all my bills by check, and I use cash for everything else. I want to be able to disappear if I ever need to."

"Holy shit. Why would you ever need to?"

"You never know. And probably I'll never have to find out. The world is supposed to end in a few months anyway."

"Good point."

Kate got up and let me have the chair. "Stay as long as you like. I'll be here for a while, so just ask if you hit a snag."

I was going to ask Agent Savage if there was a way to get rid of my information. Big Brother didn't need to know that I was late for my pap smear, though that reminded me about Dr. Isobel Lee. I plugged in the information like Kate had showed me. There were a lot of Isobel Lee's in the state of Georgia. Six of them were doctors—two specializing in gynecology. I dug deeper on both of them and was finally able to narrow it down with financial records. One of the Dr. Lees made significantly more than the other, and the deposits were being made by the same company who'd deposited the money into Amanda Whitfield's account.

Digging even further into her life, I was able to see that she'd been an infertility specialist at one time, but she had a few marks on her record and had lost funding and credibility because some of her experimental treatments hadn't turned out well for the patient.

"I guess we know what Sirin is holding over your head," I murmured. "They're probably the only place you could get a job."

She no longer had a private practice and her place of residence was listed as 227 Broad Street in Savannah. I was willing to bet Dr. Lee's office occupied one of those middle floors of the Sirin building.

I shifted my searching to Becca Gonzales and Andi Bachman, and I occasionally glanced at the phone, cracking my knuckles as I willed it to ring. I hadn't heard a peep from Nick. Not even a text message. He was probably armpits deep in dead bodies, but I was pretty sure morning after etiquette at least included a casual hello or a phone call.

Those little insecurities that had plagued me after Greg had thrown me over for Veronica were starting to surface —*Why wasn't I good enough?* or *Was I that bad in bed?*—the kinds of questions that made women raving lunatics and drove men to drink. I'd never ask the men in my life those questions, because I had pride, but I sure as hell couldn't keep them from sneaking up on me.

I turned my attention back to the job at hand, putting

Nick as far out of my mind as possible. I was fascinated by the life of ill repute. If I were Natalie Evans, I'd ask for my own reality TV show. There was sex and money and scandal in spades, so they'd make a killing in the ratings.

"Well, holy shit," I said.

I'd definitely hit the jackpot. And Noelle Price, the fourth friend in the quartet of call girls, was the icing on the cake. Especially since she was dead. I printed all the information out, practically jumping in my flip-flops with excitement. I grabbed all the papers and headed next door to Kate's office. Her head was buried in paperwork, so she didn't hear me when I came in.

I glanced up at the clock and saw it was after eight o'clock. Nick still hadn't called, but I'd passed the point of getting my hopes up where that was concerned. What did have me concerned was that Kate was still in the office when I knew damn good and well she and Mike always reserved Saturday night for their date night.

"Why are you still here? I thought it was date night?" I asked.

Kate looked up briefly, but her face betrayed nothing. "I have work. Some of us do that for a living."

"Well, ouch," I said, heading over to the Keurig to make myself a cup of coffee.

Kate winced. "Sorry. That was out of line. But I'm busy here, Addison. We can gossip later."

I just doctored my coffee the way I liked it and set the papers I'd brought in aside. We could get to that later. I took the seat across from her desk and just waited, staring patiently at her until she couldn't stand it anymore. When she finally looked up I was horrified to see the shimmer of tears in her eyes. Kate *never* cried.

"Jesus, are you okay?" I asked. "You're not dying or

anything are you?" I leaned over the desk and grabbed her hand. "Did you find a lump?"

She shook her head and the tears actually fell. Panic started to build inside of me. Kate was the calm one. The one who always knew what to do in a crisis. This was the equivalent of Diane Sawyer standing on top of her news desk on live television and screaming that the world was about to end.

"We can fix this," I promised her. "Whatever it is."

"I think Mike is having an affair," she said.

My eyes popped open wide at that news. Mike was the last person on earth I'd ever suspect of having an affair, but Kate was a pretty good judge of character, so if she suspected, then something was probably up.

"Do you need help hiding the body?" I asked. "I've always thought the bayou was a good place. Of course, we'd have to weigh him down pretty good so he didn't churn back to the surface in a bad storm. Sheriff Rafferty would probably suspect you first thing, even though he is dumber than hair."

Kate gave a watery laugh and reached under a stack of papers for one of the case files she put assignments in. A ball of dread, like weighted lead, gathered in the pit of my stomach when she placed it in front of me.

"All the information is inside," she said. "Treat it like any other case."

I wanted to jump out of the chair and say, *hell no*, but I restrained myself because I'd do anything she asked me to help her out. I only hoped she didn't regret it. I knew from experience it was a lot harder to see first hand than to suspect.

"Oh, Kate. Are you sure?"

"I need the proof. I need to be sure before I can leave him."

I wanted to ask when things had gotten bad between them. This all seemed rather sudden. But I kept my mouth shut and took the file. "I'll let you know," I promised.

"He's on duty tonight until ten. He's been working a lot of extra shifts lately," she said bitterly.

"I'll take care of it," I told her.

And if he was cheating on her I still had a tranquilizer gun I could use on him. Probably it'd be a fair deal to let Kate take her vengeance out while he was unconscious. And there'd be less screaming. I wasn't sure I was built to witness intentional violence. I sometimes wanted to throw up watching old episodes of Nip/Tuck.

Kate dried her tears abruptly and shuffled me out the door before I had a chance to ask too many questions. I guess she wanted me to go into the case with an open mind. Considering I'd already offered to help her hide the body, I was thinking it was too late. I gave her a quick hug and invited her to stay the night at my house, but she declined, locking the door behind me and heading back to work.

What she and I really needed was a vacation. I needed to whisk her away to the Keys, where she could sip drinks with umbrellas and lay on the beach as she ogled sexy Latin men in Speedos. Of course, she'd have to pay for it since it was out of my budget at the moment.

I still had some time to kill while I waited for Mike to get off work, so I swung through Dairy Queen and used the spare change I had in the center console to buy a strawberry sundae. The thing with Kate had kind of thrown me off my stride, and I'd completely forgotten to tell her what I'd found out using the search programs. As much as I hated to admit it, I probably needed to go to Agent Savage with the information. I'd have to make sure to wear my chastity belt and put chicken manure on my lips to keep him far from kissing distance.

I blared Beastie Boys from the stereo and drove back to Broad Street, parking in the same place Savage had earlier that day. The street was still busy with traffic, so I blended in easily enough, but the Sirin building was getting no action. All of the floors were dark, and no one was coming or going from the building.

I didn't have a lot going for me normally in this job, but I had pretty good instincts. Mostly. It was listening to them that was my problem. My gut was telling me anything having to do with this building was a waste of time. Natalie Evans had kept her records and businesses clean, and the dirty work wouldn't be done here.

What I really needed to get a hold of was her client list. But short of breaking into her house and searching for it, I was at a loss on how to get it.

A shadow darkened my window and I jumped in surprise as a pale, round face stared in at me. Rosemarie's face was plastered with a grin and she waved with the silly incoordination of someone who'd had one too many drinks at happy hour. Her red lipstick was slightly smeared and she had mascara under her eyes.

Rosemarie kept her hand on the car as she made her way unsteadily to the passenger side and opened the door.

"Boy, I was just thinking about you. And here you are," she said, giggling. "It's like magic. Or voodoo. Or voodoo magic."

She thought that was hilarious and laughed so hard she snorted, sending her into another fit of uncontrollable giggles.

"I was just thinking that," I said. "You're not driving, are you?"

"Of course not!" She was so scandalized by the sugges-tion I had to grin. "You're here. Now I don't have to call a cab. I've got good luck. My mama always said, *Rosemarie Valentine, you are the luckiest duck I ever did see.* I bet I could charge people to rub up against me and then they'd be lucky too."

"I'm pretty sure that's illegal in the state of Georgia."

I looked at the time and winced. There was no way I'd be able to get Rosemarie home and make it back by the time Mike got off his shift.

"Is there a friend you can stay with here in the city? I'm still working, otherwise I'd be happy to take you home."

"Oh, don't mind me. I told you I'm lucky. If you're headed out to catch vile seducers and criminals then you probably want me to ride along with you. Don't worry. I'll do it for free on account of how we're best friends."

"I appreciate that, Rosemarie."

I just closed my eyes for a second, knowing it was futile to argue. At least she wasn't wearing bright colors, so there was the possibility that she'd blend in a little better than usual. Of course, she was wearing a black halter-top that showed about three miles of white fleshy cleavage and a black skirt that looked like it belonged on a fifteen-year-old Catholic girl looking to seduce a priest.

I started the car and cursed as I navigated the one-way roads until I'd found the one that would take me to the Savannah-Chatham Precinct just a few blocks away. Mike and Nick were stationed out of the same house, by far the busiest since it was responsible for two counties, but Mike worked out of the Property Crimes division, so they didn't work together. Which was a good thing, because cops had a tendency to stick together and keep each other's secrets. It was some stupid brotherhood code as far as I could tell. Even if the brother was a douchebag.

"So what were you doing out tonight?" I asked. "Was it a girls' night out?"

"Nope. Mostly I was just trying to get laid. You can't do that in Whiskey Bayou."

This was true. The minute a woman walked in to Clampett's Bar the men knew she was fair game, and pretty much the first semi-sober guy that could get to her would be the lucky winner. Respectable women didn't go to Clampett's. Not even borderline respectable women went to Clampett's.

"I'm sure you'll find someone someday." Though I wasn't too sure her dogs would ever welcome anyone new into the family fold.

"Well, I tried," she said, disgusted. "But I kept waiting for the Jason Mamoas and Colin Farrells to walk into the bar, but all I kept seeing was the Jack Blacks and David Spades."

"That does make it difficult," I agreed. "Physical attraction is definitely a must for good sex."

"Not always. I was married once," she said, changing the subject abruptly. "Did you know that?"

Considering I'd been at the wedding, I did indeed know that bit of information. But since Rosemarie was slurring her words to the point she sounded like English wasn't her first language, I wasn't going to hold it against her for not remembering. She didn't wait for me to answer.

"He was a rotten son of a bitch," she continued. "And he was ugly as homemade sin, but he could fuck like a racehorse."

I swerved to avoid a car and wondered if I'd blacked out for a second. I tried to get the picture out of my mind of Roger Valentine pounding away at Rosemarie, but I was pretty sure I was scarred for life. Saying he was ugly as homemade sin was an understatement.

"Then I started putting on a little weight, and he told me he couldn't fuck properly if he actually had to look at me. I told him I'd managed just fine over the years by pretending he was Gerard Butler, but he didn't appreciate that much."

My mouth quirked a little and I decided being with Rosemarie was like watching a live soap opera. "Bastard," I said. "You're better off without him."

"Damn right," she said. "And anyway, it turns out I had a glandular problem, which was what was causing the weight gain. But what really put the kibosh on our marriage was when we found out I couldn't have kids. Turns out he'd been planning to populate Whiskey Bayou with his seed and forgot to tell me. We tried and tried, but according to the doctors, I've got the eggs of a ninety-year-old wizard."

I had no idea what the hell that meant, but I didn't want to interrupt her story to ask.

"Good riddance to him," she finally said, spitting into the hole in the floorboard of the car to seal the deal. "He knocked up Denise Grizzoldi before the ink was dry on our divorce papers, and now they've got six kids and she's the size of a monster truck. Serves him right. But I still hope his balls fall off and he's cursed with constant diarrhea."

I felt the need to make the sign of the cross, but I refrained. It was a hell of a curse to put on someone. One that only the Holy Mother could cure.

I parked down the street from the gated parking lot the on duty cops used so their vehicles wouldn't get vandalized while they were trying to serve and protect. I left the engine running, but I cut the lights, slouching down in my seat some so I wouldn't draw attention to myself.

Rosemarie was humming the theme to Star Trek and searching through her giant handbag for something. I took the time to look through Mike's file while we were waiting.

Mike was a big man—not fat—but just big. He was six foot six and solid as a brick shithouse. His hair was carrot red and he was a genuine throwback to Scottish chieftains, and he looked like he'd be perfectly comfortable tossing cabers across a field.

I looked over the picture of his vehicle and his license plate just to make sure I had it committed to memory, even though I passed it sitting in his driveway most mornings.

Mike was a creature of habit. Usually. He played poker on Thursday nights, he and Kate had date night on Saturday, and every fourth weekend they'd take a little trip somewhere.

But all of that stopped three weeks before. According to Kate, he'd been taking extra shifts to make a little extra money. That right there would have made me suspicious as hell. Kate and Mike were rolling in money. She made so much from the agency that Mike didn't even have to work. And they lived in the Park Hill area of Whiskey Bayou, where all the mansions sat above sea level so they didn't have to worry about flooding or sinking into the Atlantic like the rest of us did.

Kate put in the report that he'd been working past midnight most nights, and when he did get some time off, he didn't seem to want to spend it with her. He hadn't taken her to bed in over a month.

I sighed because that was a pretty good sign that Kate was probably right. When a man went that long without asking for sex, he was probably getting it from somewhere else. This is something I also knew from experience, only I'd been stupid enough at the time to think Greg was being respectful of my needs since I'd been under so much stress with the wedding.

Rosemarie found the stick of gum she'd been searching

for and was now playing Angry Birds on her phone while we waited.

"You know what would make this a whole lot better?" she asked.

"Chris Hemsworth sitting in the backseat with his shirt off?"

She blinked at me owlishly. "I was thinking cake. I could eat a whole fucking cake right now."

"That was my second choice," I said.

It was past ten and a few of the other cops getting off duty slowly trickled out of the station and to their cars. I could see Mike's white Ford F250 from where I was parked, so I knew he hadn't managed to slip by me. Another fifteen minutes passed, then thirty, and Mike still hadn't left the station. Rosemarie snored lightly beside me, her head pillowed on her breasts, and I was really starting to wish for that cake. I'd skipped dinner.

It was just shy of eleven by the time I saw Mike come out of the station. I waited until he pulled out and was a good block ahead before I turned my lights on and started to follow.

Rosemarie jerked against her seatbelt as I stopped at a red light, and she looked up, wild eyed and disoriented.

"What's happening? Do I need my gun?"

"Jesus, please tell me you don't have a gun in your purse."

"I left it in the toilet tank at home before I left for the bar. I didn't want to scare any of the men in case they caught a glimpse of it."

"Good thinking," I said, heading north on West 37th street to the Savannah Parkway. We were headed into a purely residential area of middle class tract homes and apartment buildings built in the seventies. I had a squishy feeling in my stomach. My cell phone rang, but I was afraid if I looked down long enough to answer then I'd lose Mike.

"Ooh, it's Nick," Rosemarie said. "That is a sexy beefcake of a man. I bet he knows just what to do with a woman in bed."

I figured it was probably best to stay silent. Nick had his doctorate in fornication. Unfortunately, his morning after technique needed a little work.

"I'll call him back later," I said. "Grab the camera from behind your seat."

Mike exited off the highway, and I slowed down and cut my lights again once I saw him turn onto a street lined with town homes. I stayed two blocks back, parking on the side of the road and rolling down my window. He pulled into a driveway next to a white Honda, and I took the camera from Rosemarie.

"Why does that man look familiar?" Rosemarie asked, sticking her head out her own window so she could get a better look.

Thank God the camera had an excellent zoom lens. Hiding Rosemarie was almost impossible without the two-block spread. I focused on Mike as soon as he got out of his truck, and took several shots as he walked up to the front door and rang the bell.

"Well, fuck," I said, taking the shot that had just sealed Mike's coffin.

I recognized the brunette who answered the door. I'd seen her leave the police station about twenty minutes before Mike. She was dressed in cotton boxers and a tank top. The zoom lens amplified the fact that she wasn't wearing a bra. Mike had certainly noticed too.

I fired off rapid shots until he walked inside and she closed the door behind them. I wasn't up to sneaking around the house and getting the nitty-gritty details. And I think as much as Kate wanted me to get proof of Mike's infidelity, that she probably wasn't really ready to see them either.

"I swear I've seen that man before," Rosemarie said.

"Nope, he's just another client." The last thing Kate needed was gossip, and Rosemarie had a mouth as big as a barn door. Anyway, it would only be a matter of time before it started getting out that they were having problems. "Let's get you home. You're probably going to have a hell of a hangover."

"I never get them," she said cheerfully.

I shot her a nasty look and turned the car back toward the highway. I had some thinking to do. And it was probably best if I avoided Kate until I figured out what to do. If I showed her those pictures, Nick would have another double homicide to investigate.

8

S *unday*

I ROLLED OUT OF BED THE NEXT MORNING WITH A HEAVY heart and a tension headache that was wrapping its way around my head and squeezing like it was one of those wrestlers with forty-two inch crushing thighs on Smack-down. So I did what I always do when confronted with stressful situations—I popped a couple of aspirin and baked like I was the sole contributor to the Rotary Club bake sale.

I'm not going to lie, it felt damned good to whack a rolling pin against the helpless dough of the cinnamon rolls I was making. By the time I slid them into the oven, the kitchen was covered in a fine mist of flour and I was contemplating just eating the butter by the stick. The only thing that saved me from going down that dark and dangerous road was the ringing of the doorbell.

A scowl etched my face and I felt my blood pressure

rising. I had a feeling it was Nick, and after more than twenty-four hours of post-coital bliss, followed by him pancaking on me, I wasn't in the mood to do anything but use my rolling pin as an assault weapon.

I jerked the door open and found myself face to face with Agent Savage.

"You planning on using that?" he asked, nodding to the rolling pin in my hand. "I'd advise against it. I don't think we're at the handcuffs stage of our relationship, though I'm willing to try if you are."

His dark eyes went all sleepy and sexy, and I started to close the door in his face, but he stepped inside before I could accomplish my goal. I looked around nervously, not sure what to do with him. Savage was a little suffocating. He was very male and his presence wasn't one that could be ignored. And I was at a loss as to where I was going to put him, considering I'd had sex with another man on almost every available surface in the house. I didn't want to cross-contaminate the men in my life.

"What are you doing here?" I finally asked, leading him back into the kitchen. "How'd you find me?"

He arched a brow and I sighed quietly. I was never hard to find. And after I'd seen how easy it was to get information on people the night before, I couldn't believe I'd been naïve enough to even ask the question.

"Sorry," I said. "I'm a little slow this morning. It was a long night."

"Good thing I came over," he said, sitting at the little breakfast table in the corner. "You'd have eaten all those cinnamon rolls and then you'd have hated yourself. Now I can help you ease the burden."

"You're very thoughtful."

I pulled the rolls from the oven and my eyes almost crossed as the smell of yeast, cinnamon and melted butter assaulted my senses. I might hate myself for eating them all, but it might be worth it.

"I got some new information regarding the Sirin Corporation that I thought you'd like to know."

"It turns out I have some information too. Computers are scary things."

"More than you know," he said, pulling one of the gooey rolls from the tray and taking a bite.

My mouth dropped open and excitement was gathering in places that had no business being ready to party with a man like Savage. A look of pure bliss came over his face, and I had a fleeting glimpse of what he probably looked like after achieving orgasm.

"Jesus, these are amazing. Why aren't you married?"

The feelings of excitement stopped in their tracks and shriveled back into the frozen depths of my love life.

"He decided the home ec teacher's tits were more exciting than my cinnamon rolls, but thanks for asking."

I bit into my own roll savagely and ignored his thoughtful look. We finished our rolls in silence and then I went to grab the papers I'd printed out the night before.

"So how are you learning anything new about this case if you've been ordered to stay away from investigating Sirin?" I asked, taking my seat across from him once more.

"I've got my sources. You don't do this job as long as I have without learning a few tricks on how to bend the rules and not get caught."

"So what did these sources tell you?"

"Tell me what you found first. Let's see if any of our information lines up."

I passed him the handful of papers I'd printed from Kate's office the night before.

"It looks like Amanda Whitfield isn't the only call girl to be permanently eliminated from the Sirin payroll recently.

Amanda seemed to be closest with three of the other Sirin girls—Becca Gonzales, Andi Bachman, and Noelle Price. But their quartet is down to two. Noelle Price was found dead two weeks ago in Atlanta. Apparent suicide. A couple of cops were called in, but from what I was able to find, they didn't even do a standard investigation for foul play. The medical examiner signed off on the death, and she was cremated within another twenty-four hours."

"We need to get to those other girls. I want to monitor everything they're doing. They're probably terrified at this point, and I have a gut feeling Natalie Evans isn't through with them yet. Let me make a call. I need to get someone tracking them."

Savage stepped out of the room and I helped myself to another cinnamon roll.

"Your turn," I said once he came back to the kitchen and took his seat.

I was glad I was still wearing my pajama bottoms with a stretchy elastic waist. I contemplated making a trip to get another cup of coffee, but I was weighed down by six pounds of yeasty goodness and butter. I might not move ever again, and I secretly wondered if Savage would think bad of me if I just oozed out of the chair and laid down on the floor.

Savage must have read my mind because he stood up and grabbed my coffee cup, making himself at home as he saw to the domestic chore. The rolls hadn't affected him at all. He still looked as deliciously fit as ever, and I couldn't even see the slightest hint of a paunch hanging over his belt. Bastard.

I might have said thank you as he set the coffee in front of me, but mostly I was thinking how unfair the roles of men and women were in today's world. It would be much easier on everyone if we lived in a time where Rubenesque women were worshipped, and men were trying to constantly shove food into our mouths.

"Addison," he said, arching one of those devil brows in my direction. "Your eyes have glazed over. I can't figure out if it's because you're full or you're bored."

"Sorry." I did another cursory glance of his body. "I suppose you work out."

"Every day. It gets to be a habit."

"Figures."

"Don't worry. I like a woman with curves." His grin showed a slash of white teeth against the copper of his skin and just the hint of one dimple.

"Nobody asked you," I mumbled.

This was getting embarrassing. I'm not going to lie and say I've never had luck getting the attention of the opposite sex. I can make myself look more than respectable—granted, this wasn't one of those times—but I was still having one of those moments where I thought the men showing interest in me might be a little above my hotness level. Maybe the universe was just playing a cruel joke. Maybe I should just throw caution to the wind and get as many orgasms as possible from this predicament. Unfortunately, I had a lifetime of Catholic guilt and mostly stable morals to keep me from doing such a thing.

"Are you going to tell me what you found out?" I asked belligerently.

"Natalie Evans' client list is one of the most sought after pieces of information in this country, right behind who shot JFK and how the hell Glenn Beck ever became famous. I've got a reliable source who says Natalie is very distrusting of technology."

"I don't blame her," I interrupted. "I'm rethinking my entire outlook on life after working this case."

"Eat another one of these and listen," he said, shoving

the last cinnamon roll past my open lips. "My source says she's so paranoid about people being able to hack into her files that she keeps everything written down and locked away in the safe in her home office."

"You have an informant inside the house?" That was the only way Savage could have come by information that specific as far as I knew. Not unless the Feds had the inside of the house wired, and I was thinking that was a big no-no considering they'd already had their hands slapped.

"I have informants everywhere. And that's protected information."

"So now what?"

"Technically, it would be unethical for me to search Natalie's home without a warrant. But I'm thinking a private investigator could get away with it if they managed not to get caught. Especially if there was a guarantee that the alarm would be disengaged tonight between the hours of ten and midnight while Natalie Evans is at a political fundraiser."

My mouth dropped open in shock. Talk about bending the rules a little. Agent Savage's sock rebellion had clearly gone to his brain.

"Are you out of your mind?" I stood up and slapped my hands down on the table. "I don't know anything about breaking and entering. I don't know how to crack safes or walk silently like a ninja."

He stood and mirrored my pose so we were practically nose-to-nose. "This is the only way to get that client list. Someone in that book is a murderer. Are you going to let them get away with it?"

"Oh, no. You're not going to lay the blame at my feet for this." My vision was starting to reach that hazy red of anger. "You guys are the ones who buffooned around until you got kicked off the case."

"I'm almost positive the word buffoon was never meant to be used as a verb."

"What?" I sputtered. "I'm trying to have a fight here. And you never interrupt a fight to correct grammar."

"My bad. Please continue."

"Now I don't remember what I was saying."

I ran my fingers through my hair and remembered it was in a haphazard knot on top of my head. Little specks of flour floated down in front of my face from my cooking tantrum, and I was distracted by Savage's lips. I could tell he wanted to laugh, but if he so much as cracked a smile I was going to punch him in the eye.

"I think you should start calling me by my first name. It's Matt, by the way."

"Savage fits you a whole lot better. I think I'll stick with that."

"I bet Kate would love to go along with you to search for Natalie's client list," he said changing the subject.

I was starting to get whiplash from following his conversations. "Did they not teach you how to fight properly in FBI school? I bet suspects walk all over you in an interrogation."

"I somehow manage to muddle through. The FBI has taught me many other things," he said, moving in a little closer. "And I happen to know for a fact that Kate knows exactly what she's doing when it comes to breaking and entering."

My eyes widened at this bit of news, but I guess it seemed plausible. I'd think it would be par for the course for a private detective to know about such things.

"Except there's one problem with that," I said triumphantly. "Kate is *not* a rule breaker. She's so squeaky clean you could serve dinner off her." Savage looked slightly confused by the saying, so I pressed my advantage.

"She will never agree to this. Nothing means more to her than the reputation of her agency."

I always suspected Savage was a dirty fighter. He was obviously a man who didn't like to lose. He leaned forward and took my mouth in another one of those tonsil exploring kisses, and I groaned because he tasted of hot sex and cinnamon rolls.

I managed to pull away before I ended up christening another table in my mother's house, but I was slightly dazed and huffing like a steam engine.

"I told you to stop doing that. I'm in a relationship, dammit."

It sounded like I was trying to convince myself of that information more than him. He quirked a brow but didn't contradict me.

"I dare you to ask her," Savage said, his own look of triumph settling over his features. "Kate is prime for the pickings for a little adventure and rule breaking. Especially after what I saw last night."

"Wait a minute." I slapped a hand against his chest and pushed him out of my comfort zone. "How do you know about Mike? I haven't even told Kate what I saw yet."

"Just because you're avoiding her," he said, shrugging. "I don't blame you. It's a sticky situation."

"Answer the damned question," I growled.

"Did you know you swear a lot more when you're angry? And to answer your question, I knew about Kate's husband because I've been following you. You don't think I'd just set you loose on a case like this and not keep track of you, do you? People are dying here. And you're just doing the things that I can't right now because of the politics Natalie Evans is playing."

A whole myriad of things was whipping through my mind at his confession. Indignation and anger were two I recognized right away. But another was fear. Savage had been following me around, and I'd had absolutely no inkling. Not even a twinge that there were eyes watching me. Of course, he was a professional, so that made me feel a little better.

"Just ask her," he pushed. "I'll be there as backup in case you get into trouble."

"I don't mean to snoop into your private business," I said, gathering up the dishes and taking them to the sink. "But do you get into a lot of trouble with your superiors on a regular basis? You seem to have an issue with authority."

"They're just jealous because I have better taste in socks."

"I'm sure that's it."

I looked around the kitchen and winced at the mess. I wasn't a neat cook. I'd pretty much used every pot and pan in the house, and flour and spices were sprinkled on most of the flat surfaces. Good thing my mother wasn't in town. I could leave it for later without feeling too much guilt.

"What do you have planned for the day?" Savage asked a little too innocently.

I narrowed my eyes and wondered if some of his Indian ancestors had been shamans. I had plans—but they weren't anything I wanted to share with him. Savage had an uncanny ability to wiggle his way into a situation without you being aware until it was too late.

The first of my plans was to find a new place to live if I had to do back alley hand jobs to achieve the dream. The second was to avoid Kate at all costs. I didn't want to go to her with my suspicions about Mike until I had given her the case tied up with a bow. I didn't want there to be any room for doubt if I was going to be the one to deliver life-destroying news.

My life was getting complicated. I wasn't all that good

at subterfuge. Good thing I'd had years to perfect my lying techniques or I'd have been in trouble.

"My plans are no concern of yours. Stop trying to complicate my life."

The slow stretch of the smile across his face was like being stripped of one article of clothing at a time. "I am complicating your life, sweetheart. You'll just have to deal with it. I've heard through the grapevine that you're looking for a new place to live."

"Someday I'm going to have to meet these infamous sources of yours. They must have sold their souls to the devil to know so much."

"What if I tell you I have a friend who has a little house in Savannah that needs immediate occupancy?"

"I'd say it's probably way out of my budget. I've checked the prices in Savannah. There was nothing that even came close to what I can afford."

"This place hasn't been advertised yet. Some friends of mine bought it for their mother several years ago, but she passed away last month. It's an older home, but it's in good shape, and I think you'll be surprised at the rent. My friends are in a position where they don't really need the extra income. They have rental properties for the tax deductions."

"Are you serious?" I asked, propping my hands on my hips. "This isn't your idea of a cruel joke is it?"

"I'm serious. I'd be glad to give them a call and set up a time for you to see it—"

I could tell by the slight pause in his voice that there was a *but* coming.

"What's the catch?" I asked.

He crossed his arms over his massive chest and rocked back on his heels. "I want that first date I told you about yesterday. I'm not above bribing my way into getting it."

"That's low, Agent Savage. Downright despicable."

"I told you to call me Matt—"

"I'd rather call you Lucifer—"

"And it might be despicable, but I'm going to get what I want."

I tapped my foot on the ground in indignation. He was right. I'd give in because I had to get out of this house and back on my own. I had to get out of Whiskey Bayou. It was important to get on with the next phase of my life as soon as possible and pretend like the last year had never happened. In the last twelve months I'd been left at the altar, I'd run over said fiancé, been sued, evicted and fired. I was starting to hope the Mayans were right about the whole end of the world thing.

"I'm in a relationship," I said again, just for good measure.

"And where is Detective Dempsey? He's been unusually absent."

My subconscious filled in the blank. Nick had been unusually absent since he'd gotten what he'd wanted.

"He's working a homicide. I was a cop's daughter long enough to know how those things go. He'll be back when he can." *I hoped.*

Savage arched a brow. "It's up to you then. But my deal stands."

"Fine, but here are my terms. I'll go with you, but I'm not calling it a date. We can go as friends, and if you try to kiss me again I'm going to make you a soprano."

"Don't threaten me unless you can back it up, Addison. You and I both know you like me kissing you more than you want to admit."

"I'm going to take a shower. Call your friends." I stomped towards the bathroom, angry that he'd had the last word. "And if this house isn't every damned thing I need it to be and cheaper than dirt, then your slimy deal is off and you can go back to dating your hand."

He barked out a laugh as I slammed the bathroom door. *Shit, shit, shit.* I looked at my phone and willed it to ring. It would have been a great time for Nick to call.

9

"Of course it would be perfect," I muttered under my breath two hours later.

"What was that?" Savage asked, trying to hide his smile as we walked to the front door.

The tiny house sat in the middle of an older neighborhood, surrounded by neatly mowed lawns and American made cars. It was dark blue with white trim and matching shutters, and it was so small I could almost lie down in front of it, stretch my arms up and point my toes, and reach it from end to end. But the paint was fresh and it wasn't falling down, so I let my hopes creep up a bit.

The porch creaked under our combined weight, and Savage stooped to grab the key the owners had left under the mat. He turned the key in the deadbolt and the door creaked when he push it open.

Fresh Pine Sol and hot air smacked me in the face as Savage waited for me to precede him inside. I stepped into a small square of a living room with scarred wood floors. An even smaller dining room was in the middle. A crooked brass chandelier hung from the ceiling and a big square window looked out to a patch of chain length fence smothered with hydrangea bushes.

Savage leaned against the front door as I walked further into the house, the floors squeaking beneath me. The kitchen floor was large squares of black and white linoleum and newish white appliances were freshly scrubbed. I didn't even need to see the rest of the house. There was no way I could afford this place—not in as good of shape as it was in. I mentally rearranged my checking account and pretended there was extra money stashed in places for rainy day occurrences such as this.

"How much is it?" I finally asked, dreading the numbers.

Savage rattled off a price that made me light-headed, and before I knew it I'd agreed to sign the lease they'd left on the counter and give him a check for first and last month's rent so he could deliver it to his friends.

I was in a state of shock the entire way back to Whiskey Bayou. I'd done it. I was 92% of the way toward being a free woman. I didn't want to give Savage any ideas, but I was feeling mighty warm towards him for the moment.

"I've got to drop you off and meet with some of my men," he said as we reached my mother's house.

"You have men?"

"That's what the Special Agent in Charge part of my name means."

I grabbed my purse and got out of his nicely air conditioned Tahoe into the swampy humidity of Whiskey Bayou. "Thanks for telling me about the house. Maybe you're not such a bad guy after all."

"Just a minute, Mata Hari," he said, grabbing my purse and yanking me back so I was partially inside the car. "You've got a job to do tonight. We need that client list, and I've got everything set up for you so you can get in easily.

Get Kate up to date, and be ready to rock n' roll right at ten o'clock. I'll be parked down the street where I can keep watch."

"Has anyone ever told you you're bossy?"

"All the time, sweetheart. Sometimes that's a good thing."

He gave me one of those slow smiles and a wink and pushed me the rest of the way out of the car. I was still standing there confused when he sped away.

IT TURNS OUT I DIDN'T HAVE TO GO HUNTING FOR KATE TO get her to agree to this harebrained idea of Savage's. She came looking for me, and I saw her car pull up outside the window just in time to get the camera hidden I'd used the night before.

"I got a call from Agent Savage," she said by way of greeting. "He said you needed my help on something tonight."

I noticed the duffle bag slung over her shoulder but I didn't mention it. It looked like Kate was staying the night. Or maybe the week.

"Savage is a nosy bastard. He's going to be surprised as hell when he gets my bill."

"I think Savage wants to pay you in different ways." Kate headed to the fridge and got herself a beer, popping the top and tossing it in the trash on her way back to the living room. "I saw the way he looked at you. He's hot."

"I think he might be a bit unstable," I said. "I don't know why that's attractive."

"It's the bad boy persona. Men like that are great for sex, but hell to live with. Nick's got the same vibe about him." Kate plopped down on the couch and put her feet on the coffee table. "Speaking of Nick, he can't be happy about you working with Savage so closely."

"Nick can jump off a bridge," I said, joining her on the couch. I was doing without the beer because I still felt guilty about the cinnamon rolls.

Her eyes widened. "Uh-oh. What did he do?"

"You mean besides giving me the most amazing sexual experience of my life and then not making contact in—" I looked at my watch and calculated quickly. "Thirty-six and a half hours."

Kate sighed and shook her head. "I heard he caught a bad one. You might need to give him a break on this one."

"He told me. The sex came after the dead bodies. He was able to squeeze me in. But a text message or a carrier pigeon with a note that said *I'm not dead* would be thoughtful, don't you think?"

"It's true. He could have managed something. All men are assholes."

The silence that followed that statement was extremely awkward and I fought to keep from fidgeting in my seat. I needed a distraction, and I needed one fast.

"So—it turns out Agent Savage wants us to break into Natalie Evans' house tonight and steal her client list," I blurted out. "Though I'm sure Savage would deny this if asked outright. He's a bit shady, I think."

Kate choked on her beer and I pounded her on the back until she was breathing steadily, if a bit red-faced.

"You've got to be kidding me," she said. "What makes him think I can bypass an alarm of that quality without doing a little recon first?"

My hand stilled on her back as I stared at her, wide-eyed. That wasn't the first question I'd expected to come out of her mouth. I was expecting a *hell no*, or a resounding *that's illegal*.

"Um, Kate." I took the beer from her hand and chugged back a fortifying swallow. "You're not actually thinking about going through with this, are you? What happened to protecting the reputation of the agency and following all the rules?"

"Maybe I'm tired of following all the damned rules all the time," she said, her voice hitching on the verge of hysteria.

I was pretty close to hysteria myself. I wasn't used to being the rational one.

"Maybe I want to do something reckless," she insisted, taking back her beer and downing the rest of the bottle. "Maybe if my life is going to hell anyway, I should just enjoy the ride and join in the fun. We need to get Savage on the phone. I need to know how to get past her security."

Kate stood up and started rummaging around in the duffle bag she'd brought, pulling out black cargo pants and a black t-shirt.

"Savage said the alarms would be down from ten to midnight. I think he has someone on the inside." I felt like I was standing outside my body looking at the scene playing out before me.

"That's smart. Savage is a good agent. He was a Green Beret, you know. I did a background check on him after he made contact with me. Long sleeves would be better," she said, almost to herself. "I bet there's an extra in the closet somewhere."

"I don't mean to be a wet blanket, but how are we supposed to get the client list once we're inside? Savage said she keeps it locked in a safe in her office."

"I just need to know what kind of safe it is, so I know what tools to bring. I want to go in with as little baggage as possible. Having you with me is going to be bad enough, but I could use a look out."

"Hey," I said, indignation coloring my voice. I fisted my hands to my hips. "I resent being referred to as baggage. If you're going to call this mission anything, be honest and call it stupidity. We have no experience with breaking and entering."

"*You* have no experience with breaking and entering," Kate said. "I'm a professional."

"You're a professional private detective. You are not Grace Kelly in To Catch A Thief."

"That's a great movie," she said, heading to my bedroom, no doubt to search through my closet.

"It is a great movie. But it doesn't change the fact that we're breaking the law here. No matter how noble the reason. I don't want to go to jail. I'm just starting to have sex again."

"Lucky for you he's a cop and can probably sneak in the occasional conjugal visit. I'm going to call Savage. I need more information."

I fell back on my bed and stared at the ceiling. My life was going to hell in a handbasket, and I was wondering at what point I'd be able to get back in control.

AT THREE MINUTES TO TEN I FOUND MYSELF DRESSED IN head to toe black, hidden behind a thicket of crape myrtles and sweating my ass off. Wearing long sleeves and pants during one of the hottest summers in history was just asking for trouble, and already I was finding it a little difficult to breathe. Of course, that could also be the panic.

I'd caught sight of Savage's black Tahoe parked down the street where one of Natalie's neighbors seemed to be having a pretty swinging party, and he was absorbed perfectly in the landscape. Only Kate and I looked ridiculous taking cover behind bushes and garbage cans. I could only be thankful there were no other witnesses.

"It's time," Kate said, adjusting the pack of supplies on her back.

Savage had told Kate the best point of entry was the French doors that led into the master bedroom at the back of the house. The only problem was the giant fucking wall that encased the back yard. I wasn't about to delude myself at this point. I'd been doing this long enough to know that I had absolutely no skill when it came to the more athletic parts of my job.

We were just across the narrow alley, looking at the solid stone fence that rose more than ten feet above us, when I felt the buzz of my phone in my pocket. I pulled it out, and I saw Kate shake her head as she tried to cover the light it was making with her hands.

"It's Nick," I whispered.

She shook her head no again, but I was already dropping to the ground and turning my body into the darkness so I could answer. I heard Kate sigh behind me, and take cover further back into the shrubs.

"Hello," I said as softly as possible.

"Why are you whispering?" Nick asked.

"I'm trying to work."

"Then you shouldn't have answered the phone."

"I saw it was you and thought you might need to tell me something important."

Like thanks for the sex, or sorry for pancaking on you, or I love you. *Jesus, where had that come from?*

"Nevermind," I added. "I don't need to hear anything from you."

"Have you been drinking?" he asked.

"No, I'm with Kate." And I wasn't about to tell him we'd

both taken a fortifying shot of tequila before we'd left my house.

"Oh, well that makes me feel better. You can't possibly get into trouble with Kate."

I heard Kate snicker and realized she could hear every word Nick was saying.

"You bet," I assured him. "We're safe and sound tonight. No shenanigans going on at all. Is there a reason you called?"

Kate punched me on the shoulder and signaled me to wrap it up. We were working within a time frame.

"I just wanted to let you know I'd wrapped up the case I was working. I'm going home to get a full night's sleep, but I thought I'd stop by and see you tomorrow. I'm off all day." His voice lowered to a caress that touched every nerve ending in my body. "Get a good night's sleep tonight. You're going to be busy tomorrow."

Spots danced in front of my eyes at the implication of what he had planned, and would have fallen over in the bushes if Kate hadn't steadied me.

"Wow," I said for lack of anything better. "I have to go now."

"Be safe," he said and hung up.

"I'm going to be pissed if I'm in jail instead of getting my world rocked tomorrow," I said, shoving the phone back in my pocket.

"If you're done with social hour maybe we can break into this goddamned house now," Kate said. "I've got cramps and my tequila is starting to wear off."

"I'm ready," I said, nodding at her in reassurance. I'd probably be a lot more resistant to this whole thing if I hadn't had the smooth warmth of the tequila flowing through my veins.

We stayed to the shadows and crept to the back fence. It

was built of solid gray stone and it was hot to the touch, having absorbed the heat from the sun all day. Kate laced her fingers together and gave me the go ahead to put a foot in so she could boost me over.

I wasn't sure I should be the first to go over the wall, but I wouldn't have been able to make it otherwise. I'd never been able to climb the rope in gym class. So I placed my foot in Kate's hands and we did a couple of awkward test bounces before I grabbed onto her shoulder with one hand and put the other on the hot stone of the wall.

She pushed with all her might and I went flying to the top ledge of the fence, and an unladylike *oomph* coming from my mouth as I jackknifed across the top and my pelvis took the brunt of the impact.

"Fuck, that's hot," I whispered, the blood rushing to my head as I hung over the top of the fence. I wasn't sure where to put my hands without them getting burned and I teetered back and forth like a seesaw, trying to decide the best course of action.

I slowly brought my knees up and started scooching the rest of my body to the other side. The problem was that ten feet going up wasn't all that big of a deal. But I had ten feet going down that I had no idea how to maneuver. It's not like there were bales of hay on the other side to break my fall.

"For fuck's sake, Addison. Hurry," Kate hissed.

Sweat dripped in my eyes and my boobs were squished against the rocks made of lava. I finally gathered all my strength and heaved my legs over the fence. Unfortunately, I overcompensated and started the long fall to the ground. I caught myself by the tips of my fingers and got a nice glimpse of the stars before I plummeted to the ground.

The good thing about having the wind knocked out of you was that you hardly made any sound at all. The bad thing was not being sure if your spine was broken, or if the crack you just heard was the equivalent of getting an adjustment.

A thin nylon rope landed on my stomach, and I had enough wherewithal to grab hold and brace my feet against the wall as Kate's weight pulled against it. She hopped over the side and landed on her feet like a damned cat, so silent that if I hadn't been watching her I wouldn't have known she was there.

"Sometimes I hate you," I said, rolling to my hands and knees once I was able to take deep breaths again.

"It's those cinnamon rolls you had this morning. Don't think I didn't notice the mess your kitchen was in. Maybe you should think about clean living."

"Maybe you should mind your own beeswax."

I stayed glued to Kate's back as we made our way from tree to tree, avoiding a koi pond and a metal sculpture that looked like one of Satan's kidney stones. A large swimming pool sat just outside the French doors leading into the bedroom, and the urge to yank off all my clothes and dive in was more exciting than the prospect of what we'd find in that client list.

"Stay here," Kate whispered. "Keep watch on all the entrances. I'm going to check the door."

Kate scurried off and knelt in front of the French doors, checking to see if they were unlocked before she pulled the black case from her bag. I tried to keep watch on all the entrances to the backyard like Kate had told me to do, but I was too fascinated by the lock picking set in her nimble fingers. I wondered if they'd teach me to do that stuff in classes to become a private detective. Somehow, I was thinking that wasn't a skill they wanted to teach to the general public.

She had the door open in a matter of seconds, and

when she gestured for me to join her, I ran to her side like the great loping gazelle I was—almost slipping on the edge of the pool and going in face first.

"Thank God," I said as we entered the bedroom.

The air conditioning was on full blast, and I took a minute to lean against the wall and let the sweat on my skin turn to chills while Kate locked the French doors behind us and went to check the security system.

The green light was on, letting us know it was disengaged, and she gave me a thumbs up signal to show everything was good. I would have returned the gesture, but it seemed like a lot of energy to move my thumbs at this point.

She moved to the bedroom door that led into the house and knelt down so she could see through the crack at the bottom of the door. Savage had managed to get us a set of blueprints for the house, and we'd already mapped out our route to get to Natalie's office on the second floor.

I joined Kate at the door and held my breath as she turned the doorknob slowly, easing it open a crack without making a sound. I already knew I wasn't cut out for the life of a criminal. Butterflies were dive-bombing in my stomach and I had to pee like a racehorse.

We hunched over and made our way through the long corridor. There was staff moving all over the damned house and we barely ducked into a dark room as a man in a black suit jacket walked by.

The steady pressure Kate was putting on my arm let me know more than anything that now wouldn't be a good time to make a sound. We were hiding behind a love seat, our view obstructed so the only thing we could see were his shoes as he made a second pass down the hall.

"He's security," Kate finally said. "And he's carrying."

"Carrying what?" I asked.

I could see the whites of her eyes rolling in the dark. "A gun. Try to stay out of his way."

"Right," I nodded.

Kate took a gleaming black weapon from her bag and shoved it in the front of her pants. This was going from bad to worse with every passing second. We'd now upgraded from just burglary to armed robbery.

I grabbed Kate by the shoulder before she could move back toward the door, and I shook my head frantically, trying to get her to see reason. When she decided to go off the deep end, she did it with style.

"Relax, it's a tranquilizer gun." The words were barely a whisper, floating on the air.

"I knew that," I said, relieved.

I followed her back to the doorway, and we went out quickly, heading for the second set of stairs towards the kitchen. Savage's contact had told him they were the least travelled at this time of night because most of the live in staff was in their private quarters.

I was sweating bullets—despite the air conditioning— by the time we made it to the second floor. The stairs went up even higher, but we broke off and slipped down the long hallway to the last room on the left. I kept watch while Kate worked her magic on the locked door, and then we were inside and Kate was shoving things into my hands to put away in her bag. Apparently, I was the equivalent of a thief's personal assistant.

I relocked the door and took out the small tool Kate had showed me how to use back at my place. It was like a miniature version of a submarine periscope, and I lay down on the floor and stuck one end under the crack in the door, curving it gently so I could see the entire length of the hallway when I put the other end to my eye.

I was too scared to watch Kate diddle with the safe

she'd found behind the abstract painting of a naked woman with five breasts. Time slowed to the point that I could hear every thud of my heart and count the seconds we were inside.

"Bingo," Kate whispered. "I've got it."

The words barely registered because I saw and recognized the shoes standing at the top of the landing. The security guard was back and he was making his way up the hall, poking his head in each of the rooms like he had downstairs. I had no idea if he had orders to stay out of Natalie's office, but I wasn't about to stick around and find out.

I jumped up and shoved everything back in Kate's bag, waving my hands around in indiscernible hand gestures that she couldn't possibly interpret, but I think my urgency got through just the same because she tossed me the small, leather bound book in her hands and went back to closing the safe and putting the painting back on the wall.

I put the little book in the bag and slung it across my body, and I bit my lip to make sure no stray noises of fear escaped. Kate went to the large picture window and motioned me over as she unlatched it and pushed it open with only a minimal squeak of the hinges. It was enough to have both of us pausing as we heard the doorknob rattle.

We gave each other identical *oh, shit* looks and Kate shoved me out the window and onto a steep patch of roof. A huge magnolia tree covered our escape, but it wouldn't for long. We were on the front side of the house nearest the street, and I was thinking now would be a great time for Savage to lend us a helping hand.

Kate hopped out behind me and reclosed the window, and then she grabbed my hand and we ran, using the steep pitch of the roof to climb up to the third story so there was less chance of being seen if the guard looked out the

143

window. We scaled the widow's walk and crouched low beneath a dormer, waiting to see if we'd been spotted.

I was almost ready to declare surrender and let them cart me away. Our only option down from such a height was to jump across to the closest tree and climb down. I'd already had my fair share of experiences with tree climbing, and none of them had ended well. I wasn't expecting this time to be any different.

I could see Savage's Tahoe from where we were sitting, and I dug around in Kate's bag until I came out with a pair of small binoculars. I looked through them and saw the incredulous expression on Savage's face as he stared back at me. I waved and he dropped his head on the steering wheel, banging it hard enough that I thought he might do some damage.

"Savage says hi," I told Kate, replacing the binoculars. "So what's the plan? I'm assuming it has something to do with that tree."

"Looks like the only way," she said.

Neither of us were in a hurry, but I saw Savage get out of his Tahoe and move like a shadow through the neighborhood until he stood below us.

"He's very stealthy," I commented. "That's kind of hot."

"It is. I guess we'd better go. He doesn't seem to be in all that good of a mood."

"This was his dumb idea in the first place. And it's not like we didn't get what we came for."

Savage climbed the tree like a stealth monkey until we were almost eye-to-eye.

"You go first," I said, nudging Kate.

It was a hell of a jump from the roof to the sturdiest branch, and I wasn't all that confident in my abilities. My limbs were stiff from sitting so long and my full bladder was weighing me down.

Savage gave Kate the all clear and she made a flying leap toward the thick branch. She wrapped her arms and legs around the branch and scooted towards the safety of the trunk. She shimmied halfway down the tree, staying hidden in the branches while she waited for me to take my turn.

"You're up, Addison," Savage called out quietly.

I looked down the three stories below me and looked back at Savage with sheer terror in my eyes. There was no way I could kamikaze myself onto that branch. I shook my head no, even as he scooted further out onto the branch, holding out his hand.

"I can't do it," I said back. "Y'all go on without me. Save yourselves."

He rolled his eyes and said, "Get a grip. It's twelve minutes until midnight. I don't think you want to still be here when the alarms go back on. Now jump, dammit."

I chewed on my bottom lip and did a few stretches. Maybe I should have worn my Nikes instead of my Chuck's. Not a lot of bounce in Chuck's, but they were the only all black thief shoes I had.

"This is going to have to go into my report," Savage said. "It'll say chicken in big red letters right next to your name."

I narrowed my eyes and made a flying leap for the branch, catching Savage by surprise. I wrapped my arms and legs around like I'd watched Kate do, but I ended up sliding sideways until I was hanging upside down like an opossum.

"Christ," Savage muttered as his strong arms pulled me from certain death. "It's like going on a mission with Gomer Pyle."

"Excuse me," I hissed. "Not all of us can be Green Berets. And I bet you looked really stupid in the hat."

I heard Kate snort out a laugh and I watched as Savage's mouth tightened to a thin line.

"Respect the beret," he finally said.

He wrapped his arm around my ribs and squeezed a little tighter than was necessary, in my opinion, and then he made easy work of getting both of us onto solid ground. The urge to kiss the grass was fleeting as the party from down the street began to let out and traffic picked up.

"I'll follow you back to your place," he said as we ran for cover. "I want to see that book."

I didn't tell him there was no way in hell he was getting a look at that book tonight. I just ran back with Kate to her car and hopped in, taking a pit stop by a gas station along the way so I could use the restroom.

When we got to my house, Kate and I ran inside, laughing like lunatics before Savage could get out of his car and stop us. I bolted the door behind us. Kate and I had a date with a bottle of tequila to finish.

I'd just set out the bottle and two shot glasses when Kate dropped a bomb. "So how long are you going to wait to tell me if my husband is cheating on me?"

10

M*onday*

THE WILD BLAST OF *BABY GOT BACK* BLARING IN MY EAR HAD my head jerking up and smacking on the underside of the dining room table. The details of getting under the table were hazy, but since I had a rolled up towel for a pillow and my high school letter jacket for a blanket, I was assuming I'd decided to use the table as a tent of sorts. I'm sure it made sense at one point.

I reached blindly for the phone and didn't even bother to look at the screen to see who was calling.

"Lo," I mumbled, trying to decide how to navigate through the maze of chairs surrounding me. It seemed like a lot of effort, so I laid my head back down on the towel. I might have dozed for a few minutes because I woke again to the buzz of Savage's voice nattering in my ear.

"Addison. Answer me now or I'm going to be there in the next ten minutes to put my foot through your door."

"I'm here. Don't get your panties in a twist. And stop talking so loud. My head hurts." My voice sounded like I'd spent the night swallowing shards of glass instead of tequila.

His sigh was audible from the other end, and even that felt like ball peen hammers rocketing through my skull.

"Did you get a chance to look through the client list?" he finally asked after several seconds of silence.

"Yeah, Kate and I read through the whole thing last night. We made it a drinking game." Which, as it turns out, was a bad idea. "You wouldn't believe some of the names in there. It just goes to show that the men in Hollywood don't take their marriages seriously."

"You needed a little black book to tell you that?"

"I at least had the illusion," I defended. "I assume you want to see it for yourself?"

"Yeah, but I'm tied up at the moment. Can you meet me in Kate's office at three o'clock? I want to look through that list and check out the background you've done so far. Maybe something will click and we can take a fresh look at this thing."

"Three o'clock," I mumbled. I calculated the time in my head and figured I could make myself mostly presentable by then. "Sure, I can do that."

"Keep that list safe," he said. "If anyone finds out you have it, you could be in danger."

He hung up with that ominous warning, and I decided maybe I should put the book somewhere safe until three o'clock. I navigated my way past the labyrinth of dining room chairs, knocking a couple over as I finally crawled from beneath the table and managed to stand.

An empty bottle of tequila sat on the coffee table and the remnants of a bag of Oreos accompanied it. No wonder I felt so bad. Just the thought of all those Oreos sloshing around in a bath of tequila was enough to make me turn green.

I downed a couple of aspirin and got into the shower, and by the time I got out again I was semi-human and ready for a cup of coffee. I wrapped my head in a towel and my bathrobe around my body and headed into the kitchen.

I eeped out what could only pass for a scream with my damaged vocal cords at the sight of a stranger putting dishes in the dishwasher. He looked a little startled at my appearance, and he immediately handed me a cup of coffee. I breathed in the aroma and felt the tension drain from my body.

"You're a godsend," I finally said. "The best man I know."

"Remember that," Nick said, smiling. "Kate doesn't look much better than you. I stopped into the office this morning to see if she had anything new for me, and it was like being met by the swamp creature."

He shuddered at the memory and I tried to smile, the corners of my mouth working their way up slowly. I finished the coffee and handed my cup to him silently, letting him refill it so I could start the process all over again.

My brain finally started to function and I took a good look around. The kitchen was spotless, and Nick stood with his back to the counter and his arms crossed over his chest. He was dressed in the suit he often wore when he had to speak to the media and a blue and gold striped tie. His jacket was draped over the kitchen chair, and the sleeves of his dress shirt were rolled up, exposing the sexiest forearms I'd ever had the privilege of being acquainted with.

It was starting to get hot in the kitchen all of a sudden. And very crowded.

"I—umm—I thought you had the day off. What's up with the suit?"

"I had a meeting with the mayor this morning and a press conference. The rest of the day is mine to do as I wish."

He loosened the tie at his throat, pulling it from beneath the collar with one long swipe, and he unbuttoned the top button of his white dress shirt, exposing a dark expanse of throat and a small amount of chest hair. I clenched my thighs together and tried to think of something to say, but I was pretty much brain dead at that point.

"I know just the thing for that hangover," he said.

His voice was pure silk and sex. I could hear the smile and wanted to return it, but all I could do was stare, mesmerized as his fingers undid the rest of his buttons.

"Are you trying to make me crazy?" I managed to croak out.

"How am I doing?"

"Pretty damned good. My headache's gone."

He pulled the shirt from the waistband of his slacks and had his fingers poised at his belt buckle when I couldn't stand it any longer and pounced. His lips met mine, and I forgot that I was trying to be mad at him for not calling after the last time. I didn't even think too much about the fact that I'd eaten all of those cinnamon rolls the morning before, and now Nick was about to see me naked. At least I didn't think about it too much.

Things got pretty hazy from that point on, but we actually made it to the bed this time. All I knew was that three hours later, all signs of my hangover were gone and I couldn't feel my feet. After another shower—which involved more messing around—and a quick sandwich, I was back in top form and ready to get to work. I filled Nick in on everything I'd found out about the case, and showed him the little black book we'd retrieved from Natalie Evans' home the night before.

"I don't suppose you want to tell me where you got this," he said, flipping through the pages and letting out a soft whistle between his teeth at some of the names written there.

"It's probably best if you don't know. You wouldn't get sex if I was in prison."

"I'm a cop," he said, not bothering to look up. "I'd make sure you got conjugal visits."

"Thoughtful of you," I said, looking over his shoulder. "What we have is politicians, A-list actors, eight princes, twelve rock stars, two opera singers, an underage pop star, a sultan, the governor of Georgia, and the police commissioner. Not to mention the billionaires and philanthropists. That's a long list of potential murderers."

"Fuck," Nick said, rubbing his hands over his face. "This isn't good. In fact, this is really, really bad. This morning at the press conference, I was asked about the murder of Sasha Malakov and if the gems he'd been transporting had been recovered. The mayor stepped in and gave a bullshit answer about professional thieves who'd been following the auction sites, making it sound like it was the same group of people who pulled off that diamond heist in Luxembourg last year. Christian DeLuce is making a public nuisance of himself, making it sound like we're all twiddling our thumbs while a murderer goes free, and it looks like he might be right."

"So what do we do?"

"What you've been doing. I'll help out however I can, but with this many officials involved, I've got to be careful. I'll assume it's going the same way for Agent Savage, since he's got you doing stupid ass things like breaking into Natalie Evans' private office to steal her client list."

I tried to look innocent, but I could feel the heat of guilt rushing to my face.

"Jesus, Addison. I can't believe you'd take a risk like that. I hate to even imagine how he talked you into doing it."

"Hey, that's uncalled for. Besides, Kate was with me the whole time. We were perfectly safe."

I tried not to think about the random kisses and the blackmail date I'd agreed to just in case Nick had become a mind reader since I saw him last. I pinched my lips together with indignant anger.

"Somehow that doesn't make me feel better. And what the hell was Kate thinking going along with a stunt like that? That doesn't sound like her at all."

"She's having a personal crisis. I was hoping she'd decline Savage's invitation, but she kind of ran with it."

"What kind of personal crisis?" Nick asked. His eyes were narrowed and I could see the anger he was trying to hide smoldering in his eyes.

And that's when I realized. "You already know," I said, mouth hanging open. "Of course you do. The gossip spreads faster in cop shops than in Betty's Beauty Parlor. Son of a bitch. Why didn't you say something?"

"Because it's not something you just walk up to someone and drop on them. I work for Kate occasionally and I know her only as an acquaintance on a personal level. She's a smart woman. I knew it wouldn't take long for her to find out."

"I'm going to kill him," I said, pulling clothes out of the closet and tossing them on the bed. I rummaged around in my underwear drawer and came out with a pair of black lacy underwear, tossing them on the bed as well. "I'm going to hunt him down like a dog and shove his body parts through a meat grinder."

Nick winced and squirmed on his chair, said body parts obviously cringing in sympathy.

"I'm sure Kate has a meat grinder of her own. You might let her handle this. Probably death by meat grinder doesn't allow for conjugal visits."

I glanced up and grinned. He was still in his underwear, looking rumpled and sexy sitting at my desk. I tried to ignore the sudden rush of happiness I felt just in case he could see my feelings on my face. I was afraid I was falling in love with him, and I knew from experience that the sudden rush of euphoria only lasted so long before reality slapped you in the face.

"What are these?" he asked, holding up the underwear I'd tossed. "I've never seen these before. They look fun. You should put them on."

"I plan on it," I said, yanking them from his fingers.

"And then I can take them off again."

A general look in the direction of his lap showed me he was very interested in taking them off again, but I moved out of reach and shimmied into them before he could grab me.

"We don't have time. I'm supposed to meet Agent Savage at Kate's office at three. He wants me to bring the client list."

"I just bet he does," Nick said, jaw clenched together. "Maybe I should join you for this little meeting. Just to be kept in the loop."

"Fine with me," I said, tossing my robe aside and pulling on the turquoise and lime green maxi dress I'd gotten on sale at Neiman's last summer. "But you should probably get dressed, unless you're just dying to rub it in his face that you spent the morning naked with me."

"I won't have to rub it in. He'll know. Men recognize things like that."

"Too bad they can't recognize when the toilet seat is up or when the garbage needs to be taken out."

"Some have more highly developed senses than others," he said.

WE TOOK NICK'S TRUCK INTO SAVANNAH SINCE HE'D MORE or less invited himself to stay the night at my place. And because he had air conditioning. Things were comfortable between us, which felt a little odd considering we'd spent most of our time up till now arguing.

I almost didn't see them until we'd driven right by— Noogey Winthrop and Marika Dubois.

"Stop!" I yelled, yanking on Nick's sleeve as he slammed on the brakes. It was a good thing no one was behind us or it would have been smash city.

"Are you fucking crazy? You don't just go doing that while someone is driving."

"Don't you call me crazy," I said giving him my best PMS look. "I was just taken by surprise. Pull over there and park before they see us."

"I'd be surprised if anyone *hasn't* seen us. I'm stopped in the middle of the goddamned street."

"That's why I told you to park over there," I said, showing more than adequate restraint. "I need my files."

I rummaged through my bag while Nick did an illegal turn and parked off the side of the road. I could practically hear his molars grinding together, but I didn't care. I'd just seen Noogey and Marika walk into Christian DeLuce's jewelry store. Not the usual shopping place for the destitute and impoverished.

I glanced Nick over from head to toe. Other than the flush of anger in his cheeks he looked like a successful businessman dressed in his suit. Thanks to the dress, I didn't look half bad either.

"How do you feel about a little shopping?"

"Does it involve sex toys?"

"Not unless Christian DeLuce is designing diamond encrusted dildos in his shop. Which doesn't sound like all that great of an idea now that I've said it out loud."

Nick sighed and looked at the front page of the file in my hand. "If we're going in a jewelry store you're going to owe me more than regular sex tonight. It's going to have to be chandelier sex. And it'll probably have to include dairy products."

"I was hoping you'd say donuts," I said, shoving the file back in my bag and getting out of the truck. "That'd be way more exciting."

"We'll try donuts the next time I screw up. This is your punishment. You're going to have to live with the consequences."

We walked into Christian DeLuce's store laughing, and we immediately caught the attention of a swan-like man with thinning strawberry blond hair. He was middle-aged, probably close to fifty, and his eyes were pale blue. His skin was so pale it looked like it would catch flame if he went outdoors. He smiled wanly in our direction and headed around the counter to greet us.

I looked around quickly to see where Noogey and Marika had gotten off to. They sat in a little alcove at the other end of the shop across from a saleswoman who was displaying a large selection of rings on a black velvet background. Marika was falling out of the top she was almost wearing, and Noogey was drooling into her cleavage. It was obvious to see how Marika got what she wanted.

"Detective Dempsey," the swanlike man said as he held out his hand to Nick.

"Mr. DeLuce," Nick said.

He looked so frail I was afraid Nick's handshake would crush every bone in the man's hand. He couldn't have weighed a hundred and twenty pounds soaking wet. I'd never actually seen Christian DeLuce in person. It was hard to imagine the man standing in front of me having the strength to machine some of the beautiful pieces he'd created over the years. Or having the eccentric temperament he was so well known for.

Nick put his free hand to my back and pressed slightly, warning me to keep my mouth shut for the time being. Since I couldn't think of anything to say at the moment, I was agreeable with this plan.

"Are you here about my gems?" he whispered. Though whisper might have been an understatement. I wasn't even sure where he got the energy to breathe out the words. "I've just been overcome with worry. That poor foreign man was killed trying to bring me my possessions. And now if they're not found I won't have time to design something fabulous for the spring expo. It's just tragic, I tell you."

He brought a handkerchief to his eyes to wipe away the dampness. I noticed he didn't get teary-eyed over the dead man, but he watered right up over missing a jewelry expo.

"No, I'm afraid I don't have any new information I can give you at this time," Nick said. "But I promise you we're working with the FBI as well as the McClean Agency to find out who did this and recover your property. We're here today for more personal reasons."

Christian DeLuce clapped his hands over his mouth, the tears disappearing, as what could pass for excitement spread over his face.

"Oh, an engagement. How wonderful. And to one of the

boys in blue. You're very brave, my dear," he said reaching out to take my hand in his papery thin grasp.

Nick's and my mouth dropped open in Simultaneous shock, and a burst of nervous laughter escaped before I could control it. Nick had broken out in a sweat, and I was pretty sure I was going to have his fingerprints embedded in my back from the pressure he was putting there.

"Come right this way," he said, holding out his hand with a flourish. "We normally only do fittings by appointment, but I'll make an exception this once since I know you're so busy. And don't worry," he whispered out of the corner of his mouth to Nick, "I'm sure I can find something in a cop's budget. If not, I do offer payment plans."

My feet seemed to be glued to the floor because Nick and Christian walked on without me. I was trying to decide whether or not to turn around and run out the door when Nick turned back and grabbed my wrist, pulling me toward him.

"Oh, no you don't," he whispered. "And stop laughing. This isn't funny."

I jerked my arm out of his grasp. "It's not like you can't tell him he's mistaken. You're the one letting him get carried away. And thanks so much for the look of horror, by the way. That's a sure fire way to get dairy product sex."

"Keep your voice down," he hissed. "You're becoming hysterical."

"You're right," I said, taking a deep breath. "It's not like this thing between us is serious. We can certainly pretend to look at engagement rings while I take a few incriminating photos."

"It is serious. Sort of," he said, wincing.

Sweat beaded along his forehead and he had the panicked look of a buck just before he was about to get mowed down by a semi. I could have kicked myself. Here I was thinking about love and a future together, and all the while he was under the impression that what was between us was *sort of* serious.

"Well, thanks for making that clear," I said to Nick.

Christian DeLuce was staring at us out of owlish eyes, and I gave him my picture day smile—all teeth and no personality. I took the seat he offered me and managed to sneak another look at Marika and Noogey. She was trying on a diamond engagement ring the size of a baby fist, and I could see the gleam of commission in the saleswoman's eyes.

"You don't seem like a traditional kind of bride," DeLuce said, narrowing his eyes as he dissected my entire personality in twenty seconds. "We pride ourselves at DeLuce's on finding the perfect ring for each woman. You're going to be a hard one to fit, I can tell. You're an unusual sort of woman. Unique. You'd have to be to catch the eye of our dashing detective. I swear, it's just like a movie. Very romantic."

I wasn't sure where DeLuce had picked up the Georgia accent, considering he'd lived in L.A. for the past decade, but he seemed to be adapting well to his current surroundings.

"Just bring whatever you think will do," I said politely. "I'm sure you know best."

Nick was sitting to the right of me, an odd look on his face, but he was providing me the perfect cover to take photographs of Noogey and Marika.

"Listen, Addison. I didn't mean all of that to come out that way. DeLuce just took me by surprise."

"Move a little to your left," I said, ignoring him. I used the camera on my phone to snap several shots of the salesperson filling out a purchase ticket. "Gotcha, you bastard. Lean forward like you're going to kiss me."

"Addison, listen to me," he whispered, moving into position to do as I'd asked. Nick nuzzled against my neck and kissed a spot that had chills dancing along my skin. I had the phone hidden under his arm and a direct line of sight to Noogey and Marika.

Noogey took out a thick envelope from his pocket and gave it to the saleswoman, and when she opened it, I got a picture of the crisp bills inside. Noogey was going to pay for what he'd done to his wife. I'd make sure of that.

"Addison," Nick said again. "You can't possibly be mad about this. We're not ready for marriage. We don't even know each other all that well. Sometimes I'm not even sure we like each other. I thought we were just having fun at this stage of the relationship. I mean, I enjoy being with you. That's why I'm with you—"

He was winding down, digging the hole deeper, and I was starting to feel a little sorry for him. "No harm, no foul, Nick. Like you said, it's nothing serious. We're just having fun, right? And if this is nothing serious, it's not like we need to be monogamous."

Nick leaned back so he could see my face, and he narrowed his eyes at that statement. "I don't want to date other people. I have enough trouble keeping up with you. I couldn't imagine adding another woman to the mix."

I flashed him a smile that was cold as ice, but it was the best I could do under the circumstances. I was about thirty seconds from bursting into tears, and I was thinking it'd be best if I just got up and walked down to Kate's instead of spending another second with Nick. We probably both needed a little time to think. Clearly I had different ideas of what a sexual relationship entailed than he did. It was time to take a step back and evaluate.

"You're overreacting, Addison. What we have is good. Just leave it at that."

I pushed my chair back to get up, but Christian chose that moment to come back in, a black tray covered in silk in his hands. He presented it in front of us, and then whipped the black cloth off with a flourish.

A group of five rings lay nestled in the black velvet, and my eye was immediately drawn to the one in the middle. The band was thick silver and in the center sat a cluster of freshwater pearls the size of caviar surrounded by a circle of black diamonds. It was unique in every way, and it was perfect.

I pushed my chair back all the way and stood up. "I don't think these are for me, Mr. DeLuce. I'm sorry we've wasted your time."

My eyes were dry, and I tightened my grip on my purse strap so I wouldn't be tempted to reach out and try it on.

"Oh, no, my dear. I'm sure one of these is just right for you. Maybe this one here," he said, picking up the one I'd been admiring and taking hold of my hand. He slipped it on my finger, and I was almost dizzy with the want. Too bad the fake groom didn't feel the same way.

"It's beautiful," Nick said.

I shot him a glare I hoped was strong enough to wither his junk and tried to take off the ring to hand it back.

"I'll tell you what we'll do," DeLuce said. "Why don't you wear it for a couple of days and see how you like it? If it's not to your satisfaction then you can always come back in and make another selection."

I was just opening my mouth to apologize and decline his invitation when Nick piped in.

"That's a great idea," he said. "We'll take it."

11

I walked at a brisk pace down the two blocks of cracked sidewalks until I stood in front of the agency. Nick was somewhere behind me. I hadn't stopped to look, and we hadn't spoken a word since I'd walked out of DeLuce's. I looked at the bare place on my finger and knew I'd done the right thing by giving it back. There was no reason to carry the farce on longer than necessary, and I'd gotten the shots I'd needed of Noogey Winthrop.

I headed straight back to Kate's office, ignoring Lucy and wishing I hadn't eaten the entire bag of Oreos the night before. I could have used a couple or ten right about now.

"Can I load these photos onto your computer?" I asked Kate, holding up my phone.

Kate didn't look so good. She had a green pallor to her skin and she was sweating slightly, even though the temperature in the office was turned down to frigid settings.

"Sure. What did you find?"

"We ran into Noogey Winthrop at DeLuce's Jewelry

Store. He was buying a big-assed engagement ring for Marika. I've got him cold."

I downloaded the pictures I'd taken of the fat envelope of cash in Noogey's possession, and wondered not for the first time why people with money thought they could get away with anything without paying the consequences.

"This is good timing," Kate said, leaning over my shoulder to see the evidence. "The grand jury is set to meet on his case at the end of the week. I'll have these delivered to the prosecutor's office and contact Mrs. Winthrop."

"That'll be a fun conversation," I said, wincing at the thought of Kate having to relay to the old Mrs. Winthrop that there was about to be a new, much younger Mrs. Winthrop.

"This job is nothing but fun and games," Kate said with a heavy sigh.

Nick stood against the doorframe and watched us out of unreadable eyes, while I did everything possible to avoid his gaze.

"Agent Savage is running a little late," Kate said to Nick. "Why don't you clear out the conference room and we'll meet in there. It's too cramped and stuffy in here." Nick nodded and left, and I let out a slow breath of relief.

"It's a meat locker in here, Kate. Maybe you should go home. You don't look so good."

"I don't feel so good. It's what I deserve for horking down booze and Twinkies."

"We had Twinkies? I don't remember that."

"You threw yours up. It wasn't pretty. What's going on with you and Nick?" she asked. "Things seem a little tense."

"I don't want to talk about it. I just want to get this done and start making plans to move into my new place. I don't want to think about Nick."

We walked into the conference room just after Agent

Savage, and he grabbed a pen and pad from the shelf by the wall. I ignored Nick completely, choosing to take the chair furthest from both men. I was starting to think with the kind of luck Kate and I had with the opposite sex, that maybe we ought to just have sex with each other. Of course, I'd miss the whole penis part of that equation, but I saw on a late night infomercial that they could be bought easily enough. It was worth looking into.

"Did you find out anything about Noelle Price's death?" I asked Savage.

"Nothing you didn't already know. If there was anything to find, they destroyed the evidence with the rest of her remains when she was cremated."

I passed Savage the client book we'd retrieved from Natalie the night before, glad to be rid of it. Something about that book made me very nervous, and it wasn't like I was likely to forget most of the names I'd read in there.

The tension in the room was also making me nervous. I was out of knuckles to crack and I'd taken to shredding the paper in front of me into confetti-sized pieces. Nick was silent and brooding. Savage was downright gleeful since he'd noticed the tension between me and Nick right away. Kate looked like she was ready to vomit, and I was trying to ignore it all by mentally decorating my new house.

"I noticed something in the research you did on Natalie Evans from the copies you gave me," Savage said. "There's something wrong about her profile that I can't put my finger on, but my gut is screaming. I've passed it along to a guy I know. He should be able to tell me if my hunch is right. And if it is, we've got bigger problems facing us then just our government. If they find out what we're doing, we're as good as dead."

"I haven't had enough coffee today for death threats," I said.

"I wouldn't mind dying right about now," Kate muttered. "Wish they'd hurry it up."

"You think this goes above and beyond a bunch of stolen gems?" Nick asked, steepling his fingers in front of him. "It makes sense. Whatever Natalie's goal is has to be worth the risk of getting caught. She's calling in a lot of favors now that we suspect her."

"I think we could all have our asses handed to us by the time all this is said and done," Savage confirmed. "We need to keep our eyes open and stick together for the time being. I've put in for a few days vacation time. What are the chances of you doing the same?" he asked Nick.

I was actually surprised that Savage had it in him to be so cordial to Nick and extend the proverbial olive branch so they could work this case. It meant he took his job seriously and didn't mind using whatever resources he could to solve a case.

"After the weekend I just put in, I could take a couple of days," Nick said. "What do you have in mind?"

"Something crazy," Savage said, smiling. He turned to look at me. "Are you up for doing another little job?"

The urge to look at Nick and gauge his reaction was overwhelming, but I somehow restrained. I could feel his anger launching itself at me across the table as soon as the request left Savage's lips. Probably looking at Nick was a bad idea at the moment.

"Not if it's like the last little job you had me do," I told him. "I'm out of tequila."

"You should be able to do this job without too much liquid courage," he said.

"Don't you think it's a little risky to keep using an untrained civilian for these little jobs you keep coming up with?" Nick asked.

"I think I'm utilizing all of my resources. And you know

as well as I do that if I didn't have her doing these jobs for me, then she'd be out on her own mucking things up. She's too nosy not to be in the middle of it."

"Hey, I resent that," I said, leaning up in my chair and bracing my arms on the table. And maybe it hit a little too close to home. I did have a knack for getting into trouble when left unsupervised.

Nick just sighed and gave me an unreadable look. "You're right. Go ahead," he said to Savage.

"I like how y'all are talking around me like I'm not even here," I said. "There are things I could be doing today, but instead I'm here helping you out of the goodness of my heart."

"We're paying you," Savage said.

"I haven't seen the money yet. And believe me, I could use it. I need to be moved into my new place before my mother gets home. That's not going to be a fun conversation, believe me."

I knew somewhere deep inside that my mother was hoping I was moving home for good. She'd been pretty lonely since my dad died, and she'd missed having someone to take care of. I knew Vince wouldn't move in for good any time soon because the gossip would be too much for my mother to handle. She'd barely been able to function hearing all the gossip about me recently. It was the hell of small town life. You lived under a constant microscope.

"You're moving?" Nick asked.

"I didn't have time to mention it," I said, blushing even though I told myself I was an adult and shouldn't be embarrassed if a room full of people knew I'd spent the morning having unbridled sex.

Nick's grin was slow and intimate. "I'll help you pack."

"Maybe if we can get back to business I can have lunch

at some point today," Savage said, not nearly so smug now after seeing the smile Nick just gave me.

I felt kind of bad for Savage, because he was a pretty interesting guy and there was no question he was handsome, but I just didn't feel the zing with him like I did with Nick. The lack of zing with Savage could be because I hadn't gotten the chance to get to know him yet. I knew from experience that chemistry wasn't always instantaneous. Of course, having that instant zing with Nick was obviously getting me nowhere, and there was always the possibility of it dying a slow and painful death.

"Sorry," I told Savage, not sure what exactly I was apologizing for.

"My men have been keeping tabs on Becca Gonzales and Andi Bachman," he said. "Now that we have the client list, we can begin to narrow down the suspects of who the girls are escorting and how they're laundering the stolen gems."

"How are we supposed to keep track of that?" I asked. "Natalie didn't write down who she paired her clients with. And she wouldn't try to sell those gems to just anyone. It'd have to be someone who could keep their mouths shut and who wouldn't want to risk the exposure of a scandal."

"I know, and I don't think Natalie will be so stupid as to put another one of her girls in danger. But she'll try to unload the gems just the same. They're a hot ticket now and she'll want them out of her possession."

"How are we supposed to catch her?" I asked.

"According to our intel, the girls are informed of their next job by phone. They're not given names. Only the location of the meet and what the dress for the evening will be. We need to find out who those girls are meeting and catch Natalie in the act of trying to sell the gems. If we can get her on that, then we can bring her in and make a deal with her for the names of who killed Amanda Whitfield and Noelle Price. Of course, we're going to try to hang her on the murder of Sasha Malakov as well, so she's not going to have a lot of bargaining room, but we won't tell her that right away."

"We need to have access to those girls' phones," Kate said. "If they're using secure phones, there's no way to listen in on their conversations without tampering with the phones themselves. It's the only way I know how to intercept their clients."

"Exactly," Savage said. "Becca Gonzales has an appointment tomorrow afternoon at The Green Door spa. So do you," he said, looking at me. "I want you to slip this little device inside her phone. Just pop out her SIM card and replace it with this one. Once you do, we'll have complete access to her conversations as well as anything she has stored on the phone."

I'd pretty much stopped listening after he'd told me I had an appointment at The Green Door. First of all, even when I had money, I was too poor to go to The Green Door. And second, they were booked months in advance. I hated to break it to Savage, but this was a plan doomed to failure, even though I'd almost be willing to do anything for it to succeed.

"That's a lovely plan," I said on a sigh. "But The Green Door has a waiting list a mile long for clients who aren't regulars. There's no way you could get me in."

"It's already been taken care of." The corner of his mouth quirked up in a private smile and his dark eyes melted like chocolate. "I told you when we met yesterday that I had connections."

I didn't like how the look in Savage's eyes made it seem as if we were the only two people in the room. It was too familiar and much too intimate for the short time we'd spent together. He made it sound like we'd been having secret liaisons behind Nick's back.

And I guess technically, we had been meeting, but the subject of those meetings hadn't come up the last couple of times I'd seen Nick—mostly because his tongue had been down my throat. And I didn't accidentally want to let it slip that Savage had kissed me. Though the more I thought about it, if Nick wasn't up for a serious relationship, then there was no reason why Savage couldn't kiss me if he wanted to.

This shit was too complicated to figure out and my headache was starting to return.

"I'm telling you no one gets an impromptu reservation at The Green Door," I insisted. "I don't care who you are."

"One of the techs had a miraculous last minute cancellation and was able to squeeze you in. Believe me, your name is on the list. Show up tomorrow at one o'clock and it'll all work out."

"And how am I supposed to get to Becca's cell phone? I've heard that place is like Fort Knox when it comes to privacy. They have too many celebrities stripped down to their skivvies on any given day."

"Let's just say one of the techs owes us a favor. You should be able to get to Becca's phone in the changing area where all the lockers are. The attendant will be busy doing something else for the few minutes you need. All you have to do is exchange the SIM cards before you go on to your own treatment room."

"What treatment did you schedule me for?" I asked. I was hoping like crazy it was a massage. I had so much stress gathered in the back of my neck and shoulders I was beginning to feel like Quasimodo.

"I just told my contact to give you whatever they had available. Beggars can't be choosers," Savage said, arching a brow. "You'll only be there for one treatment. The government doesn't have the budget for that place."

"Not many people do. I'm surprised you're allowed to do this at all."

"I haven't turned in my expense report yet. I like for things like this to be a surprise," he said. "There are several high ranking FBI directors on that client list. I figure they're going to be so busy cleaning up the mess from the fallout that they won't even notice my receipts."

"Good thinking." I pushed back from the table and grabbed my purse. "Well, if that's all for the day, I think I'm going to head home. I've got packing to do and a couple of things to take care of. Thanks again for finding me the house," I told Savage. "I talked to your friend on the phone and everything is taken care of. She said I could move in as soon as I wanted."

"I'm glad it worked out," Savage said, cutting his eyes to Nick. "And let me know if you need help moving. He's not the only one who can help you pack."

My eyes widened in alarm and Kate snickered, but quickly turned it into a cough. I was pretty sure I heard Nick growl from behind me. I thought the best course of action would be to escape before the first blood was shed, but Kate had a different idea.

She caught my hand before I could walk out. "If you work tonight I want you to call me. No matter how late it is. No lame excuses this time."

The green pallor of her face only stood out more with the directness of her gaze. I'd been giving her nothing but noncommittal answers every time she'd asked about what I'd seen Mike doing. She knew I was stalling, and in truth, I was. I didn't want to do this particular job, especially since Nick had all but confirmed Mike's guilt.

I nodded once and continued out to the street. It was

then I remembered I'd ridden in with Nick. I heaved out a sigh and turned around to go back in, but he stepped through the door and held my gaze for a minute.

"You know I'm probably going to have to kill that man before this is all said and done."

"Why? Because he's poaching on your territory? That doesn't sound like the reaction of a man who's sort of involved in a serious relationship."

We stared each other down, and if I'd had the money I would have headed straight for the nearest Dairy Queen. No wonder people started letting their bodies go after marriage. Stuffing my face has been the only thing I've wanted to do since facing the relationship drama. I couldn't imagine what it would be like living with it twenty-four seven.

"I'll take you home if we can call a truce for ten minutes," Nick finally said. "And you've got that crazy look about you. I think it'd be a good idea to take a detour by Dairy Queen on the way."

He had a look in his eye I couldn't really interpret. It might have been indigestion. Or it could have just been me. I had that effect on a man. But he knew me well enough to know when I needed ice cream. That sounded like a serious relationship to me.

Neither of us spoke after we got our dip cones and drove into Whiskey Bayou. I hunched down in the seat, hoping no one would see me and stare. I'd managed to go three days without being reminded that I'd been fired from the only job I'd ever known. And I'd managed to do it mostly sober.

My mother was bound to get phone calls once she got back home about Nick's truck being parked in the driveway all night, but that seemed pretty minor in comparison to all the other gossip about me at the moment.

"This has the potential to be an awkward situation," Nick said, driving right past my mother's house. If he drove very much further south we'd be up to our wheels in swamp.

"I don't know why you'd say that," I said. "Everything seems perfectly normal to me. Where are you going?"

"Just thought we could use a change of scenery. I am on vacation after all. Or at least I will be after I call it in. It's been three years since I've taken any vacation time. I plan to enjoy it."

He pulled the truck just to the edge of the bank of the bayou under a weeping willow that hid us partially from view. He left the car on so we didn't die of heat stroke and unbuckled his seat belt so he could turn towards me.

"I've changed my mind," I said. "This is awkward. Especially since it looks like you've got a gun in your pocket, even though I know you didn't put on a weapon this morning."

"It's your underwear. I've been thinking about it under that dress all day."

"You seriously can't be flirting with me right now. I don't know if you've noticed, but I'm pissed at you."

"I noticed, but that's still hot for some reason. I think it's because anger makes your nipples hard."

"Then they must be like tiny knives right now."

"Come here," he said, pulling my rigid body against his until I was sprawled across his lap.

"Let me go, you Neanderthal. Why is it that none of the men I know can fight properly? You can't just manhandle me into submission."

"You can't seriously be mad about what happened today. So I panicked a little. Sue me."

"You panicked a little?" I asked, eyebrows raised.

"It was a gut instinct. I've been down that road before."

Once upon a time when Nick was fresh out of the military and a rookie cop he'd been married to a woman he harbors no warm or nostalgic feelings for at all. I relaxed a little because his reaction in DeLuce's store was starting to make sense.

"Right, well, maybe it had more to do with you treating me as more of a fuck buddy than a girlfriend."

He held me tighter when I tried to pull away. "You're right. I'm sorry. Chalk it up to a moment of insanity. I'm only a man."

I rolled my eyes and tried to find a comfortable position with the gun in his pocket poking me in the hip. His fingers pulled at the stretchy fabric of the top of my dress, and his eyes got that look that meant we were about to reach the point of no return.

"And what we have between us is serious," he said. "I'm feeling very serious right now."

I didn't want to give in too easily, but I was feeling pretty serious at the moment as well. And he was right. What we had between us was good. We still had a lot of growing to do.

"It'd be almost a sin to not take advantage of this moment," he said, pushing back the seat so his legs stretched all the way out. "We've got a nice secluded spot and I've got good shocks on my truck. What more could you ask for?"

"To not have the sheriff become as familiar with my body parts as my gynecologist," I said automatically. "The sight of Sheriff Rafferty looking through the window is enough to wither me right up."

He nipped at my lower lip and all the synapses in my brain started to sizzle. I couldn't remember why I'd been mad or the points I'd wanted to bring up about our rela-tionship. I just wanted his hands on me. Now that we'd finally gotten past months of foreplay to the real deal, it seems I was turning into some kind of sex maniac.

"I'm not easy, you know." I shifted so he could push my dress around my hips and I could straddle his thigh. My flip-flops had fallen to the floorboard and his hands were hot on my waist.

"I've waited four months for this. Believe me, I know."

"It seems to me that if I'm going to risk my reputation by getting caught, the least you can do is help me pack up my stuff and move. Think of all the rooms we'll have to christen in my new place."

He pulled the elastic down on my top and hummed low in the back of his throat at the sight of my breasts. My eyes crossed as he took a nipple into his mouth and I ripped frantically at his dress shirt, flinging buttons so I could feel his skin against mine. He was wearing way too many clothes and we both fought to get his belt undone and relieve the pressure behind his zipper.

The glass was appropriately fogged and we were both panting for breath by the time the last of our clothes was shed.

"I'll make you a deal," Nick said, his fingers tightening on my hips as I sucked on his earlobe.

"I'm dying here," I whimpered. "Why are you talking?"

"I'll help you pack *and* I'll pay for a moving company to unload your stuff if you'll do that thing I like. Otherwise, this is going to last about four seconds."

I knew how he felt. I was ready to implode and he hadn't even gotten inside me yet. I think I might have been turned on by the possibility of getting caught. I'm not really sure what that says about me.

I smiled and kissed my way down his chest until my

head rested in his lap. "You drive a hard bargain, Detective Dempsey."

"Sweetheart, you have no idea."

No one could ever say Nick Dempsey wasn't a man of his word. After our roadside canoodling, followed by a few hours of packing, takeout pizza, and another canoodle, Nick decided he was pretty much spent. He called his captain and arranged to take a few vacation days, not mentioning the fact he was working off the books with a renegade FBI agent, and then he passed out in my bed watching Duck Dynasty.

I'd had a pretty full day, but to me, orgasms were like downing energy boosters, so I was revved and ready for action. The piddly amount of clothes and other things I had in my room were already packed in boxes, the kitchen was scrubbed and all signs of my wild weekend were gone. I had nothing else to occupy my time other than work. I couldn't get Kate and Mike out of my head.

It was a quarter to ten and I dialed Kate's number, almost hoping she didn't answer. Luck wasn't on my side.

"I thought I'd go out and do a little surveillance work tonight," I told her in lieu of a greeting.

"Better hurry. He'll be off work soon."

"I'm heading out the door now," I said.

I looked in on Nick to make sure he was asleep, and left him a note on my desk. I borrowed the keys to his truck and slipped out of the house. I figured he wouldn't have left them hanging out of his pants pocket if he didn't want me to have access to them. And after I'd done that thing he liked, he should probably give me carte blanche from now on as far as borrowing his stuff.

"Are you sure you want me to do this, Kate? Maybe you should be the one to take this."

"That's the last thing I need to do. I'm armed, remember."

"Good point."

"I need to know, one way or the other so I can get on with my life."

"I'll be in touch."

We disconnected and I slid into the driver's seat of Nick's truck, inhaling the heated scent of leather and man. This was a much better idea than taking my Volvo on a stakeout. And the fact that it was black would help me blend into the darkness. At least that's the story I was sticking to.

I was cutting it close as far as getting to the station in time to follow Mike when he left, and he was just getting into his truck when I parked in my spot down the street. I did like I had the time before and waited until he was at the stop sign a block away before I turned on my lights and followed behind him.

I didn't have Rosemarie chattering beside me this time and the silence was beginning to get on my nerves, so I checked to see what Nick had in the CD player. My mouth dropped open as something with a lot of strings and brass shredded the speakers. Apparently Nick was multifaceted. I'd never once considered he'd be a fan of classical music.

The problem with classical music was that it was impossible to sing along with, so as I trailed behind Mike, I found myself making up lyrics to go along with the music. I had a lot more respect for Elmer Fudd's *Kill The Wabbit* after testing my lyrical chops on whatever was coming out of the speakers.

I couldn't take it anymore and finally ejected the CD, feeling more human as Maroon 5 smacked me in the face.

We'd been driving a long time, longer than the trip had taken the night before to his lady cop's house. I frowned as I followed him out of Savannah and into Chatham County. Surely Mike didn't have more than one lady. That seemed like overkill. He had to know Kate would castrate him at best if she ever caught him cheating.

He pulled into the driveway of a little Spanish style bungalow, and I quickly parked behind a van and killed the lights. I grabbed my binoculars and focused in on Mike as he got of his truck and reached in the back for a black duffle bag. I was guessing he was planning on making this one an all-nighter. Asshole.

I waited until he rang the doorbell and a plump older woman came to the door. I wouldn't have categorized her as a cougar, but she was probably ten years older than Mike, and she looked like everyone's favorite Sunday school teacher. Those were always the wild ones behind closed doors.

I put the camera strap around my neck and slipped out of the truck, locking the doors behind me. I wasn't exactly dressed for stealthing—cutoff shorts, a tank top and my flip flops—and I wasn't so sure about my ability to convince anyone who saw me that I was a tourist passing through after ten o'clock at night.

The little bungalow sat next to an empty lot on the right and another little bungalow on the left, and it had a nice sized fenced in yard. I was just glad the house wasn't two stories. I was tired of climbing trees.

I made my way around to each of the windows, trying to find any crack in the blinds or curtains so I could see in, but they were closed up tight. I was going to have to try the back yard. I was also tired of climbing fences, though this one wasn't nearly the same caliber of obstacle as Natalie Evans.

"Stupid, Mike," I grumbled, kicking at a bush as I made my way around the side of the fence that bordered the empty lot. "Nothing but trouble. Never should have gotten you that barbecue set for your birthday."

I went to the far corner of the fence and used the posts to shimmy up the side so I could look over the top. A big yellow lab sat at the ground on the other side with its tongue lolling out and a curious look on its face. He didn't bark a warning but he did run and go get his tennis ball and bring it back to drop on the ground.

"You're the worst guard dog ever," I whispered. "What if I was a burglar?"

The dog didn't have an answer for that, so I brought my camera up so I could use the zoom lens to see if there was any activity through the back windows. The kitchen window was small but there weren't any curtains or blinds to hamper my vision. I couldn't see in the room without being there up close and personal. There was a set of French doors that was also open, but it was pitch black in the room they led into so I wasn't having any luck there either.

"Damn." I was going to have to take my chances crawling over the fence. The dog chose that moment to give a soft *woof* and I shushed him, promising I would throw the ball if he'd stay quiet. This particular event would have had a completely different ending had Rosemarie's dogs been the one staring at me from the other side instead the golden ball of fluff.

I slung the camera over my shoulder and made a lot of unladylike noises as I pulled myself up and climbed over the fence. I had splinters in my fingers and thighs, but I managed to drop down to the ground with passable grace and agility. The dog picked up the ball again and wiped a stream of slime across my leg.

"Right. We made a deal."

I took the tennis ball gently and hurled it to the other side of the yard, and then I made my way around the perimeter of the fence and house until I got to the kitchen window. I'd barely gotten a peek into the lowly lit kitchen before the dog was back, nudging the backs of my legs.

"This isn't working out for me," I told the dog. "Run slower next time. I've got a job to do." I threw the ball again and turned back to the window. The lights in the main part of the house were on, but I couldn't see much past the little breakfast hutch with the roosters painted on it. I'd never understood the point of decorating a kitchen with fowl.

I ducked down and crept along the wall, deciding to double check the living room windows for visual. I had my nose pressed against the window and my hands cupped around my eyes to see in when I heard the distinct sound of a gun cocking from directly behind me.

"Don't shoot," I croaked out, putting my hands up in the air in surrender.

"Addison?"

I recognized Mike's voice and breathed out a sigh of relief. He wouldn't shoot me. At least I didn't think he would. I looked down at the dog, and gave him a dirty look. He was standing beside me holding the ball, quiet as a mouse.

"You were supposed to give me a warning that someone was here," I said. "That's the last time I throw a ball for you, buddy."

"What are you doing here?" Mike asked. "You're lucky you didn't get your damned fool head blown off. This is private property." He put his gun back in his holster and put his hands on his hips. He loomed over me and was properly intimidating with his scowl, but I had justice on my side.

"Don't you take that tone of voice with me, Mike McClean. I happen to be working. You're the one who shouldn't be here."

"Working? You're following me?" he asked incredulously.

"You have some nerve pretending like I'm the one in the wrong here. I always thought you were a good man. I never would have thought you'd have that kind of betrayal in you. You're breaking Kate's heart by taking up with these bimbos, and you don't even care who knows it. Working extra shifts and making trips to strange women's houses in the middle of the night. Just be glad that it's me here instead of Kate. She was afraid she'd end up shooting you."

"Kate thinks I'm cheating on her?" he whispered. I could see his face pale even in the darkness.

"Wrong, mister. She *knows* you're cheating on her. You can't stand here and deny it. Especially since you've been caught red handed."

"The hell I can't. I would never cheat on Kate. She'd kill me."

"Yep, your time on this earth is limited." I brought the camera up and took a spur of the moment photo. "I guess I'll be going now. My work here is done. I'm disappointed in you, Mike. I always thought you were different."

"Wait," he said, grabbing my arm before I could leave. "I swear to God I'm not cheating on Kate. You've got to believe me. I need to get home and explain to her. You can't tell her about this until I've had a chance to explain."

"She's my best friend, Mike. I can't lie to her if she asks."

"That's fine, but I'm not cheating on her. And there's no way you have any photos of me proving I am because it's just not true. Give me the benefit of the doubt here and let me make this right. I'd never hurt Kate. I love her."

I sighed and wondered what the hell I was supposed to do. I knew I should have never gotten in the middle of this. I was going to have to make an executive decision. I could give Mike time to talk to Kate. It's not like this needed to be hashed out on my end tonight.

"Fine," I finally said. "Go home to your wife. Stop being stupid and communicate with her. I'm going home now."

I headed back to the gate and preparing to climb back over.

"Why don't you just use the gate?" Mike asked.

I sighed and headed towards the front gate that was clearly unlocked. "Don't push your luck, McClean. Don't push your luck."

T*uesday*

"SO WHERE'D YOU GO LAST NIGHT?" NICK ASKED THE NEXT morning as I made waffles.

I'd thought I'd gotten away with my sneakery since I was able to slip into bed beside him without waking him.

"How'd you know?" I loaded waffles onto a plate and put them in front of his at the table.

"I would've had to be dead not to know. You make a lot of noise. You're probably going to have to work on that if you're serious about getting your P.I. license. I'd hate for you to get caught because you can't keep from talking to yourself while on a job."

I winced and thought of my experience from the night before. Technically, I'd been talking to the dog instead of myself, but Nick was right. I was uncomfortable with long periods of silence. I wondered if Mike had actually heard me talking or if he'd just had that cop's sixth sense that someone was watching the house.

"I was following Mike," I told him. "Kate wants to have all the facts before she decides what to do." I stared jealously at his stack of waffles drenched with syrup and looked down at the single one I'd allowed myself. Life was unfair.

"Or she could just ask him outright what's going on," Nick said.

"He wouldn't be sneaking around if he wasn't doing something wrong. And Kate knows there's no point in trying to open communication when the other person is lying right from the start."

"That's bullshit. She knows he's up to something but she doesn't confront him? Communication is a two way street, babe."

"Don't you dare defend him."

"Oh, I'm not. He's been a dumbass for getting involved with that group, but I'm talking about their relationship."

"It's weird you suddenly have the urge to talk about relationships. Are you feeling okay?"

"Very funny. I'm just saying, let's suppose I start sneaking around and you know I'm lying about it. What would you do?"

"I'd shoot you in the ass with a tranquilizer gun. But I get your point. She should have pinned him down the moment she noticed something going on. It's gotten out of hand."

Somehow my plate was empty and I didn't remember eating, so I stole one of Nick's waffles and was a little more generous with the syrup this time.

"It's a good thing you have good metabolism," Nick commented. "Wonder how long that's going to last?"

I narrowed my eyes. "Excuse me? What's that supposed to mean?"

He grinned and licked the syrup off his fork. I was a little envious of the tines.

"Nothing. I like a little extra something to hold on to. You'll get no complaints from me."

"I feel like I should be offended," I said, eating the rest of the waffle in short order. "What did you mean when you said Mike shouldn't have gotten involved with that group? What group?"

He stared at me like I was crazy. "I thought you'd been following him. The fact that we've set you loose in Savannah is a terrifying thought. How do you not know what Mike's involved in?"

"You should be grateful I'm not armed right now."

"I don't think I'd be worried if you were," he said, smirking.

"Would you like to put a wager on it?" I asked.

"I'm not going to bet with you over whether or not you could shoot me."

"As much as I like the sound of that right now, I'm talking more of a friendly competition. Kate said I had to get my concealed to carry license before she could hire me full time. This is a good chance to practice."

"Kate is out of her damned mind," he said, shaking his head. "But it's probably better you practice with me there than some poor unsuspecting fool."

"Then it's a bet," I said, crossing my arms over my chest. "What does the winner get?"

"I'd like my every sexual fantasy fulfilled."

"You haven't gotten that yet?" I asked, eyebrow raised. "We're running out of options as far as unexplored territory. If you're bored, it's probably not a good sign for our future."

"Bored is the last thing I am since I met you. And believe me, baby, there's a lot we haven't done yet. Once I win, I'll show you."

"You're going to be eating those words when I'm crowned champion. I hope you're prepared to do some manual labor. My new house has a nice big yard that needs to be mowed, and I'd like some planter boxes built under the windows. I'll make you a list."

He smiled and got that challenging look in his eyes that would mean good things for me later, but I wasn't going to be distracted from my original topic of conversation.

"Are you going to answer my question?" I asked. "Who is Mike involved with? Kate hired me to prove he was cheating on her. That's all I was looking for whenever I followed him around. I assume by the look on your face that I've missed something important."

"Mike wouldn't cheat on Kate," Nick said. "He's too scared of her, which is why he's sweating bullets all the time now. Mike has been known to enjoy gambling. He sticks mostly to the races and the fights, but he'll bet on anything in a pinch."

I knew this about Mike. I'd never seen a man in my life yell at a horse at the track like he could.

"His habit turned into a problem along the way and he ended up losing more money than he had. Unluckily for him, Big Sal Angelo was there to bail him out. Now he's paying a hundred percent interest on his debt to Big Sal so he doesn't end up with his kneecaps being extracted through his asshole."

"Holy shit," I said. "Kate is going to go ballistic."

"Which is why you should officially stay out of this from now on."

"I told him last night I'd give him a chance to explain to her before I talked to her."

"He caught you following him?" Nick said, laughing. "I bet that went over well."

"He knew he didn't have room to bargain with me."

"You're lucky he didn't shoot you and bury your body."

"Mike would never do something like that."

"Men that desperate will do a lot of things, sweetheart. Remember that. Which is why you need to keep your distance from Savage. That man wants you bad."

"I don't have any more room for lunatics in my love life. You're all I can handle at the moment."

He leaned over the table and kissed me, licking along the bottom of my lip before he explored the inside.

"Mmm, syrup," he said. "Very sweet."

"Too bad you've got the movers scheduled to come at eight. We could fool around for a little while if we weren't moving boxes."

"Sweetheart, I'm multitalented. We can do both with plenty of time to spare."

BY NINE O'CLOCK, I WAS AS RELAXED AS PUDDING AS I watched the movers. They stacked my boxes in the back of their truck next to the furniture they'd retrieved from the storage building I'd rented. Dating a cop had its advantages apparently, or maybe Nick just had inspiration to bribe them to move quickly, because within the next hour they'd unloaded everything in my new house and put it in the appropriate rooms.

"This is a good space," Nick said, looking around. "Lousy security. You'll need to change all the locks on the doors and add a deadbolt."

"Thanks, daddy. I'll make sure and do that."

He raised his eyebrows at me. "Kinky. But I'm willing to play along if you are."

"In your dreams."

We set my bed up and put on fresh sheets because Nick insisted that was the most important thing, but everything else was going to have to wait until later.

"I've got to start getting ready for my appointment at The Green Door."

Nick checked his watch and nodded. "You okay with doing this?"

"I don't really have much choice. And I get a spa day out of it. As long as I don't wet my pants in fright I should be able to muddle through somehow."

"That's the spirit," he said as I went to shower. "But maybe you should take an extra change of clothes just in case."

THERE WAS SOMETHING ABOUT THE WEALTHY THAT WAS JUST hard to explain. Maybe it was the way they carried themselves, or the air of authority they used in nodding their head at the help. All I knew was that they recognized their own. And I wasn't it.

I figure me walking into The Green Door was the equivalent of Oliver Twist asking for more scraps from the table, and I was surprised no one tried to rush me back out into the street once I passed through the infamous green doors.

A cool rush of air and an immediate feeling of calm swept over me as I stepped inside. There was a certain scent in the air that made me want to lay flat out on the floor and take a nap and the sound of rushing water seemed to come from all directions. The décor was a mix of Return to the Blue Lagoon and a Japanese massage parlor that offered happy endings, but it seemed wrong for me to judge too harshly since they'd obviously made a success of themselves.

"May I help you?"

The voice coming from behind a sleek bamboo counter belonged to Minnie Mouse's long lost twin. And if I'd been brought up wealthy, I'd have probably been schooled on how not to show a reaction when faced with something out of the ordinary.

As it was, I gaped into the face of a dragon beast of a woman with drawn on eyebrows and a beehive that added another foot to her already substantial height. She had to be well over six feet tall and she filled out the pale grey scrubs she wore without much room to spare. She wasn't fat. She was just big. And I hoped to God she wasn't the one who'd be giving me my massage. I liked my vertebrae exactly where they were.

"I have a one o'clock appointment. Addison Holmes is the name."

She pursed her lips and typed my name into her computer. "Yes, your treatment has already been paid for. My name is Jasmine. Come with me. I will give you a tour."

I barely contained a nervous snicker at the mention of her name. She looked more like a Helga or a Beelzebub. I was about twenty minutes early for my appointment. I wanted to have plenty of time to get a lay of the land, and I wanted to already be in position when Becca Gonzales arrived.

Savage had assured me just before I'd come in that Becca was about ten minutes away. He'd had a man keeping watch on her.

I followed Broom-Hilda through a heavy wooden door that had to weigh a ton, because even she strained under the pressure of getting it open, and she led me through an arched hallway where there were artfully placed bamboo arrangements and paintings depicting Japanese women at various stages of their bath.

"This is our changing room," she said, narrowing her gaze at me as she sized me up from head to toe. I had to stare at her just to make sure that squeaky voice really was coming out of that body. It was damned weird.

She opened a large cupboard and handed me a brown robe from a neatly folded stack, a small package of disposable underwear and a pair of flip-flops. My arms were piled high and I followed her further into the bowels of the place where there were dark paneled lockers in rows and full-length mirrors every time you turned around. The mirrors were especially exciting to me because I'd always wanted to see myself naked from every direction in unflattering light.

"You can put your belongings in a locker. Once you've changed, just follow the golden path into the relaxation area." She pointed to a shiny golden swirl that started just beyond my feet and grew wider like the yellow brick road. "I hope you find your time at The Green Door gives you serenity and balance."

"I hope that too," I said, nodding in agreement. "I could use a little balance in my life."

Jasmine left me to my own devices in the locker room, and I stared awkwardly at the slender Asian woman sitting in a director's chair in the corner of the room. She looked scared as shit, and I was willing to bet she was the tech who owed the FBI a favor.

I wasn't really sure about the protocol. Should I strip down and treat the woman like invisible help, or should I strike up a conversation and pretend like I got naked in front of strangers all the time? It was a quandary to be sure, and I decided to err on the side of caution.

"Is there a restroom close by?" I asked.

"Right over there," she whispered.

"Thanks."

The bathroom doors were built to look like they were part of the walls and it took me a minute to figure out how to open it, but once I was inside I realized I'd found the perfect solution. If I stood just right I could see out into the locker room area.

I got undressed quickly and donned my paper underwear and flip-flops, tying the robe tight around me. I heard the squeaky voice of Jasmine welcoming Ms. Gonzales back to The Green Door, and I held my breath as I got my first up close glimpse of Becca Gonzales. She was a paler version of Eva Longoria, though with a little more bust and a lot more volume to the hair. She dumped her purse into one of the top row lockers.

I got my answer about the whole nudity protocol because Becca stripped down naked as a jaybird and pulled her paper underwear over lady bits that were bare as a plucked chicken. She pulled her hair in a high knot on her head, hung her clothes on the tiny hooks inside the locker, and then followed the yellow brick road to the next area.

I glanced over at the attendant sitting in the corner and swore she was staring straight at me. She lowered her gaze and then got up from the chair, picking up a stack of towels and moving out of the room so I was left all alone.

I wiped my damp hands on my robe and fished the SIM card and paperclip Savage had given me out of the zipper pocket of my purse. I could do this. Probably.

I went straight to the locker Becca had chosen and opened it up like I had every right to be there. I ignored my shaking hands as I dug inside her purse for the phone, and I cursed my inability to be able to get a hard case off of an iPhone quickly. I poked the paperclip in the little hole and her SIM card popped out, and I quickly made the exchange.

By the time I had everything back in her locker and my own clothes stored, I was sweating like a pig and I needed a hit of something—a chocolate fudge sundae or a flagon of whiskey—I wasn't going to be too picky.

I followed the yellow brick road and passed the attendant on my way out as she was going back to her post. Now I could spend the next seventy minutes having someone pound the tension out of me.

I SHOULD HAVE BEEN MORE INSISTENT TO KNOW WHAT I WAS getting into when Savage said he'd gotten the first treatment they had available. G.I. Joe was right—knowing was half the battle.

My nether lips were now as naked as Becca's, and it felt like someone had taken a blowtorch to my privates. And I especially liked how my technician had lubed me up with aloe as if that were going to take the pain of having all the hair ripped from my body.

I walked out of The Green Door like I'd been sitting on a horse for the last week and was thankful to see Nick parked just down the street. He gave me an odd look as I waddled to his truck, and I whimpered at the thought of having to hoist myself inside.

"Are you okay?" he asked.

He waited patiently while I settled myself inside and put on my seatbelt, and then he put the truck in gear and tried to find a break in the traffic so he could pull out.

I turned the air conditioning vents so they blew right at my crotch and I sprawled back in the seat.

"I don't want to talk about it," I said. "Have you ever sat on your own balls?"

He slammed on the brakes, causing an oncoming car to honk and shoot him the finger. He looked at me with incredulity and horror.

"Not to my knowledge," he finally said.

"You'd probably know it if you had. I bet they'd swell to the size of grapefruits. It'd be hell to walk around with that swinging between your legs."

"Jesus, did they give you funny vitamins in that place? Do I need to report them to vice?"

"Nah. That was just my own way of using metaphor to make a point. I'll let you infer from it what you will. I need to change clothes and take some Ibuprofen before we go on to our afternoon activities. And maybe get a cold pack."

"What afternoon activities? I thought you wanted to unpack."

"There's plenty of time for that. We have a bet. And don't you try to get out of it."

"Hmm," he said, pursing his lips. "I kind of thought you were kidding about the shooting range. I'm not sure how comfortable I am with you having a gun in your hand. I've already got the t-shirt for that experience, and I'd prefer not to go back to darker times."

"Don't be such a baby. Are you scared you're going to lose?" I waggled my eyebrows and made chicken sounds.

"I'm afraid I'm going to end up with a bullet in my back. You're a scary woman."

"And don't you forget it. Take me to the range you go to. Maybe if we're surrounded by other cops you'll feel safer."

"I'm not taking you anywhere near other life forms. I

know a private place that has plenty of room. If you're dead set on being humiliated this way, then that's what we'll do. Do you even know how to shoot a gun?"

"Of course I do. I'm the daughter of a cop, for Pete's sake. My dad used to take me out when I was little. It'll be just like riding a bike."

Two hours later my privates were starting to feel more normal and I was pretending to listen to Nick as he explained all the rules about gun safety at the range. He'd taken me somewhere about thirty miles out of Savannah and there wasn't anything around us but a field of dead grass, a big red barn and the blazing sun.

The barn didn't have any frills. The entire back wall was missing and divided up into sections for shooters to aim at the targets set up in the field. The place was completely deserted except for me and Nick and a wizened little man that looked like Little Jimmy Dickens.

"Are you trying to kill me? It's seven hundred degrees out here," I said, putting on the protective glasses he gave me. I was wearing a strappy tank top and cut-off shorts, but it didn't do much to relieve the heat.

"Did you hear anything I just said?" Nick asked.

"You bet. Shoot the target. Not you. Why does that man keep staring at us?"

"That's Harvey Dodd. He's run this place for close to fifty years. And he's not staring at us. He has one glass eye and it kind of fixates in one place. Don't let it bother you."

I stepped up to my lane and put on the ear protectors that hung from a nail. Nick had set up both of our targets at a hundred yards for the first round, and he mirrored my actions in the lane next to mine.

I bent over and did a couple of stretches before finally taking the .9mm Nick had procured for me in my hands.

"You realize that your finger does all the work, don't you?" he asked.

"Just getting loose. It's all in the stance. Are you sure you don't want to back out? I won't think any less of you."

His lone dimple winked as he grinned at me. "You're going to like my fantasy," he said. "I hope you're not shy."

I narrowed my eyes and got in position, raising my weapon. "Whenever you're ready, cowboy. Make my day."

IN ALL HONESTY, NICK WAS A PRETTY GOOD SPORT ABOUT the whole thing. I probably should have mentioned that my dad and I had been out shooting a lot, and that I'd been outshooting cops for most of my life. My dad used me as kind of a parlor trick whenever he and his friends got together.

I glanced at Nick nervously out of the corner of my eye. I don't think he'd blinked since we left the shooting range —just a glazed stare into the distance as he navigated his way back to my house. It probably hadn't helped that Harvey Dodd had laughed so hard that he'd had to hold in his glass eyeball.

I wasn't really sure how to handle the situation, so I just kept quiet and hoped Nick wasn't too disappointed in having his fantasies dashed. In all honesty, he'd probably be able to talk me into them anyway as long as it didn't involve margarine or barnyard animals.

Nick's phone rang just as he pulled into the driveway behind my Volvo. My heart lightened at the sight of the little blue house and all I could think was *mine*.

I tried to eavesdrop on Nick's conversation but he was pretty much keeping everything on his end to one-syllable answers.

"I'm on it," he finally said and disconnected. "I'm going to have to drop you and leave."

I sat there expectantly but he didn't say anything. "Well?" I finally asked.

"I was wondering how long it would take you." He finally made eye contact after our little wager—which I was starting to think was a bad idea because men were finicky creatures when it came to losing to a woman—and drummed his fingers on the steering wheel in impatience.

"That was Savage. He wants me to follow up on a couple of leads for him. I'll catch up with you later."

"Maybe you could bring dinner if you get back in time. I'm not set up for cooking yet."

"Will do." I got out of the truck and he waved before backing out of the drive and going to do whatever secret things Savage had put him up to. I unlocked my front door and reveled in the creaks and groans as the house settled around me. I tossed my bag on the dining room table and got a bottle of water out of the fridge because I was dehydrated as hell after our little outdoor adventure. I headed into the master bedroom, shedding flip-flops and clothes along the way and leaving them in a pile.

The sight of my naked body took me briefly by surprise. I looked like one of those hairless cats but without the wrinkles. The good news was the pain was mostly gone. I fell face first into the bed and immediately drifted off to sleep. It had been a long day.

The simultaneous buzz of my cell phone and the knocking on the front door jarred me out of sleep an hour later. I was stiff in unusual places and I groaned as I crawled out of bed and tried to find some clothes to put on. Almost everything was still taped up in boxes, but I found a pair of cotton shorts and a t-shirt. I couldn't remember where I'd put my bra, so whoever was at the door was going to get a show.

Fortunately it was just Kate.

"Wow, you look terrible," she said, coming inside. "Got some sun, did you?"

So that's what was wrong. My skin felt like it had been stretched and dried out like animal hide. I wasn't burned that I could see, but I was a lot darker, and I could feel the heat seeping from my skin.

"I appreciate the observation. You look better than the last time I saw you. Must have gotten rid of the Twinkies." She was dressed in her perpetual jeans and t-shirt and shoulder holster, and she looked the place over as she moved to the couch that sat haphazardly in the living room. I hadn't gotten around to arranging the furniture yet.

"Yep, and a few other things I didn't know I'd eaten. I owe you an apology," she said suddenly. "You were right about not making you do the dirty work. I should have pinned him down right from the start."

"That's what friends are for, baby. I take it he came home and told you what was going on?"

She dropped her head against the back of the couch and sighed. "Yeah, I still don't know what I'm going to do. He was working extra shifts to make more money, and he was taking little repair jobs after shift for women who didn't have a man around to do the work for them."

I thought about the off-duty cop who'd met him at the door and decided to stay silent. I believed Mike when he said he wasn't cheating on Kate, but that woman had been on the prowl.

"I do know if I see Big Sal Angelo walking down the street that I'm going to run him down with my car. Bastard was trying to bleed Mike dry. I gave him the money to settle his debt, but Mike's going to have to see someone about his gambling problem. We can't afford another bailout like this one. And he's putting his job on the line."

"Everything will work out," I said. Kate and Mike were a good unit, despite his recent dumbassedness.

"How'd it go at the spa?" she asked. "Were you able to make the switch?"

"I was awesome. Stealthy as shit."

"Amazing," she said, her smile telling me she didn't believe me for a second. "How was the treatment? Everything you ever hoped for?"

"If you mean was having all the hair ripped out of my genitals in barbaric fashion everything I've ever dreamed of, then the answer is no."

Kate barked out a laugh and doubled over as her whole body started to shake.

"It's not funny. If it wasn't totally weird I'd show you what they did."

"Thank you for showing restraint. I'll have to use my imagination." She wiped the tears from her eyes and flopped back against the couch. "Look on the bright side, I bet Nick is going to love it."

"Maybe. Or maybe he'll just get hungry for Kentucky Fried Chicken. You never know with men."

Kate left to go back home and told me to come into the agency the next day because a couple of new cases had come in. This was good, because I needed as much work as possible, and the summer had been a little light for my pocketbook.

I hadn't had time to go by the unemployment office and fill out the paperwork to start drawing checks, but I'd get to it. Eventually. Going to the unemployment office made my recent firing a little too real. And I was still doing a pretty good job of being in denial. I was happy to stay there for a while.

I was left at loose ends now that I was by myself, and I'd had enough of a nap to give me a little energy. I put it to good use by rearranging all the furniture and hooking up the electronics. I called the cable company so they could send someone out, and the phone company for wireless Internet. A girl had to have the necessities in life.

I put a rug I'd gotten half off at Pier One in the living room and another under the dining room table. I'd see if Nick was available to hang some curtains and a few pictures. He did owe me manual labor after all.

My phone rang from the bedroom and I saw Savage's number on the screen. There was a part of me that thought about not answering. I was almost positive Savage was bad for me. He fed my need for adventure and my propensity for danger. He was becoming my enabler. And he was starting to grow on me.

"What's up?" I answered.

"The device you planted is active. We just got our first hit. How do you feel about going to the movies tonight?"

I stubbed my toe on my desk chair and caught myself on the corner of the bed, running through a litany of swear words as my eyes teared up from the pain.

"Some day you're going to have to explain what you find so repulsive about me," he said. "I don't normally get that kind of reaction out of women."

"You just have a tendency to take me by surprise. Maybe you should incorporate a little subtlety into your pick up lines."

"You don't really strike me as the subtle type. You just used every curse word ever invented and a few I've never heard. That's a strong reaction to a man."

"I stubbed my toe, okay? Geez."

"That's okay then. And I wasn't asking you to the movies for my sake, anyway. Becca has two tickets to the ten o'clock showing at Bridgeport Tavern. I thought it would be a good idea for you to see who her guest is."

"Right, I can do that. No problemo."

Bridgeport Tavern was like the Taj Mahal of movie theaters. They served a six course dinner and wine pairing included in the price of the movie, and their popcorn had real butter. It was expensive as hell, and I didn't have room on my credit card for a ticket.

"Is the FBI covering this?" I asked.

"Just turn in your receipt the next time I see you."

I stayed silent, trying to figure out how to break the problem without seeming like a loser. Nothing came to mind so the silence gradually became awkward.

I heard him sigh just before he said, "I'll have the ticket waiting for you at the counter."

"I can't go by myself," I said, horrified.

There was nothing sadder than going to the movies and seeing the people who sat all alone. Especially women. That was a stigma that was hard to get rid of, and at a place like Bridgeport Tavern, I'd stick out like a sore thumb if I went by myself.

"Seriously?" he asked. "What's wrong with going to the movies by yourself? I do it all the time."

"Because you're a man. Women do not go to movies alone. It makes us look like we're so desperate we're trolling for theater pickups. And let's face it, that never turns out well for anyone."

"Jesus," he said. "You're making my head explode. Fine. I'll have two tickets waiting for you."

He hung up and I sprinted into the shower so I'd have time to do full hair and makeup. The Bridgeport Tavern wasn't a shorts and t-shirt kind of place. I'd seen women wearing cocktail dresses and men in tuxedos there before. Or at least the one time I'd been.

I hopped back out and dried off, and I realized I hadn't invited anyone to use the second ticket. I knew Kate was a no go. She had enough to deal with in her own life, and she'd told me they had some things to do this evening.

I dialed the number quickly before I could think too much about it.

"Are you up for a ten o'clock showing at Bridgeport Tavern?"

"Hell, yeah," Rosemarie said, squealing in my ear so loud I had to pull the phone away.

It always took me a little by surprise when Rosemarie opened her mouth. She looked like everyone's favorite Sunday school teacher, but she talked like a doxy. Or whatever people called doxies nowadays. Let's just say that Rosemarie had many sides. When she wasn't in school, she liked her clothes tight and her men large and black. I was pretty sure she had multiple personalities, because when she was teaching next door to me once upon a time, her voice was sweet and southern and her clothes came right out of the Sally Field collection.

"Okay then," I said. "I can pick you up or meet you if you'd like."

"Why don't I pick you up? No offense, honey, but your car doesn't exactly scream Bridgeport Tavern. I kind of miss the Z."

No shit. I kind of missed it too. I rattled off my new address and disconnected. Now I was depressed on top of everything else. I blow dried my hair and let it curl around my face, and I took extra time with my makeup, going a little dramatic on the eye makeup to make up for everything else that was going wrong. A little makeup could make a girl feel human again.

I dressed in a black, halter style sundress and accessorized with chunky silver and turquoise jewelry. I slipped on a pair of black sandals and then called the credit card company so I could get an account balance just in case. The robotic voice on the other end didn't come back with good news, so I settled for scrounging around in my other purses for loose change. It would also act as a weapon in case I needed to clonk anyone in the head with my purse.

It was a good thing Rosemarie was driving, because it would have sucked to run out of gas in the Bridgeport Tavern parking lot. She knocked on the door and I went to answer.

"Let's get movin'," she said. "If you get there too close to the start time you don't get your food as fast. And then people hate you because the waiter is standing in front of the screen, delivering your food during the movie."

Rosemarie was decked out in more circumspect clothes than normal. She wore a sarong type dress in neon blue that fastened over one shoulder and hung all the way to the floor. It was like Aphrodite meets Violet Beauregarde.

"You go here a lot?" I asked, locking up the front door and heading to the yellow Beetle.

"About once a month. I like to go by myself and sit in the back so I can watch all the couples sitting in front of me. It's like a game. I try to guess who's on a first date, or who's cheating on their spouse or who's having a fight. And then there are those women who come in with some man they hardly know just so they don't have to be by themselves. It's pathetic, I tell you."

"Hmmm," I said.

"I hardly ever go to the movies with a man. It's just weird. They always want to hog the Milk Duds and cop a feel in the dark—like squeezing my tits behind a giant box of popcorn is going to get them in my pants later on."

"Interesting approach." I tried not to sound bitter at her assessment. She was hardly a professional on human behavior. The woman fed her dogs off plates at the table every night at dinner for goodness sake.

"So what are we going to see?"

"I don't exactly know. The tickets were given to me at the spur of the moment," I lied. "I don't even know what's playing."

"I hope it's that movie with the dog. I've heard it's hilarious."

"I hate watching movies with dogs," I said, squenching my eyes as Rosemarie rocketed down my street and turned on two wheels as she accelerated towards the highway. I probably shouldn't have bothered doing my hair as I was pretty sure it had exploded around my head in fright.

"Why? It's a comedy."

"It doesn't matter," I said. "Anytime a dog is in a movie and he plays a major part, then you know he's going to die. It's one of those screenwriter rules or something. Look at Turner and Hooch or Old Yeller."

"Dogs are people too," Rosemarie said somberly.

Which, in my opinion, was part of Rosemarie's problem. We drove the rest of the way in silence, mostly because I was praying, and we pulled up to the curb a good forty-five minutes before the movie started. Rosemarie gave the valet her keys and a tip, and I managed to unpeel myself out of the car, only slightly surprised to not see the indent of my body in the leather seats.

I picked up the tickets at the front counter and saw that it was, in fact, the dog movie we were there to see. I wanted to get into the theater and get a table in the back so I'd have a good shot of Becca Gonzales when she came in. I'd opted to leave the camera at home, but I had my cell phone to take pictures of her mystery date.

"This is a good seat here," Rosemarie said. "It's the perfect angle so we can see everyone as they're eating. You'll like this game. I promise."

That cover worked for me. I didn't want to tell Rosemarie that I was working. She had a tendency to take things a little too far.

Our waiter came up and we ordered drinks as he told us what the different courses for dinner were. I hoped to God the price of the ticket included gratuity, otherwise our waiter was going to get a new tube of Chapstick and a half pack of gum for his tip.

Savage texted me and asked if I'd made it all right and I texted him back, telling him to stop hovering. He sent me a frowny face in response that made me laugh.

Becca Gonzales came in about ten minutes before showtime, and her date wasn't anyone I recognized right off. He was a few years older than Becca, but he looked like he could afford her. The price of his sport coat could have fed a third world country.

I held my phone up and acted like I was still texting and took a quick picture, and I sent it to Savage.

Recognize him? I added to my message.

No, but I'll put him through facial recognition and see if I get a hit. Watch them closely. And let me know if they leave the theater.

Yes, Master.

Will you get mad if I say I like the sound of that?

Will you get mad if I smack you in the head the next time I see you?

I like a woman with a little fight in her.

I shook my head and put the phone away when our first course came. And then the movie started and I forgot about everything.

I leaned over to Rosemarie halfway through and whispered, "See! I knew this was going to happen. That fucking dog is going to die, and it's going to destroy me."

"It'll be fine," Rosemarie said, her lips already quivering. "He's such a good dog. They won't kill him off. You'll see."

The people at the table next to us turned and shushed us and we slunk back in our chairs. By the time the movie was over, I had my head down in my arms and I was sobbing like I'd just lost a family member. Come to think of it, I'm not sure I've ever cried that hard at a human's death.

Rosemarie was whimpering beside me, but I couldn't break away from my own grief to check on her. I was in a state, and nothing beyond medication was going to get me past it for the next little while.

My phone buzzed on the table and I reached blindly for it.

"H—hello?" Another sob escaped before I could control it.

"What's wrong? Are you hurt?" Savage's voice was urgent.

"They killed him. He got shot right in the head. It was terrible. Right in the head."

"Boom," Rosemarie said from beside me. "It was a fucking big gun too."

"Stay where you are," Savage said. "I'm coming to get you. Who got shot?"

"Ar—Arnold," I sobbed.

"I'll be there in a minute. I'm assuming the police are on the scene?"

"Why would they be? It's not like anybody cares. He dived in front of a gun to save a life that wasn't even worth saving."

"What the holy hell are you talking about?" Savage's voice was tight and controlled. "Who's Arnold?"

"The dog. This is all your fault."

"Are you telling me you're fucking crying over a movie?" he exploded. "Where the hell are Becca and her date?"

"I'll have you know it wasn't just a movie, you insensitive brute. It changed—"*sob*—"My—"*sob*—"Life."

I looked up to see the theater empty except for the cleaning crew standing against the wall, watching me and Rosemarie like a sideshow. Becca was gone.

"Oh, shit," I said, wiping my eyes with a napkin so I wouldn't smear my makeup. "They're gone."

"You lost them?" he said softly and then hung up without saying goodbye.

Rosemarie and I supported each other on the way out and she handed her ticket to the valet to retrieve her car. The young man went off to get it, giving us both a wide berth and an odd look. A big black Tahoe pulled up in the space in front of us and I backed up a step behind Rosemarie as Savage got out of the vehicle.

"Holy mother of God," Rosemarie whispered, her eyes wide as she got a load of Savage up close and personal. "My prayers have been answered."

"Don't count on it," I said. "Looks can be deceiving."

Savage's smile was tight as he stalked toward me, and his dark eyes were like black fire.

"It wasn't my fault," I told him, holding up a hand to ward him off. "It was that stupid movie. How was I supposed to know what would happen?"

"You were supposed to watch the mark. Not the movie."

"The whole time?" I sputtered. "Why didn't you say so?"

Savage clamped his back teeth together with a snap and grabbed on to my arm. "I'll take you home. It's on my way."

"You always have all the luck," Rosemarie said.

"I was just thinking that," I said sarcastically as Savage

pulled me toward the truck. "This is kidnapping. Unhand me, you scoundrel."

"A brute and a scoundrel, huh? You better watch out or I'll show you how brutish I can be."

"That's so romantic," Rosemarie said, her hand over her heaving bosom. "Don't worry about me, Addison. I can see you're in good hands."

"He could be an axe murderer. You don't even know him."

"But I'm an excellent judge of character. My great-grandmama was a gypsy and she had the sight. Just remember to keep your knees together if you want to keep your virtue in tact."

Savage barked out a laugh and almost loosened his grip enough for me to get away. "Don't keep them together on my account."

"Let me go. You can't just cart me around like a child."

"Believe me, treating you like a child is the last thing on my mind."

I pinched my lips together and scooted to the far side of the car in case he got any ideas, and I shot Rosemarie a dirty look as she waved us goodbye. I started to relax a little when Savage drove through a Dairy Queen and ordered me a Blizzard.

"What's this for?" I asked. "Not that I'm not grateful. I need about ten pounds of this after tonight."

"I figure if you're putting that in your mouth then you're not talking. It's a win-win situation for everyone."

"Flattery will get you nowhere."

He smiled and the tension slowly seeped out of his shoulders. "I got a hit on the picture you sent me. The guy's name is Jason Lyle. He's the youngest son of Congressman Lyle."

"Eww." Congressman Lyle had been on the list of Sirin clients. "Like father, like son?" I asked.

"Not exactly. From what I was able to gather, the younger Lyle and Ms. Gonzales have been seeing each other pretty frequently. I'm under the impression that he doesn't really know what she does for a living."

"That'll be fun."

Savage turned onto my street and pulled into the driveway behind my Volvo. He left the ignition running but got out to walk me to the door.

"Thanks for bringing me home."

"Like I said, it was on the way." He took the key from my hand and unlocked my door, going in first to make sure everything was okay. Once he was satisfied he turned and looked at me.

"So how serious is it between you and the cop?"

I swallowed and wiped my damp palms on my dress. "Serious enough to make that an awkward question."

"Hmm," he nodded, smiling slightly. "Cause I would have sworn that there was a little tension between the two of you."

"It's complicated."

His smile had alarm bells ringing in my head and he moved closer so I had no choice but to back against the wall. My only thought was that I couldn't let him kiss me again. Not if I wanted to preserve my sanity.

"I can work with complicated," he said, running a finger from my shoulder down to my wrist. I gasped and my eyes widened as I started to feel tingles I swore hadn't been there between us the last time we were in such close proximity. His body was huge and hard, and he had the kind of dominating presence I should have found smothering, but I still had the overwhelming urge to lean up and nibble at the little scar on his chin.

He took hold of my wrist and leaned forward ever so slightly, giving me plenty of time to call him off. I took a deep breath and tried to get my tongue working.

"Don't kiss me," I finally said.

The corners of his mouth turned up in a smile and he brought my hand up, his dark gaze never leaving mine, and he pressed a kiss to the palm of my hand.

"See you tomorrow," he said, and walked out the door, closing it behind him.

I fell against the wall and banged my head against it a few times, hoping it would knock some sense into me. "Shit, shit, shit."

That pretty much summed it up.

1 3

W*ednesday*

I DIDN'T HAVE A RESTFUL NIGHT'S SLEEP. I CAN'T IMAGINE why.

So at the ungodly hour of whenever the sun decided to peep through the blinds in my window, I got out of bed and shuffled to the kitchen, cursing the fact that I hadn't unpacked my coffee maker or the all important grounds the night before. I finally found them in a box labeled *linens* and set it up before I ripped through the bag with my teeth and ate the grounds dry.

I took my first cup into the shower with me and stood there staring at the tile in a half daze, impressed by how clean the grout was. The lady who'd lived here before me must have been a cleaning demon, because everything was scrubbed to within an inch of its life.

I shut the water off and dried haphazardly, throwing on a pair of white shorts that I was sure to spill something on at some point in the day and a black and white polka dotted sleeveless blouse. I braided my hair wet and didn't bother with makeup. There was no amount of concealer that could fill in the bags under my eyes.

I was contemplating breakfast when there was a hard knock at the door. I could see Nick through the small square window and he winked at me as I stood there staring at him, trying to decide if I was up for the eventual sparring between us. Being with Nick took a lot of mental energy.

I finally gave in and opened the door, standing back to let him in.

"Hey, it's starting to look like a house in here," he said. "Very cozy. It suits you."

"Thank you. It's every woman's dream to be told by a man that she's cozy."

"No, really. It's a good house. And you do have that giant TV. I've missed that since you've been living with your mother."

"You can go now," I said, heading back to the kitchen.

"Relax. I want you for your body too."

He laughed as I threw the spoon I'd used to stir my coffee at his head.

"So much violence. You've got a lot of anger inside you, babe. Maybe you should see someone about that. Violence is never the answer."

He rushed in to grab me before I could find something else to throw, and I pretended to put up a little resistance as he pressed me against the counter and played space invaders. I'd found out the two times we'd been together that Nick was very much ready for anything first thing in the morning, and the proof of that was drilling into my stomach.

His magical mouth found mine, and the resistance I

tried to put up turned into compliance. I twined my arms around his neck and moaned as his teeth nipped at my bottom lip. His tongue rubbed against mine in a slow, lazy dance and I wrapped my leg around his hip, searching for relief from the pressure he always managed to build inside of me.

"Good morning," he finally said, breaking the kiss and nibbling along my jaw.

"It's turning out to be."

"Can I have some of that coffee?" he asked, leaving me to go to the machine.

I was a little miffed he wasn't interested in finishing what he started. I was in a bad way, and I wasn't above tackling him and restraining him with his handcuffs so I could have my way with him.

"So I went to meet with Savage's man yesterday," Nick said, taking his first sip. "Damn, you make good coffee."

Oh, yeah. We were supposed to be working. Sometimes I got distracted from the main goal. What can I say? I was easily tempted. The Catholic Church hadn't been able to beat that sin out of me.

"What did you find out?"

"Savage noticed something unusual in the background check that was done on Natalie Evans. It was a thorough check, though too clean for my liking. No one has an image that clean. But dental records don't lie."

"I'm not following you."

"Savage is ex-Special Forces. He recognized some of Natalie Evans' dental work. During the cold war, Russia didn't have the same materials for fillings and crowns that the US did. The work is actually very distinctive. And after talking with Savage's man, it's so distinctive that he's a hundred percent positive that she spent her childhood and teenage years in the Soviet Union."

"That seems like it should be bad for us."

"It's very bad for us. Especially if Natalie Evans is a double agent. And it explains why so many people are trying to get in our way here."

"So what does that mean?" I fished out a frying pan from a box, intending to cook breakfast since it didn't look like we would be canoodling any time soon, but I remembered my refrigerator was empty except for ketchup and beer. All the food was still at my mother's house. I let the skillet drop and decided another cup of coffee was enough to sustain me.

"It means we can narrow down our searches. Part of the trouble with following the money trail is *finding* the money trail. We've got men working on tracing from the other end, seeing who Russia's most generous patrons are."

My cell phone rang and a horrible pressure starting building at the base of my skull. That could only mean one thing—it was my mother on the other end of the line.

I stared at it and ignored Nick's silent laughter as I debated, but I was afraid she'd keep calling, or send a policeman to track me down to see if I was lying on the side of the road somewhere, or calling hospitals to see if they had any Jane Does. This had never happened to me before first hand, but these were her constant fears. I'd managed to make it to adulthood mostly untraumatized.

"Hello," I said.

"Addison, this is your mother. I just wanted to let you know that Vince and I are back from the Bahamas."

"Oh, good. Did you have a nice time?"

"It was beautiful. Not that I saw much past the hotel balcony, but the skyline was very nice."

I pressed a finger over my eye, hoping the images of my mom having sex on a hotel balcony weren't permanently burned into my skull.

"I'm glad we came home when we did. I assume you're with the police giving them a statement."

"Umm, no. Why would I be?"

"Someone has stolen all of your things. God knows what's gone of mine. I've sent Vince around to see if he can tell."

"Yeah, I should probably explain about that."

"You can do it over breakfast. I know you never eat right when I'm not around. Why don't we meet at the Good Luck Café? Vince said he's got a craving for their pancakes."

I was pretty hungry. I just wasn't sure I was hungry enough to share a meal with Vince and my mom together after the images of the balcony.

"Listen, I'm with Nick right now and I don't—"

"Oh, good. Bring him along. See you in a few minutes."

She hung up without giving me a chance to come up with any more excuses, and I looked at Nick, quirking a brow as I devised a plan. He gave me an odd look and started backing away.

"I don't trust that look in your eyes," he said. "I think I need to go. I'm pretty sure I have a lot of other stuff planned for the day."

"Yeah? Like what?"

"Guy stuff. I don't want to bore you."

"I've got a deal for you."

"Not even the promise of wild monkey sex with you and the Doublemint twins could get me to hang out with your mom and Vince."

"She told me to bring you. You wouldn't want to disappoint her, would you?"

He was starting to look a little panicked, and he tugged at the collar of his t-shirt. "Tell her I'm getting sick and I don't want to pass on my germs."

"Don't you want to hear the deal I'm willing to offer?"

"Nope. Not really."

I smiled and started unbuttoning my shirt, smiling as he backed up another step and bumped into the refrigerator.

He cleared his throat once as the shirt dropped to the ground and I was left in a turquoise lacy bra that left very little to the imagination. I used to belong to an underwear of the month club back when I could afford groceries and other stuff, so I had quite a collection of undergarments.

"The panties match," I said, unbuttoning my shorts.

"This isn't going to work. I'm tougher than this."

"I haven't shown you my surprise yet." I dropped the shorts to the ground and stepped out of them, revealing the tiny triangle of turquoise lace.

"Sweet Jesus." He took a step forward before he remembered he was holding out. "You're right. The panties do match."

I arched a brow and toyed with the front clasp of my bra, flicking it open and holding the cups in place just to tease.

"I don't know why women think that sex will get them what they want when it comes to men. No one ever gives us any credit for standing up for what we believe in."

"It's so true," I agreed. "You're a paragon of virtue." I let the straps fall from my shoulders and the cups slide away slowly until the bra dropped to the ground with the rest of my clothes. "Are you ready for your surprise?"

"I hate to tell you, but it's not much of a surprise." His voice was huskier than normal and the fit of his jeans was starting to look pretty uncomfortable. "You forget I've been here before. I've seen and conquered. I have the scratches on my back to prove it."

I stuck my finger beneath the elastic straps of the panties, lowering them inch by inch until they slipped from my grasp and fell to my ankles. I stepped out and put a hand across my belly, barely skimming the newly bared area with my fingers.

I was a little nervous to see what Nick would think about my new landscaping, but one look at his face made every minute of the torture from the day before worth it.

He fumbled with his belt buckle, never taking his eyes from my roving fingers.

"Nevermind," he croaked. "I'm surprised. What do you want? Whatever it is, I'll do it. I'm your slave for life."

"Maybe you'd better show me what you've got to offer first. You might need to convince me you're up to the challenge."

I turned around and put my hands on the counter, bending over slightly, and I shot him a sultry smile over the corner of my shoulder. His nostrils flared and his pupils dilated so the blue of his eyes was no longer visible. He dug in his pocket for a condom and growled low in his throat as he ripped at the front of his jeans. And when he came up behind me and slid inside to the hilt, my eyes crossed and I barely noticed my head banging against the cabinet door.

———

TWENTY MINUTES LATER WE WERE BOTH PRESENTABLE AND headed into Whiskey Bayou to meet my mom and Vince. The expression in Nick's eyes was satisfied and lazy, and I was slightly freaked out because I knew anyone who looked at me would be able to tell what I'd just done. I couldn't get the stupid grin off my face, no matter how hard I tried.

"It's no use," Nick said, pulling into a parking spot just outside the Good Luck Café. "Everyone is going to know."

"Perfect. I might as well be wearing a damned sign and really give all the gossips something to talk about."

"That might be overkill. They usually have plenty to talk about where you're concerned."

Which was another reason I was dreading this breakfast. I was going to be smack dab in the middle of gossip central. I'd kept a pretty low profile the past few days. The problem with small towns—especially small southern towns—was that people didn't mind coming right up to you and asking you straight out about the horrific things in your life. They just peppered it with a bunch of *Bless your hearts* and *You poor things* while they were soaking up every nuance like a sponge so they could pass it along with the right amount of flair to whoever was filing their nails or selling them plywood at the hardware store.

"Let's get this over with. I'm starving."

Nick put his hand on my lower back—warm and solid —as he opened the glass door for me and we walked into the café. All talk stopped immediately as heads turned to look in our direction.

"I think you tricked me," Nick whispered next to my ear. "I'm not sure your surprise was worth this."

"Too late now. Just smile and pretend everyone's naked. That's what I do."

"That's sick. You need help."

"It's a coping mechanism, for crying out loud. Lighten up. There's my mom and Vince."

I headed to the back corner of the restaurant where my mom had procured a booth that afforded us at least a little bit of privacy. The problem was I'd have to sit with my back to the door, and I'd have to be really careful about what I said in case someone snuck up behind me and tried to eavesdrop.

"Hi, mom. Vince," I acknowledged, looking over my mother with a critical eye as I sat down across from her. "You look fantastic."

"Oh, thank you, dear. The beach agrees with me I think."

And she did look amazing. The lines of grief that had etched their way across her face after my father's death were gone, and there was a healthy glow about her. Probably a lot like the one I was sporting at the moment. I shot a look at Vince and he raised his eyebrows at me, smirking before he continued to read his menu.

We waited to start our conversation until we'd placed our order.

"I wanted to tell you that my things weren't stolen from the house," I said, pouring a healthy amount of cream into the most Godawful coffee I'd ever had. "I found a new place up in Savannah. Nick helped me move everything yesterday."

"And is Nicholas living in this new house with you?" my mother asked, narrowing her eyes at Nick.

"No, maam," he said, smiling the charming smile that always got him out of trouble. "I was just helping."

"Good, I'd hate for the gossips to get hold of that. They're already talking enough because the two of you aren't engaged yet. You're getting to that age where it's almost too late, dear."

"I'm only thirty."

"That's like a hundred and twelve in Whiskey Bayou years. Not that you should rush into anything, especially since your young man seems to have commitment problems. No offense, Nick."

"None taken," Nick said, smiling tightly.

"Leave the kids alone, Phyllis," Vince said. "They'll do things in their own time."

"Which is all fine and good, but I'd like grandchildren before I die."

My eyes widened in alarm. My mom had never voiced the need for grandchildren before. I wasn't even sure she liked kids. I mean, I knew she loved me and my sister, but my mom was kind of a flake. I was always terrified she'd lose one of us. Getting my driver's license was the best day of my life.

"It's a lovely house," I said, breaking in before things could get weirder. Nick's hand was gripping my thigh so hard it would leave bruises and I could tell he was mentally counting to ten. "It's just exactly the right size and it's close to the agency."

"Which brings up another question," my mom said, as our food was served.

Jolene Meador, the owner of the café, was taking her own sweet time putting our food in front of us, hoping she'd overhear something worthwhile. But we'd all been around the block enough to put on our company smiles and wait until Jolene had no choice but to head back to the kitchen.

"How are you going to afford this house?" she asked. "You don't have a job. You've been doing just fine staying with me. There's plenty of room."

She had an odd look in her eye that I wanted to question, but I thought it might be prudent to keep the conversation on track just this once.

"You remember what happened to Lois Gluck?" she asked. "She got laid off from the distillery just after she'd scraped every penny she had together to buy that shanty down by the railroad tracks. She ended up having to sell one of her kidneys to make ends meet. And I heard she sold her ovaries on the black market to some woman who couldn't get pregnant. Not that Lois's ovaries were in that good of shape to begin with, so I don't think she even got top dollar."

Nick was shaking with laughter beside me, and I nudged him with my knee to get him to shut up.

"Don't let that be you. I don't want a daughter of mine walking around town without her organs. It's just not natural."

"I promise I won't sell my organs. I've still got another month before my teaching contract is up. I'll get one more paycheck, and then I can start drawing unemployment. I've got enough to get by until I can get hired on at the agency full time."

My mother pinched her lips together and we all ate, speaking in stilted tones until I remembered she'd had an ulterior motive behind this whole breakfast.

"So what's up?" I asked. "What did you want to tell me?"

I chose that unfortunate moment to take a drink of coffee.

"Vince and I got married while we were in the Bahamas," she said, beaming like the blushing bride she was at Vince.

I choked on the coffee and some of it came out my nose. Nick pounded me on the back while he gave his congratulations to the happy couple.

"Say something, Addison," my mom said. "Isn't this exciting."

"Pretty exciting," I said, my eyes so wide I was surprised they didn't pop right out of my head. "Congratulations, you crazy kids."

"And look on the bright side," Nick added. "Maybe you don't need grandchildren. Maybe you can have another of your own. You're still young enough."

My mother beamed at Vince and I had the sudden urge to stick my fork into Nick's hand. But he'd assured me that violence was never the answer, and I was going to go along with that theory for now. Mom was in her early fifties, so I was pretty sure I wouldn't have to worry about welcoming a new sibling to the dysfunctional fold.

But pretty sure wasn't the same as a hundred percent sure.

14

The rest of the morning was kind of a let down after breakfast. Nick and I left the restaurant pretty soon after that embarrassing moment, and we were just getting in his truck when my cell phone rang.

"What's up?" I said to Savage.

"I need you to meet me at the agency. We've got something big. And we've got to move fast."

"We're on our way," I said and disconnected. I relayed the information to Nick and he headed back to Savannah, and the urge to do something drastic dissipated with every mile between us and Whiskey Bayou.

"I thought that went well," Nick said, biting the inside of his cheek.

"Shut up. You did that on purpose to get back at me for making you go. That's the last time I give you any surprises."

"Act in haste, repent in leisure. My grandpa used to say that all the time."

"I'm sure he meant it for an occasion such as this one."

"If you knew my grandpa, then it probably was. He was

a wily old bastard. Was married six times and had fourteen children. His youngest was born when he was almost seventy."

"Genetics is a weird thing. It terrifies me."

"I've met your family. It terrifies me too," he said.

We got to the agency in no time, but had to park a block over because the traffic was so bad. It was high season in Savannah, though why anyone would want to come look at a bunch of cemeteries and old houses during the hottest month of the year was beyond me.

Lucy wasn't behind her desk when we walked inside the agency. In fact, it was downright quiet inside. There was usually this constant buzz of activity and the murmur of voices, but that was all absent.

I saw why when we went into the conference room to meet with Savage. Most of Kate's agents were inside, sitting around the twelve-seat table. Lucy was pouring coffee and delivering it around the room and Kate was talking to Savage quietly.

Everyone looked up when we came in, and Nick and I took two empty seats at the opposite end of the table from Savage. I was having trouble looking Savage in the eye. I hadn't forgotten what he'd said the night before, and I wasn't really sure how to handle the matter. What I was sure about was that this case needed to end so Savage and I could part ways before he remembered he had a first date to claim.

"Thanks for getting here so fast," Savage said. "It was lucky the two of you were together. Saved me an extra phone call."

My head snapped up to meet his eyes, wondering if there was a hidden message in there somewhere, but his face was perfectly blank except for the eyebrow he had quirked.

"My mother invited me to breakfast," I said. "I needed reinforcements." I didn't think it would help matters to mention the christening of my new house. "So you said you got a hit on Becca's phone?"

"Yeah, at about eight o'clock this morning," Savage said. "The call came in from the Sirin offices and informed Becca she had a new client who was interested in obtaining her services for business purposes. She's to get a key from the front desk at the Marriott and go directly to the penthouse suite at 7:00. The transaction will be complete by 8:00 and then dinner will be served. The woman kept calling it a business meeting to cover her tracks and told Becca that attire was semi-formal. She said her services had been paid for in advance for an entire night. Becca didn't say but two words the entire phone conversation."

"Geez," I said, suddenly uncomfortable. I shot Savage an irritated look, not sure what I expected him to do about it, but just knowing something needed to be done. "Why the hell would she agree to meeting a complete stranger like that? In a hotel room? The whole thing is just skeezy."

"Money," Nick said. "Money is almost always the bottom line. She's pulling in five figures for a full-night's work."

Savage threw up his hands and smiled. "I'm just repeating what was said during the phone call. Don't look at me like I'm the guilty party. I hear you're one of those who likes to shoot first and ask questions later."

I looked at Nick, but he refused to meet my gaze. "It was just a tranquilizer. There are some people in this room who have a tendency to overreact." Everyone was staring at me with rapt attention. "Sorry. Please continue."

"Whoever was making the call from the Sirin offices didn't go into too many details, but she did say specifically that Becca was to be a facilitator for a business transaction. It was mentioned that this is a two million dollar deal and to do whatever necessary to make sure the business was completed to the client's satisfaction. Further instructions will be given once Becca is in the hotel room."

"Well we obviously can't let her go," I said. "And we can't let those gems exchange hands."

"I've already had a man pick Ms. Gonzales up, and he's holding her in a safe house for the time being. I've also confiscated her phone."

"That's clever of you," I said, a plan hatching in my mind. I looked up at Savage and saw the gleam in his eye. We were on the same wavelength. It was everyone else in the room that seemed to have a problem.

Kate had laid her head down on the table and Nick was giving me a death glare so strong I could feel it through the side of my brain. The other agents in the room were trying their best to pretend they weren't there or make direct eye contact.

"So," I said.

"So," Savage answered. "With Becca out of commission we need someone to go in and take her place. We can bug the room and set up surveillance with a team one floor below. I can have another team watching Natalie Evans, and if the exchange is made how I think it's going to be made, we can pick her up for questioning and confiscate the stolen gems."

"Piece of cake," I said.

"I hear the phone ringing," Lucy said, leaving the room abruptly.

"I've got to—"

"—doctor's appointment"

"Root canal—"

Voices clambered over each other as the other agents gave their excuses and fled the scene.

"You and I are coming very close to having a problem," Nick said.

At first I thought he was talking to me, but when I turned to blast him with my opinion I saw he was looking at Savage, and it wasn't a friendly look.

"Anytime, anyplace. But you know as well as I do that my orders override your personal feelings. We'll do this however we need to so we can get the job done and go home. If you have issues with that then I have no problem cutting you out of the loop completely."

"You're more than welcome to," Nick said.

He was stone cold in his reply. There wasn't even a hint of the anger I knew was boiling under the surface. A quiet Nick was not a good sign. I moved my chair over slightly to get out of the line of fire just in case.

"But *you* know as well as I do that I can make things harder on you. I won't be bothered by playing dirty."

Savage's smile was sharp as a blade and Kate looked like she wanted to put her hand on her weapon just in case things got out of hand.

"You can try," he said. "Or we can see this through and be done with each other. You're call, Detective Dempsey."

"She doesn't go in alone," Nick said. "I want a man inside the room. And I want in on the bust."

"Easily done," Savage said.

"Hey, I'm sitting right here. Don't I get a say in this?"

"No—" they both said in unison.

"All righty then," I said. "You guys let me know when you've got the details hashed out. I need to go shopping. I'm fresh out of semi-formalwear."

I decided to take advantage of the situation and walked up to Savage, holding out my hand. He turned those dark eyes on me, and he quickly banked the fire of his anger. I appreciated the gesture, because an angry Matt Savage was disturbing. He raised a brow in question and looked at my hand.

"Credit card," I said. "It's the least the FBI can do to catch a group of dangerous criminals."

Savage rolled his eyes and reached into his back pocket for his wallet, taking out a silver credit card that carried his name.

"This is my personal card. Try not to go crazy."

"Hey, talent like mine doesn't come cheap. I'll look every bit as good as Becca Gonzales by the time I'm through. Kate's going to help me." I grabbed Kate by the arm and hustled her to the door before the conference room turned into the OK Corral. "You boys have a good time bonding."

AT SIX O'CLOCK I HAD ON UNDERWEAR WORTHY OF A HIGH-class call girl and my head between my knees. I'd been close to hyperventilating for half an hour.

"Whose idea was this?" I asked for the millionth time. "This doesn't seem at all safe. Maybe we should get someone else."

"This was your idea," Kate said. "And it isn't safe. Maybe one day you'll stop opening your mouth as soon as a thought pops into your brain."

"Hmmm," I said. The dizziness was mostly gone and I picked at a piece of loose thread on the bedspread, deciding if I left my head between my legs too much longer I was probably going to suffocate. I didn't know how guys did it.

I flopped back on the bed, wishing I had Marky-Mark

to look upon and ask advice like in my old room. It was easier to breathe lying down. The boning from my lingerie was no longer cutting off the circulation to my innards.

Kate was sprawled at the other end of the bed. "Look on the bright side. You got some really awesome clothes out of the deal. And maybe you could try this getup on for Nick later. That would probably go a long way in soothing his temper."

"I've already used that approach once today," I said. "Do you think there's a limit?"

"Not so far as I've noticed. I think as long as you're naked and semi-willing, then you can get things to turn in your favor when it comes to dealing with a man."

I put my hair in hot rollers and spent a few minutes looking at myself in the mirror. The corset was black lace and only hinted at the skin beneath. It also did a damned good job at sucking in the cinnamon rolls, Twinkies, ice cream and Oreos I'd gorged on the past week. When I thought about it like that, it was almost enough to make me sick. What can I say? I'm a stress eater. And I'd had more than my fair share over the last few days.

The panties were briefer than I'd like, but I wasn't actually planning on stripping down. I was assuming Savage would bust in and put things to a halt before it got that far. And I'd forgone the garters because there was no way in hell I was wearing stockings in this heat.

Mostly I was wearing the underwear because Kate was right. I had a whole lot of making up to do where Nick was concerned.

I did a full makeup job and dusted bronzer over my neck and shoulders before slipping on the black strapless sheath I'd bought earlier. Kate helped me zip it up in the back and I waited until the very end to take the hot rollers out of my hair. I was dealing with a hundred and twenty percent humidity, so it was a little bigger than normal. I evened it out by putting on another coat of lipstick and long silver dangles at my ears.

"That's as good as it gets," I finally said.

I looked over and Kate was asleep on my bed. She'd opted to be in the surveillance room with Nick and a couple of other FBI agents. I personally thought Kate needed a vacation. She was burning her candle at both ends.

Savage picked us up a little early, and he did a mostly good job of keeping his gaze above my neckline. It was kind of hard to blame him. The corset pushed my breasts up to impossible heights, and I kept catching glimpses of them from my peripheral vision.

Kate took her own car and followed behind us, and Savage put his hands around my waist and lifted me into his Tahoe. I was grateful, considering there was no way I'd be able to lift my leg that high without ripping the dress.

I kind of leaned back against the seat so I could draw air into my lungs a little easier, and decided then and there that I was cutting all sweets out of my diet. My spleen was starting to go numb.

Savage narrowly missed a parked car while glancing over at my décolletage.

"They're pretty good, huh?" I said.

"They'll do. I hope the poor bastard isn't old. I'd hate for him to have a heart attack. Adds more paperwork."

I was kind of hoping he *was* old. Even I could probably outrun a senior citizen. And I could probably knock him over if I had to.

"We've already got a team set up on the floor below the penthouse suite," he said as we turned onto Randolph Street and headed straight for the Marriott. "I've spoken with the manager and all but delivered death threats to make him keep his mouth shut. I don't want Natalie Evans getting word of this before we can pick her up, and she has the uncanny knack of having all the right people in the right places."

"Where are you going to be?" I asked, picking invisible pieces of lint from my skirt. I was trying to figure out how I was going to get my head between my knees in this dress if I had another moment of panic.

"I've already been in the room. There's a second bedroom on the opposite side of the living room. I've got sensors placed so I'll be able to watch on a hand-held device. I've got your back."

"Okiedokie."

Savage pulled up at the glass front doors and a bellman opened the door for me. I walked as casually as possible into the lobby, wondering if everyone in sight thought I was a prostitute, and ducked behind a potted palm when I recognized Harry Brewer and his wife heading towards the elevator. Harry was one of only three postmen in Whiskey Bayou, and he had no compunction about reading through people's mail, so I had no doubt he'd love to get a hold of this bit of information to pass along. Just my luck.

I waited until they'd disappeared up the elevator before making my way to the front desk and the manager. Apparently, he'd been waiting for me, and Savage had done a good job of intimidating him because a fine sheen of sweat dotted his upper lip and his eyes were wide as he stared at my cleavage in fascination. I gave him my name and he produced a key to the top floor.

I got on the elevator without company, and slid in the key card to access the top floor. I slouched against the mirrored wall, trying to relieve the pressure in my feet and chest. The next time I had to dress for seduction, I was just going to go au natural beneath my clothes instead of winching myself in a contraption that required the strength of a thousand men to get on. This little scheme wasn't going to work all that well if I passed out in the man's lap before the diamonds could be exchanged.

I teetered down the hallway and was just about to slide in the key card when the door jerked open and Savage pulled me into the room.

"Good grief, what's taking you so long? Can you not feel the sense of urgency here?"

I narrowed my eyes and poked him in the chest. "Listen, buddy. I'm doing you a favor here. You don't want to push me right now. I can't feel my toes and my lungs are being strangled by whale bones."

He looked slightly taken aback at that bit of information, and he got distracted again by my heaving bosom.

"The client will be here in less than twenty minutes, and I just got word from downstairs that they've got interference on the visual connection. There's no time to fix it. There's only audio, so you're going to have to make sure you're giving them an accurate picture of what's going on up here. Got it?"

"You bet."

"Here's Becca's cell phone. They'll be calling soon with final instructions on the exchange. Don't say anything past hello. We don't want to give ourselves away."

"Right," I said. I took the cell phone from Savage and we only had to wait a couple of minutes before it buzzed in my hand. He nodded at me in encouragement.

"Hello," I said.

The voice on the other end was brisk and impersonal. Male this time. And he didn't bother with social niceties.

"Once you've secured the payment from our client then you'll call this number." He rattled off a phone number and Savage handed me a pen and a piece of hotel stationary so I could copy it down. "Tell the client to call down to the front desk and have them send up a bottle of champagne. The product will arrive within a few minutes. The client will set the briefcase outside the door as an act of good faith. Once the transaction is complete you will conduct business as usual."

The caller disconnected and panic seized me. There was so much potential for a colossal screw up on my end of things that I started to hyperventilate again. Little black dots danced in front of my eyes and it suddenly became imperative that I get out of the contraption of torture.

"It was a man this time," Savage said, oblivious to what was happening inside me as he took me by the arm. "What were your impressions?"

"I think I'm going to die," I said instead.

"That's a little dramatic, don't you think?"

"No," I said, wheezing. "My guts are being squeezed out the bottom of my feet like a tube of toothpaste. You've got to get me out of this thing or things aren't going to be pretty."

"Shit, Addison. There's no time. I've got to take cover."

"There's time," I insisted. "Help me or suffer the consequences."

I reached behind me and yanked at the zipper of the dress and the material fell to my waist, revealing the contraption below. I heard Savage suck in a breath, but I didn't care about his reaction. I just needed to breathe.

"Just untie it and loosen the strings," I said. "Kate doesn't know her own strength. She's trussed me up like Mammy did Scarlet in Gone With the Wind."

To give Savage credit, he was a man of action and not one to sit back and let an opportunity pass him by. He untied the knot Kate had made and used his fingers to loosen the strings. Little by little I was able to draw in the all important air that would keep me on both feet instead of passed out in a heap on the floor.

"Oh, shit," Savage said. And before I knew it he'd yanked my dress all the way down and tossed me on the couch. "Look sexy. He's here." Savage disappeared into the room behind me and closed the door quietly.

"Oh, God." God wasn't much interested in helping, because the door clicked to signal it had been unlocked and the handle rattled. I was sprawled on the couch in the most unsexy way possible, and I quickly tried to get in a pose that screamed "seduction" instead of "mentally unstable."

I laid down on my side and propped my head on my fist, crossing my ankles and hoping I wasn't about to come face to face with Brad Pitt or something. I tried to get rid of the grimace on my face and channel a look of seduction, but all I manage was a wobbly smile and a whole lot of heavy breathing. It would have to do.

The foyer was blocked by a wall, so I couldn't immediately see anyone, but I heard the footsteps as they fell against the tile. And then there was silence as he stepped to the carpet and came face to face with me.

I didn't recognize him. Thank the Lord. But the bad news was he definitely wasn't old, and he looked to be in pretty good shape. I wasn't going to have much luck outrunning him if push came to shove. He was movie star handsome, and why the hell he'd need to hire an escort service to see to his sexual needs was beyond me. He probably had women tripping all over themselves to get into his bed. He was tall, dark and handsome in a classic sense, but you could see the power he wielded as if it were a part of his skin. This was an important man.

"Well, hello," he said, propping a shoulder against the

wall and running his gaze from the tips of my stilettos all the way up my body.

"Hello, yourself."

"This is a pleasant surprise," he said. He set down the duffle bag in his hand at his feet and unbuttoned the single button on his suit jacket before taking it off and draping it across the back of a chair. He loosened the tie at his neck, but didn't make any other moves.

"What fun is business if there's no pleasure in it," I said.

Holy crap. I didn't even recognize the voice that was coming from my mouth. It's like I had multiple personalities or something, and I didn't find that as disturbing as I should have. I was like a super spy. And apparently I was good, because Mr. Noname's nostrils flared and he picked the briefcase up and came towards me.

"That's a lovely sentiment," he said. "I agree. I'd much prefer to get the business out of the way so we can get to the pleasure."

"Surely you're not going to leave me in the dark." He quirked a brow in question and I said, "Your name. What should I call you? Or are we going to be passing strangers for the next twelve hours?"

He smiled, showing a slash of white teeth and a slightly crooked incisor that was charming in its appeal.

"Robert Duncan," he said, setting the bag on the coffee table. "And you're Ms. Gonzales, I presume?"

"I am." I moved slowly, putting my feet on the floor with deliberation as I stood up and let him get a full view of me.

"Very nice," he said appreciatively. "It seems I'm going to owe Natalie a favor since she's obviously sent me her best."

My mouth tilted up at the corner in what I hoped

passed for a smile. "Why don't you bring your burden to the table," I said, gesturing to the heavy antique table.

I followed him to the table because there was no way in hell I was going to let him walk behind me. My underwear was drafty to say the least, and my corset was loosening more and more by the minute since Savage hadn't had time to secure the strings.

Robert set the bag on the table and unzipped it. I kept my mouth firmly closed and a look of impassivity on my face as he pushed it toward me. Just another day at the office, Addison. Two million dollars in cash. No big deal.

"Why don't you call down for champagne while I make sure everything is good here," I told him. "I think you'll be surprised by what they bring you."

He smiled and took my hand, laying a soft kiss to my fingers. I resisted the urge to wipe it off once he walked to the phone and turned my attention instead to the fat stacks of cash bundled together with rubber bands.

I counted the money and then put everything back inside, zipping it closed.

"They'll be here in a few minutes," he said, returning.

"Excellent. Why don't you set this in the hallway? My employer would like an act of good faith."

"Two million dollars is a lot of faith when I'm left with nothing to show for it."

I took a step closer and whispered, "You've got me."

His eyes darkened and he took the bag and set it outside the door. Damn, I was good. I had a fleeting thought that I probably shouldn't get too excited. Things hardly ever went right when I was involved, and there was still a lot of room for catastrophe.

I had a moment of panic when Robert came back into the room, and he was pulling his tie from beneath his collar and working at the buttons at his cuffs. He probably thought he was an expert at the whole seduction thing, but I felt like I was more like a specimen under a microscope when he looked at me rather than an actual person, and it was starting to creep me out. The fact that he was so attractive only made the feeling stronger.

"How about some music?" he asked.

"I'd love some music." I said a quick prayer, hoping he wouldn't ask me to dance. My moves pretty much were limited to the running man and the sprinkler.

He turned on the stereo and classical music—something soft and dreamy—filled the air. A knock at the door sounded a few seconds later.

"Ah, that will be our champagne. And other things, I presume?"

I nodded and he went to answer the door. I limped back over to the couch and kicked my shoes off just as all hell broke loose. A deluge of gunshots echoed through the room. Furniture splintered and glass shattered under the hail of bullets. I saw Robert stumble backwards into the room, his white shirt soaked with red, and I jumped behind the couch just as a piece of flying glass hit me in the leg.

There were harshly ordered commands and I peeped around the couch in time to see three men open fire on Robert at point blank range. He crumpled to the floor, and I slapped my hand over my mouth to keep from screaming.

More shouts came from the hallway and the three men turned around and opened fire. That's when Savage grabbed me from behind and rolled me to the nearest closet. He got me to my feet and pressed me into the wall, protecting me with his body as the fight outside seemed to go on forever. I had no idea what had just happened, and even worse, I didn't know if that was the cops that had drawn the gunmen's fire at the end. My worry for Nick ratcheted up a few notches and I felt the tears gathering in my eyes.

"Everything will be all right," he assured me. "We've got plenty of backup."

I let out a sigh of relief at that reminder, but that didn't take away the worry for Nick. My eyes were wide and my pulse was pounding under my skin. I found myself almost hypnotized by the blackness of his eyes, and it was then I realized I was wrapped around him tighter than a blanket. It had been pure reflex to grab on as tight as I could and not let go. My fingers were cramped and digging into his shoulders and my leg was around his waist as I tried to crawl up his body.

"My leg hurts," I whispered. "I think it got cut by the glass."

"We'll get it checked out," he said against my ear, his lips barely moving. "Relax. And be ready to move on my say so. Someone else is in the room."

He pushed me harder into the wall, his body shielding mine, as he brought the gun in his hand up and pointed it at the closet door. I bit my lip hard enough to taste blood, and I took comfort in the way he put his free arm around me. I fit against him easily—too easily—and it was something I'd have to think of later. Preferably when I had clothes on.

I heard the crunch of glass as footsteps made their way across the room. Then there was nothing but silence, and I knew whoever was out there stood just on the other side of the closet door. Savage and I both held our breaths as the knob jiggled once before it turned.

Light flooded the closet and I squenched my eyes closed against the glare, not having any desire to actually see my death up close and personal. I waited for the sound of gunfire and for hot metal to rip through my skin, but there was nothing but tense silence.

I cracked my eyes open one at a time and immediately wished I'd left them closed. Nick stood in the doorway, his weapon pointed steadily at Savage as his glacier blue eyes met mine. He was alive. I felt the breath leave my body on a sigh of relief, and then realized he wasn't as excited to see me as I was to see him. His gaze was glued to our compromising position, and if looks could kill I'd be six feet under.

"It's not what it looks like," I croaked out. "I swear."

"Gee, doesn't that sound familiar." His voice was harsh, and the lines of his mouth were pinched. "Just remember that payback's a bitch, sweetheart. Too bad I don't have a tranquilizer gun."

I pushed Savage away and felt lightheaded all of a sudden from the adrenaline rush. He steadied me and I stumbled out of the closet, gulping in deep breaths of air just as I heard Nick say my name with some alarm. I couldn't seem to get my bearings. My head was fuzzy, and it was like everyone was talking to me from underwater. And my leg felt like it was on fire. I listed to the side and remember Nick's arms coming around me just as the lights went out and I fainted.

15

T*hursday*

"RISE AND SHINE, SLEEPING BEAUTY," NICK SAID.

That sounded so familiar I almost smiled, but it hurt too bad so I stuck with grimacing. I cracked my eyes open one at a time stared at Nick. I must have fallen asleep after the doctor had come to see me. I'd been admitted to the hospital overnight for observation, but I was ready to get out of there. I was dressed and just waiting for my release papers so I could go home and suffer in the privacy of my own house.

"The nurse brought the bullet they took out of your leg by. It's in a jar there on the table. The doctor thought you might like a souvenir."

I grimaced and didn't bother looking at the bullet. The pain was all the proof I needed.

"So fill me in," I said. "Who were those men?"

"Russian loyalists. Natalie Evans was picked up and charged with murder and collusion, and the FBI is investigating the possibility of espionage. She killed Sasha Malakov.

"We were right about her funding her homeland by selling off the stolen gems. She doesn't like the current party that's in control and she thought if she sent the opposition enough money, then they could take control. She's been using her influence in politics for years to siphon American money into their hands. And this isn't the first time she's used priceless gems as a way to get quick cash for her cause."

Nick messed with one of the flower arrangements that was sitting on my bedside table, and I wondered briefly when it had arrived.

"It turns out things didn't go how Natalie planned. She had her own spy with his own agenda working under her at Sirin, and he was the one who orchestrated the shooting in the hotel room and killed Amanda Whitfield. He planned to take the cash for himself and send the Tear of Ivan back to Russia where it belonged because he believes their heritage shouldn't be sold to the highest bidder. We were able to confiscate the money and the gems, and the gunmen are being held without bail. Natalie was very forthcoming with information once she realized no attorney in the world could get her out of prison without some kind of deal."

"So she'll get off anyway?" I asked.

"Not necessarily. It turns out she was funding the old communist party, and the current government wasn't too happy to find that out. They'll be more than happy to take care of her if we'll hand her and the Tear of Ivan over. And to make the loss up to Christian DeLuce, they'll be sending over some other museum quality goods as an act of good faith."

"So everything worked out in the end, huh?" I said.

He stared at me somberly and I got a bad feeling in the pit of my stomach.

"I've changed my mind about thinking it's a good idea for you to get your P.I. license. This isn't a profession meant for a woman like you," he said. "You're not hard enough for the job, and you're going to get yourself killed if you keep putting yourself in the middle of these situations. I can't deal with that hanging over us all the time. I need you to be safe. To live a normal life. There are other teaching jobs out there you could apply for."

I smiled sadly and broke eye contact as the urge to cry seemed to come out of nowhere. I cleared my throat and licked my dry lips once before deciding what to say.

"You know, I was engaged to a man once who saw this image of me. He had in his mind from the start exactly the person he wanted me to be, without ever getting to actually know the real me. He needed me to be the wife of a prominent businessman. To not have too many serious thoughts and to be a good hostess or dinner companion when he had clients over. He wanted to me go to my little teaching job so I'd have something to keep me occupied and come home and be a doormat that didn't interfere in his life or do anything controversial. During that time I turned into this robot of a woman that I didn't even recognize."

I found the courage to look him in the eyes, because I wanted him to know that I was nothing but serious about what I was about to say.

"I love you," I said and would have laughed at the alarm in his eyes if the whole situation hadn't been so sad. He opened his mouth, but I held up a hand. "No, don't say anything. I'm telling you I love you, and I'd do almost anything you ever asked of me, but I'll never let myself become that woman again. Not even for you. If you can't handle the real me then that's your shortcoming. Not mine. I need someone who will support me always. Not just when it's easy."

Nick stood and braced his hands against the side of the bed, his head hanging down as he gathered his thoughts. He looked up at me and he had his cop face on, his eyes devoid of any emotion.

"The sad thing, Addison, is that I'm pretty sure I love you too. And I'll be glad to support you through anything else. But you putting your life on the line constantly for no good reason isn't something I can get behind. I can't be in a relationship where I'm spending all my time worrying about you. I have enough of that to deal with in my own job."

"Well, I guess we know where we stand then," I said, not backing down. I wanted to find the anger that I knew I should be feeling at his ultimatum, but I couldn't manage to dredge it up. Mostly I just felt heartbroken.

"I guess we do," he said softly. "You're supposed to be discharged soon. Can I give you a ride home?"

I laughed a little tearfully but refused to let them fall. "No, I'll have Kate come get me."

He nodded once and moved to the door. "See you around," he said.

I turned my head so I wouldn't have to watch him walk away.

KATE WOULD HAVE COME TO GET ME, BUT SHE WAS testifying in court and wasn't able to leave, so I called

Rosemarie and asked if she'd mind. I'd taken another pain pill before we'd left the hospital to take the edge off. Between my leg and Nick, I was content to spend a couple of days in a drug-induced haze until I was back to my old self.

Rosemarie parked her yellow Beetle in front of my house and launched herself out of the driver's seat to come around and help me out. My crutches were hanging out the window and she pulled them out before opening the door for me. My attention was distracted by a jogger running toward us who looked an awful lot like Savage.

He was wearing black athletic shorts and nothing else, and sweat gleamed on his chest. His hair was damp and his muscles gleamed bronze in the sunlight.

"Sweet mother," Rosemarie said.

"Amen, sister," I said.

I turned and put my feet on the pavement, trying to decide the best way to maneuver myself up, when Savage slowed his pace and walked up to us.

"You need some help?" he asked.

"I wouldn't mind a hand."

He got me under both arms and pulled me gently to my feet, holding me steady until I could get the crutches where I needed them. I'll admit my brain was fuzzy, otherwise it wouldn't have taken me so long to ask the obvious question.

"What are you doing here?" I asked. "Don't you have your own neighborhood to jog in?"

He stepped back to give me some room and grinned. "This is my neighborhood. I live in that house right over there." He pointed to the little white house that was across the street and over one from mine, and I closed my eyes, wondering why I'd been put on this earth for other people to torture.

"Of course you do," I said. "I think I need another pain pill."

I hobbled my way up the sidewalk and ignored his soft laughter.

"See you around, neighbor."

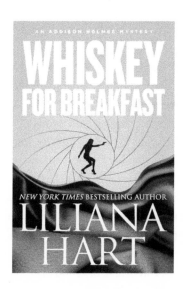

Prologue:

I'm not the kind of person to dwell overmuch on the details, but even I knew I couldn't talk my way out of my current predicament if I got caught.

I looked both ways down the deserted alleyway to make sure I was alone. A dumpster and crumpled trash that rolled across the cracked pavement like tumbleweeds was my only company. I'd gotten lucky—the moon was only a sliver in the sky and not enough to make me visible to any passersby. I was still new at this whole breaking and entering thing.

I opened my brand new Kate Spade clutch and pulled out the black cloth packet of lock picking tools I'd bought online. I'd had to practice my new hobby incognito because my best friend and boss, Kate McClean, sometimes got an eye twitch when she knew the lengths I'd go to research my job.

My name is Addison Holmes, and I'm a private investigator in training for the McClean Detective Agency. That basically means I spend most of my time spying on adulterers, making coffee, and being babysat by my trainer since I have a tendency to get into trouble whenever I'm out on my own. But in my defense, I usually managed to get the job done. I had the scars to prove it.

I'd been practicing my B&E skills by watching YouTube videos and using the back door of my house as a test dummy. It had only taken me three tries before I'd managed to click the tumblers into place, which was terrifying considering I was a woman living alone and there were more talented lock pickers than I out there. I couldn't really afford better locks, so I kept a chair pushed under the door and my gun under my pillow.

It was fortunate the back door of the clinic I was trying to break into couldn't afford better locks either, but it still took a good fifteen minutes before the lock gave. The night air was cool, but I was sweaty as a stripper's G-string because of nerves. I had to rub my hands on my shorts twice before I could turn the knob. I cursed as I thought about fingerprints, so I quickly wiped off every surface I'd touched with the hem of my Bon Jovi T-shirt, pulled a pair of rubber medical gloves out of my purse and snapped them on.

I slipped into the clinic, closed the door at my back and then bit back a yelp when the air conditioning unit came on with a rumble.

"Shit," I breathed out. I relaxed and decided I should've gone to the bathroom before I'd left the house. My bladder couldn't take the stress of illegal activity.

The clinic smelled of Lysol and antiseptic and it was long and rectangular in shape. Ugly gray brick on the outside, metal roof, and white industrial blinds were on all the windows so those who frequented the clinic had ultimate privacy.

The reception desk divided the rectangle into two parts —offices on the left and the patient rooms toward the right. Even the thought of what happened in those rooms made me throw up in my mouth a little. There wasn't enough Lysol in the world to cleanse away what happened in there.

The door I'd entered was on the side with the offices, and I passed through a long narrow hallway with white floors and wood paneled walls. The lights were off and the only reason I could see at all was because of the red nightlights spaced every twenty feet or so in the ceiling.

I stifled a nervous giggle at the thought that I'd once seen a horror movie that reminded me an awful lot of my current situation. I reached into my purse and pulled out my gun just in case there were zombies. At least I'd worn tennis shoes instead of high heels in case I had to make a run for it.

I'd wasted enough time building up my courage so I set forward with determination. I snuck past two bathrooms and a water fountain and wondered if it was against the criminal's code to sneak into the bathroom and relieve myself. But with my luck, that's when the SWAT team would break down the doors and the Enquirer would be standing there to take pictures.

I pulled the strap of my purse over my body and held the gun in a two handed grip. In my mind I was just like Laura Holt from Remington Steele, only curvier and without eighties hair. I made my way to where the hallway met the main area, squatting low and peeping around the corner to make sure I was alone.

The place was silent as a tomb and I crossed in front of the reception desk without even a squeak from my sneakers. My stealth abilities had improved by about a hundred and fifty percent since my first day on the job. Which wasn't saying much. It was the same thing as saying a kindergartner could finally use the paste without eating it.

My heart was thudding a hundred miles a minute and the red glow from the lights was creepy as shit. My goal was fairly simple: I needed to get into the locked room I'd noticed on my first visit to the clinic and search the files. The room was at the end of the opposite hall past the patient rooms, made to look more like a janitor's closet than anything else, but I'd glimpsed the rows of file cabinets during my tour a couple of days before.

I was halfway down the hallway when I heard a horrible moan. My heart stopped and I turned around to run back from the way I'd come when I heard it again. And though it *was* horrible, it wasn't a death moan. I'd heard a few of those sounds over the past months. Back when I was having regular sex I'd even moaned like that myself. From the increasing volume I was guessing she was enjoying herself, whoever she was. Either that or she was declawing a cat without anesthesia.

To say my curiosity was piqued was an understatement. I'd never been very good at listening to the part of my mind that told me I shouldn't stick my nose where it didn't belong. I made my way closer to the sounds, hurrying my steps because it sounded like she was winding up for the finale, and I noticed the door was open a crack and light flickered from beneath.

I meant to be quiet. I really did. But the sight that greeted me was enough to draw a gasp from my lips. A pair of familiar blue eyes met mine and widened in surprise. My own eyes narrowed and I felt sick to my stomach as I took in the scene. It was worse than I could've imagined.

The woman reached a climax shrill enough to break glass and the tension ratcheted up the temperature several degrees. A pregnant silence followed her cataclysmic orgasm, and I realized if I didn't breathe a little slower I was likely to end up hyperventilating.

"I should've known you'd show up here," Nick Dempsey said, closing his eyes and shaking his head in disbelief. "I don't suppose I could talk you into turning around and going back home so I can get this straightened out."

I raised a brow and cut my eyes to the loaded weapon in his hand. "No, I don't think so."

He sighed and put his gun away, reaching over to turn the TV off and the X-rated flick that had been playing. The smells of old sex and new death assaulted my senses, and I swallowed back the bile that rose at the sight of the body at Nick's feet.

"At least you put on gloves when you came in," he said, nodding at my hands. "I'd hate to think you smudged the prints of whoever broke in."

"Someone broke in?" I asked, guilt sending a rush of heat to my cheeks.

"You didn't see the front door shot to shit and standing open when you came inside?"

"Umm…sure I did. How could I have missed that?"

CHAPTER ONE

Friday, Four Days Earlier…

"Fif—ty…"

I flopped back onto my yoga mat with a thud and a *whoompf* of expelled breath, and I stared longingly at the cup of coffee I'd placed at the edge of the kitchen counter for inspiration. Too bad I didn't have the energy to get up and get it, not to mention it probably wasn't all that hot anymore.

"Go-go-gadget arm." I flung my limp hand out toward the coffee cup, but much to my continual disappointment, that saying never worked.

My abs burned like fire, and it felt like someone had rearranged my intestines. I stared at the clock for a few seconds, waiting for my vision to come into focus, and I groaned at the time. "Fifty sit-ups in eight-minutes and fifty-two seconds. A personal best. But still pathetic, Addison."

It was never the first thirty sit-ups that gave me any problems. I could do thirty in about two minutes. It was the last twenty that had me using every creative curse word I'd ever heard as the daughter of a cop. I couldn't seem to get over the hurdle. And my time was running short.

A couple of months ago I'd lost my job as a teacher in the small town of Whiskey Bayou where I'd been raised. It hadn't come as that big of a surprise since I'd gotten caught stripping at a gentleman's club in an act of desperation to bring in some extra cash. It hadn't mattered that I'd been the worst stripper ever born or that I'd only managed to hold the job for the minute and a half I'd been on stage. It had been long enough for my principal to see me and snap off a couple of photos.

I'd like to think I could've bribed or blackmailed him into keeping my secret safe, but by the time I'd made it to the parking lot he was already dead. I fell over him quite literally, and the rest, they say, is history. Once the police became involved there was no way my secret wouldn't get back to Whiskey Bayou and the residents there who thrived on gossip as if it were mother's milk.

Needless to say, my financial situation hadn't improved since the loss of my job. My unemployment benefits were only good for another couple of months, and I had regular rent payments I had to make and all the bills that went along with living in a house. Not to mention credit cards I was still paying off from a wedding that never took place.

It was a good thing I'd been moonlighting at the McClean Detective Agency to bring in a little extra cash before my unfortunate dismissal from James Madison High, otherwise I never would've had the opportunity to talk Kate into hiring me full time. I wasn't exactly a full time employee yet. I did contract work and a lot of background checks—spying on adulterous spouses and the occasional case of fraud. Savannah, Georgia was a hotbed of lust and debauchery if the cases that crossed my desk everyday were anything to go by.

I'd basically caught Kate at a low moment when I'd convinced her to hire me on as a full time private investigator. The only stipulation for my employment was I had to pass all the tests at the top of my class.

I'd spent the last couple of months taking the Citizen's Police Academy classes once a week, studying manuals thick enough to use for kindling, practicing my shooting at the range, and…exercising. I'd passed my conceal to carry test with flying colors, mostly because my dad had taught me how to shoot when I was still in diapers. A cute little H&K my mom and her new husband had bought me as a congratulations gift sat in my purse on the counter. Though if anyone had tried to break in at the moment I would've been too tired to grab it.

The written exam I had to take the week after Christmas would be a piece of cake as well. I was an expert researcher and test taker thanks to my degree in history. I could recite rules and regulations out the wazoo. The problem was my mind didn't always want to follow those rules and regulations. Sometimes a situation called for thinking on your feet instead of going by procedure. I just made sure to leave the thinking on your feet parts out of any reports I had to write for Kate. Bless her heart, she was a rule follower through and through. She always had been, even when we were in grade school.

The only section of the test I couldn't quite seem to master was the physical fitness portion. At the rate I was going, I wouldn't pass at all, much less be in the top of the class. The requirements were a two-mile run in under thirty minutes, followed immediately by fifty sit-ups in five minutes, followed by 10 pushups in however long it took you to do them. And those were just the minimums.

I rolled over onto my hands and knees, thinking I probably needed to run my yoga mat through a car wash since it was soaked with sweat and smelled of things that no southern lady should ever smell of.

A whimper escaped my mouth, and I crawled from the living room to the kitchen where my cold coffee waited for me. I managed to use the drawer handles as a way to lever myself to a standing position. My hands shook like a wino's in a dry spell, but I managed to wrap them around the cup and bring it to my lips, only spilling a little down the front of my sports bra.

The cobwebs started to clear little by little and I groaned as I realized I still had to fit in a run. I'd finally made it to the mile mark without having to stop and throw up in someone's yard, so I was at least making progress on that front.

I grabbed the binoculars from my kitchen drawer and went to stand at my front window, just like I did every morning. I cracked the blinds just the slightest bit and then put the binoculars to my face. They were already adjusted exactly how I needed them to be.

When I'd rented this house a couple of months ago, it was at the suggestion of a very sexy FBI agent I'd been working with at the time. His name was Matt Savage and I'd never met anyone whose name fit more perfectly. He looked like the love child of The Rock and Pocahontas— dusky gold skin stretched over sharp features and muscles that would make any woman sit up and take notice. I'd taken notice all right. But as much as I liked Savage and as much as I was curious to find out what he looked like under those black suits he always wore, I'd decided to keep my distance.

Savage was a nice guy, but he wasn't someone who'd be great for the long term. He liked to play fast and reckless, and there was an element of danger about him that not even I was comfortable with. And that was saying something.

But when he'd made the suggestion about the house I was currently residing in, I'd had no idea he lived just across the street. This caused me a lot of anxiety. Mostly because I was currently single and every time he got in a five-mile radius my hormones started to sing. So I'd gone out of my way to make sure I had as little contact as possible. That didn't stop him from coming over with takeout or mowing my lawn like clockwork every Saturday, but I was still trying to make an effort.

Men like Savage were no good for small town girls like me. And as odd as it seemed as a woman in twenty-first century America, I still had hang ups about casual sex. I couldn't do it without there being some kind of emotional attachment or hope that something long term could come from it.

I held the binoculars up to my face and watched Savage's house for a few minutes. He liked to run first thing in the morning before he went to work, and I tried to coordinate my schedule so he was already gone before I took my turn through the neighborhood—mostly because I didn't want him to witness my resemblance to an arrhythmic heffalump.

There wasn't a car parked in the driveway, but that wasn't unusual since he normally parked in the garage. The blinds were all closed up and I couldn't see any lights on throughout the house. I let out a relieved breath and scanned the street in both directions just in case he was still out running, but I was pretty sure the coast was clear.

It was on my second scan down the street that I got a weird tingly feeling at the back of my neck. Usually that was my internal warning that something bad was about to happen, but considering the results of my morning workout, it could've been nerve damage as well.

I don't know what made me glance at my neighbor's house—the one directly to my right. It was a little square of a house almost identical to mine, only it was painted canary yellow with white shutters. I'd never even met who lived there or seen them for that matter since my work hours were on the odd side.

The binoculars stopped of their own volition and straight into a large square window with slatted blinds that were all the way open. Another pair of binoculars stared straight back at me, wide blinking eyes magnified through the opposite end of the lenses.

"Jesus," I screeched, stumbling back a step and tripping over a rug so I landed on my ass. My lungs heaved as I tried to suck in oxygen and figure out what had just happened.

Obviously my neighbor was a peeping Tom. The only problem was technically so was I, and I couldn't exactly make accusations. I crawled on hands and knees back to the windows and closed all the blinds.

A knock at the door had me biting back a scream, but I realized I needed to get a grip. I was supposed to be a professional for Christ's sake. Adrenaline gave me an added rush of strength and I vaulted myself toward the kitchen and pulled my gun out of my purse before skulking to the door and looking through the peephole.

I didn't recognize him, but I had a sinking feeling I was about to meet my new neighbor. He was probably an inch shorter than me and had a face soft with baby fat. His eyes were very round in his pudgy face and I couldn't tell if he had eyelids because he didn't blink. At all.

Black hair stood in wild tufts around his head and a pencil thin mustache I was pretty sure he'd drawn on sat just above his lip. He wore khakis that were at least a size too big and a Star Trek T-shirt, and his binoculars hung around his neck.

I stood as still as possible, wondering what I should do, and praying he'd get tired of waiting and go back to his own house. He kept staring at me through the peephole, never blinking, and when my fingers cramped I realized I was squeezing my gun too tight.

"I can hear you breathing," he finally said through the door.

I let out a sigh as I unlocked the deadbolt and undid the chain, but I didn't bother to hide my weapon.

"You're Addison Holmes," he said, and I was slightly taken aback by the fact that he not only had been spying on me but also knew my name. "Agent Savage speaks highly of you, but I had to see that you would fit in for myself. We don't just take anyone off the street you know."

"I have no idea what you're talking about."

"Neighborhood watch." It was then I noticed he had a folded T-shirt in his hand and a dayglow orange vest, and he shoved them both at me. "I've been watching you since you moved in, and I could tell this morning that you have a good eye for what's happening in the neighborhood. We try to keep crime to a minimum here. I'm Leonard Winkle, but everyone calls me Spock. I'm the president of the NAD Squad. It's your turn to host tomorrow since you're the newest member. We'll be here at 9am sharp. Wear your shirt. Mrs. Rodriguez likes cranberry muffins."

With that he turned on his heel and headed back across the small expanse of lawn that separated our houses.

"What the fuck?"

I closed the door and locked it up tight. I put my gun back in my purse and tossed the ugly vest on the counter before holding the shirt up in front of me so I could see what it said. NAD was spelled in giant block letters in the same dayglow orange as the vest across the front of the shirt. And underneath it was the word SQUAD in much smaller letters.

"NAD Squad," I murmured. I turned the shirt around so I could read the back. "Neighbors Against Delinquency. Of course that's what it means."

I tossed the shirt on the counter and poured another

cup of coffee, deciding to take it into the shower with me. Running wasn't going to happen this morning. In fact, I was contemplating just crawling back under the covers and starting the whole day over again. Unfortunately, Kate was expecting me at the agency for a meeting.

She'd called me the night before driving back from the airport and reception had been spotty, but I'd caught the words sperm and billionaire, so it was enough information to have me sufficiently intrigued. Though a part of me was wondering if Kate was trying to set me up on a blind date.

ABOUT THE AUTHOR

Liliana Hart is a *New York Times, USA Today, and Publisher's Weekly* Bestselling Author of more than 40 titles. After starting her first novel her freshman year of college, she immediately became addicted to writing and knew she'd found what she was meant to do with her life. She has no idea why she majored in music. Since self-publishing in June of 2011, Liliana has sold more than 4 million ebooks. She's appeared at #1 on lists all over the world and all three of her series have appeared on the *New York Times* list. Liliana is a sought after speaker and she's given keynote speeches and self-publishing workshops to standing-room-only crowds from California to New York to London.

Liliana can almost always be found at her computer writing or on the road giving workshops for SilverHart

International, a company she founded with her husband, Scott Silverii, where they provide law enforcement, military, and fire resources for writers so they can write it right. When Liliana and her husband aren't spending time with their children, they're living the life of nomads, traveling wherever interests them most.

If you enjoyed reading *Whiskey Sour*, I would appreciate it if you would help others enjoy this book, too.

Lend it. This e-book is lending-enabled, so please, share it with a friend.

Recommend it. Please help other readers find this book by recommending it to friends, readers' groups and discussion boards.

Review it. Please tell other readers why you liked this book by reviewing it. If you do write a review, please send me an email at lilianahartauthor@gmail.com so I can thank you with a personal email. Or visit me at http://www.lilianahart.com.

Connect with me online:
www.lilianahart.com
lilianahartauthor@gmail.com

ALSO BY LILIANA HART

The MacKenzies of Montana

Dane's Return

Thomas's Vow

Riley's Sanctuary

Cooper's Promise

Grant's Christmas Wish

The MacKenzies Boxset

MacKenzie Security Series

Seduction and Sapphires

Shadows and Silk

Secrets and Satin

Sins and Scarlet Lace

Sizzle

Crave

Trouble Maker

Scorch

MacKenzie Security Omnibus 1

MacKenzie Security Omnibus 2

Lawmen of Surrender (MacKenzies-1001 Dark Nights)

1001 Dark Nights: Captured in Surrender

1001 Dark Nights: The Promise of Surrender

Sweet Surrender

Dawn of Surrender

The MacKenzie World (read in any order)

Trouble Maker

Bullet Proof

Deep Trouble

Delta Rescue

Desire and Ice

Rush

Spies and Stilettos

Wicked Hot

Hot Witness

Avenged

Never Surrender

JJ Graves Mystery Series

Dirty Little Secrets

A Dirty Shame

Dirty Rotten Scoundrel

Down and Dirty

Dirty Deeds

Dirty Laundry

Dirty Money

Addison Holmes Mystery Series

Whiskey Rebellion

Whiskey Sour

Whiskey For Breakfast

Whiskey, You're The Devil

Whiskey on the Rocks

Whiskey Tango Foxtrot

Whiskey and Gunpowder

The Gravediggers

The Darkest Corner

Gone to Dust

Say No More

Stand Alone Titles

Breath of Fire

Kill Shot

Catch Me If You Can

All About Eve

Paradise Disguised

Island Home

The Witching Hour

Books by Liliana Hart and Scott Silverii

The Harley and Davidson Mystery Series

The Farmer's Slaughter

A Tisket a Casket

I Saw Mommy Killing Santa Claus

Get Your Murder Running

Deceased and Desist

Malice In Wonderland

Tequila Mockingbird

Gone With the Sin